# About th

ALAN BILTON is the author of two novels, *The Known and Unknown Sea* (2014), variously compared to Charlie and the Chocolate Factory, the 1902 movie, A Trip to the Moon, and Dante's Inferno, and *The Sleepwalkers' Ball* (2009) which one critic described as "Franz Kafka meets Mary Poppins". As a writer, he is obviously a hard man to pin down. He is also the author of books on Silent Film Comedy, Contemporary Fiction, and America in the 1920s. He teaches Creative Writing, Contemporary Literature, and Film at Swansea University in Wales.

www.AlanBilton.co.uk

# ANYWHERE OUT OF THE WORLD

a collection of short stories of the
deeply mysterious and the utterly absurd
by

## Alan Bilton

**Cillian**Press|

First published in Great Britain in 2016
by Cillian Press Limited. 83 Ducie Street, Manchester M1 2JQ
www.cillianpress.co.uk

British Library Cataloguing in Publication Data.
A catalogue record for this book is available from the British Library.

Paperback ISBN: 978-1-909776-16-6
eBook ISBN: 978-1-909776-17-3

Cover: Night lateral canal and bridge in Venice, Italy
© Olgacov | Dreamstime.com

Slightly altered versions of some of these stories originally appeared elsewhere, and are
reprinted here with the kind permission of the publishers.

'The Alphabet's Shadow' in *A Flock of Shadows* (Parthian)
'Execution of an Orchestra' and 'Filling' in the *Swansea Review*
'Two White, One Blue' in *New Welsh Review*
'Letting Charlie Go' and 'Love in an age of austerity' in *Planet*
'No Refund, No Return' in *The Lonely Crowd*
'The Pool at Weine Street' in '*Sing, Sorrow, Sorrow*' (Seren)

*"This life is a hospital where every patient is possessed with the desire to change beds;*
*One man who would like to suffer in front of the stove,*
*And another who believes that he would recover his health beside the window.*
*It always seems to me that I should feel well in the place where I am not,*
*And this question of removal is one which I discuss incessantly with my soul"*

**Baudelaire**

For Pamela,
With all my love

# Contents

# Walla Walla, Washington

*"The more elaborate his labyrinths, the further*
*from the Sun his face"*
**Mikha'il Na'ima**

# 1

The guy who picked me up from the airport was a Native American fella by the name of Charlie. The first thing he did was shake my hand, take my bags and run his hands over the fabric of my suit. "Polyester," he said solemnly. I tried telling him it was a wool mix but he wouldn't believe me. The seats smelled of Febreeze and the radio was very loud.

"This is INXS," he said, pointing to the radio.

"Um, yes."

"Yes," he said sagely. "Yes, it is."

Charlie had thick, knitted eyebrows and a tremendous lump on the side of his head. When he spoke it sounded as if the words were being dragged from the bottom of a deep, dry well.

"Walla Walla means 'Many Waters'."

"Really?"

"Many waters."

I tried to think what to say next. We'd pulled out from the airport onto a long flat road across the plains. "Is Walla 'many' or 'waters'?"

"Very good irrigation. That's why there are so many vineyards."

"Mm." I gazed at the dusty back country sceptically. A few specks of snow blew across the dirty grey sky.

"Nearly two thousand acres," he said. "A hundred wineries. Very good soil."

"Maybe I ought to…"

"Fire water?"

"Ah…"

"Did you say fire water?"

"No."

"Okay."

The road was very long and very flat. Huge trucks rumbled past bails of barbed wire, a line of silos, a completely empty billboard. When we passed a farm a yellow dog chased us half-heartedly, its bark strangely hoarse. O, the prairies! On one side a graveyard of machine parts, on the other a trestle table of forlorn looking pumpkins, surrounded by a scribble of flies. Mm, I thought: *this* the Wild West?

"I'm giving a paper at the college," I said.

Charlie didn't answer. The air-freshener by his head was in the shape of Britney Spears.

"Um, that's why I'm here."

"Yes."

"A paper."

"Paper."

"Do you want to know what it's about?"

"You have paper?"

"Well…"

"We have paper. You think people here don't have paper?"

"No, I…"

"You're in the wrong business, mister. You need to get yourself a *franchise*. Do you understand? A *franchise*. That is where the money is."

12

He paused. More and more flakes were falling. The sky looked curdled.

"My brother runs a golf franchise out by the winery. Pulls in forty thousand dollars after tax…"

"Um…"

"*After* tax…"

"That's… great."

"Yes," he said. "Yes, it is."

We narrowly missed a truck coming the other way but I didn't say anything.

"You come a long way?"

"Um, the UK. Ah, England."

"England?" Charlie whistled through his teeth. "You come a long way to sell paper."

"Well…"

"Is that where they killed Princess Diana? A very pretty lady. What's wrong? Don't you think she was pretty?"

"I…"

"I'm not saying anything, mister. That's just what I heard…"

Spits of grey sleet fell from the gloomy sky. One enormous sign advertised dieting by hypnosis, a second a motel chain called Goonies. We passed an outcropping of rock which looked exactly like a hat.

"You see that rock? That's where my mother-in-law fell ill. Retching."

"The one like a hat?"

"Not in her hat. On the ground. Green."

"Ah," I said, watching the rock disappear behind us. "Is it cursed?"

"Cursed?" Charlie's lump throbbed menacingly.

"I mean, is it a cursed, um, rock…"

More flakes were falling now, but still Charlie didn't switch on the wipers.

"Gastro-enteritis," he said.

"Right."

We passed a second rock. It was shaped like a spoon but I didn't say anything.

Snow was sticking to the windscreen like cardboard. There was just one small port hole and Charlie peered at this intently. Every time we hit a bump on the road, Britney Spears jiggled.

"You see there?" he said pointing to a vague stain on the back seat. "Very sick. Green."

"I see."

"Not in her hat."

"My mistake."

"How could she be sick in her hat?"

"Well, quite."

"She has no hat."

"I'm sorry…"

"There is no hat at all."

Walla Walla Washington.

We passed a line of limp flags, some guy in a cowboy hat, a BMW dealership. The closer we got to town, the more solid everything seemed: squat buildings, fat farmers, heavy hats. The main street was pretty much as you'd imagine. The barber had a sale on beards. Seventh Day Adventists were holding an onion festival. Traffic signs dangled over the road as if they'd just been hung.

"You heard of Adam West, mister?" Charlie asked me.

"The guy that played Batman?"

"That's right."

"Yes, I've heard of Adam West."

"Good."

"So…"

"People *should*."

"Yes…"

We stopped at a red light, next to a poster advertising the Walla Walla Sweets: a blue onion with a baseball bat sang 'How Sweet You Is' above a group of cheerleaders. Across from a hunting store one sign showed the way to the roller derby park, the other the state pen.

"Is it a big prison?" I asked. "I mean, there are signs everywhere…"

"Two thousand staff, one thousand offenders…"

"Really? That seems…"

"You want to get yourself hanged, it's either here or Delaware."

"Right."

"Hangman lives just across the road from me. Very big hands. Nice kids. Don't get into an argument with his wife."

Charlie fell silent but I didn't complain; the seat belt catch was broken and I busied myself trying to fit the two pieces back together.

"Here or Delaware," I said and nodded.

The college was about a mile out of town, wooden white cabins arranged around a block of newer-looking buildings like wagons in a circle. The snow was pretty heavy now, falling slantwise on the running track, the lecture theatres, an odd, pyramid like church. The sky was the colour of tea. The lake was the colour of milk.

"Well, this is me…" I said, struggling with the bills in my pocket.

"This is where you'll be giving your papers… college papers." Charlie shook his head sadly. "Why sell college papers? A franchise, stock, that's what you need… some kind of trade…"

His teeth made a funny whistle and he pulled over to the side of the road. For a moment he seemed to be listening to some kind of static echoing his head. "I will come and get you," he said. "Do you understand?"

"Well…"

"I will come and get you," he repeated, and with that he handed me a card. I wasn't sure about where he was putting the stress, but I took the card anyway.

"Day or night…"

"Ah…"

"I will get *you*…"

Then Charlie – and Charlie's lump – were gone.

# 2

The moment the cab pulled away, the light faded, the snow came down, and the campus seemed to recede like the tide. It was like nothing I had ever seen before; the trees broke up, the pavilion vanished, and before I knew it everything had fallen apart into blobs and blurs. One minute I was taking a short cut across the playing field, the next I was staggering across an endless expanse of nothing, eyes gummed shut, lips frozen, my case snarled up in the muck. And the horizon? There was no horizon – only white. It was as if somebody had painted over my glasses for a joke. First no this way and then no that; how was I supposed to find the faculty building in this? Over one shoulder football players came and went, one minute towering over me, the next no bigger than dolls. A row of blackened trees danced like a chorus line. The straight lines of a goal post broke up into a scribble. Beyond my suit I was lost; inside my suit also. Great banks of snow blew over me, filling my pockets, my nose, my socks.

"Ah, hello?" I said. "Is there anybody there?"

But why would there be anybody there? Every step seemed to plant me deeper in the ground.

"Hello? Hello? Um, is this the Arts faculty?"

All of a sudden I saw something inexplicably round and black fall from the sky and the next thing I knew I was face down on the turf, a tremendous ringing in one ear, something cold and wet in the other. Momentarily I had no idea what was going on. There was movement all around me, but where the lines were going I couldn't really say.

"Sir? Sir, are you alright?"

I tried opening one eye but only the ball was in focus: everything else was snow and earth and blur.

"Sir? Sir? Oh sir, what have you done?"

Before I could reply an enormous helmeted figure was looming over me, his head as smooth and rounded as a hard-boiled egg.

"Um, you don't happen to see my glasses do you?" I asked. "I can't see a thing without them…"

"Sir? Sir your head is hurt very bad. Here, let me help you…" The voice sounded African rather than American and his helmet was as big as the moon.

"They're a reddy-brown with a kind of oval lens…"

"This way, please, your head is very sore…"

To the accompaniment of yells and jeers ("Man *down*!") the footballer and his egg picked me up and helped me across the field, plopping me down at the bottom of some cold, wet steps.

"I'm very sorry to interrupt your game," I said. "I'm sure you were having a splendid time…"

"Sir? Sir, I think your ear is broken…"

"You and your… brothers…"

"Sir?"

"Your tribe…"

"Sir, your face is a funny shape. Please let me get help…"

"No, no, I don't want to be a bother. Is this reception? You're very kind. I'll be fine now. Thank you ever so much, I'm so awfully sorry…"

"Professor, I really think you should sit here and…"

His voice was very soft, like a hospital doctor imparting bad news.

"You've been far too kind already…"

"Sir? Your suit is very thin and very cheap…"

"I'm fine, I'm fine…"

On the other side of the doors it looked like some kind of lobby or reception, though without my glasses I couldn't be one hundred percent sure.

"Well, thank you again…"

"Sir?"

I didn't look back.

"Sir? Sir, wait…"

Ignoring his cries, I struggled to my feet and crawled up the steps and through a set of double doors. Inside there were tables, a chairs, an office of some kind. Through the ringing in my ears I heard movement someplace (things were still kind of hazy) and then a low, feminine voice.

"Hi, hi, I'll be with you in a minute."

I climbed back to my feet and tried to pull my suit back together. When I looked back through the doors the egg and the other stick figures had vanished.

"The snows," I whispered. "The Snows of Kilimanjaro…"

"Hello?"

"Ah, I'm Professor Milton, I…"

"Sorry, Professor…?"

Oddly, the voice didn't seem to come from the body behind the desk but someplace off to my left.

"Um, Milton. M.I.L…"

"Professor Milton? I'll be with you in a moment. I'm just getting together your paperwork…"

As I crept closer to the girl on the desk, I realised she was, in fact, a coat-stand.

"Did you have a good trip? You're lucky to get here before the snow came…"

"Um, yes I am…"

I hovered uncertainly, a weird pulsing on one side of my brain.

"So how did you get here? Drive?"

"Ah, no, no, I got a cab…"

"Walla Walla has cabs? Oh, hold on, I need to photocopy this… You've had your schedule, right?"

"Ah, yes, everybody has been tremendously helpful…"

When I looked down I realised I was emitting melt water all over the desk. There was a big puddle by a clip board and I was dripping onto a stack of white sheets. When I tried to wipe it away a muddy print appeared in the centre of the papers and when I wiped this an even bigger smear appeared on top.

"You can have a bite to eat with the faculty and then the lecture is at seven. Have you seen the posters?"

"Posters?"

My hands seemed coated in some kind of clay from the playing field. Whatever I touched turned to khaki. Shuffling the papers together to hide the stain, I somehow knocked over a coffee mug instead.

"I've just made a coffee – d'you want one?"

"No, no, m'okay…"

The coffee seemed to mix with the mud and the snow. I footered around with the papers but nothing seemed to soak up anything.

"I won't be long. I just need to process your tax and insurance…"

"You take your time…"

I squinted and surveyed the scene through purblind eyes. It wasn't pretty. Papers were scrunched into balls. The coffee mug was on its side. The whole desk was turning brown, like some kind of finger painting or dirty protest. "I'm fine here…" I ran my fingers through my hair and tried perching awkwardly atop the mess. Hot coffee trickled through my seat.

"Oh, no, everything's here. I'll just need your signature and… Professor Milton?"

The voice entered the room but all I could make out was a hazy pink circle and a tiny red blob. The circle paused and hovered in front of me.

"Professor Milton?"

The voice wavered and I watched the red blob open and close; it seemed to be considering whether to scream or call the cops instead.

"Ah, Professor Milton," it finally said uncertainly. "So – how are you?"

The circle turned out to be Hanka Levenstein, my campus guide and academic point of contact. Ms. Levenstein was a postgraduate teaching assistant in Advanced Linguistics and (from what I could see) small, round and fuzzy as a peach. She seemed a little worried about my mishap on the sports' field but – through gritted teeth – I assured her the swelling would go down with time.

"And your ear?"

"Ear?"

The lecture was scheduled for seven and I had a good hour or so before I had to go and meet the other faculty members. I asked Hanka if I could go to my room to change and she ran her hand over my suit and said, "Mm…"

"Your paper is in the Kretscher Hall, right next to the Havstad Alumni Center. Have you seen it yet? By the Acme Arts Pavilion?"

"Ah…"

"Don't worry, I'll take you there in plenty of time. Do you have any special dietary, spiritual or physical needs?"

"Diet?"

"Professor Milton, are you *sure* you're okay?"

Hanka led me back out into the snow, crossing a strange angular courtyard before heading in the direction of the white colonial-style

21

buildings I'd spotted from the cab. The path was very narrow and the snow very wet.

"Is that a totem pole?" I asked.

"Hm? Oh, yeah, yeah…"

"Does it look like it's leaning to you?"

"Well…" Hanka's pink dot moved a little closer. "Maybe from where you're standing…"

Past the totem pole we passed a glass cafeteria, a huge, squat library, and then wandered out into another maze of white paths and brown, brick squares. Ms. Levenstein smelled, not unpleasantly, like a freshly-cleaned stationery cupboard.

"So – you from Walla Walla?"

She laughed. "Me? No, not exactly…"

"Washington State?"

"I'm here doing my research on the papers of Mikha'il Na'ima – you know, *The Book of Mirdad*?"

"Ah…"

"Well, he wrote here – in Walla Walla Washington. '*Ask not of things to shed their veils. Unveil yourself and things will be unveiled…*' I mean, you've heard of him, right?"

"Mm…" We passed more snow, blocks, abstract sculptures. Without my glasses *everything* was an abstract sculpture. "I guess… is he of your persuasion?"

"My persuasion?"

"Um, your tribe. The tribe of Israel…"

"I'm from Delaware not a tribe…"

"Delaware?" Something chimed enigmatically in my brain, but my ear was aching too hard for me to process it. In the meantime Hanka's dot was glowing angrily.

"No Professor Milton. He's not from my tribe…"

"Oh, I didn't…"

We passed some kind of fuzzy mural, an indistinct seating area, blobs and dabs. There were thick black stripes but none of them seemed to join up.

"And you sir? What's your paper on?"

"Mine? Um, it's…"

At that moment a gang of students abruptly pushed past us, hollering and laughing and pelting each other with snow. I repeated the title but Ms. Levenstein didn't seem to catch it.

"It sounds very, ah, interesting…"

I smiled and made a dismissive gesture with my hand. "Oh, it's not very good…"

"Really? Well, okay. Anyway, here we are." We'd stopped outside some kind of cabin, Hanka's soft pink dot floating in the air.

"This is the key – you've got the run of the whole place so make yourself at home. There's no number, but your place is pretty easy to spot, right? Shall we say I'll see you in fifty?"

"Fifty?"

I stared up at the small wooden cabin, its ramshackle veranda buffeted by the wind. O, how would this survive a storm?

"I'm sure you need to, well, freshen up…"

"You've been very kind Miss Na'ime…"

"Levenstein."

"Yes."

Her balloon bobbed up and down.

"Yes it is."

The cabin was like something out of *Little House on the Prairie* – all wood and rugs and chequered throws. The seats were very soft and the towels very coarse. The walls were decorated with what looked like some kind of indigenous art, but, to be honest, it was kind of hard to tell. Without my glasses anything beyond the end of my nose might as well have been half way round the world.

In the bathroom I gingerly washed my face, taking care not to stare too closely at my reflection; there was a huge bruise on one side of my head and my left eye was closed up like a dog's arse. My hair was sticky with clay but I was too tired to do anything about it right now; instead I stuck the wiry strands back down and wiped the worst of the mess onto a clean towel. It was only when I went to find a fresh shirt that I realised my bag was missing – and with it my toothbrush, my socks, my talk...

Immediately a jolt of fear ripped through me; how would I give my paper now? I must have dropped my bag on the sports field when the big black shape fell from the sky. But how was I going to find it now? I thought mournfully of my belongings left abandoned in the gloom, bereft amongst the snow, the mud, the football players. Ho, what a predicament, what a catastrophe! Outside the window, the snow fell sideways, the campus as empty as a whiteboard...

My first instinct was to wait for Ms. Levenstein: but then her people had already seen such trouble, why make more? Instead I picked up my shoes and poured the melt water into a sink. The emptiness beyond the paths terrified me, but the idea of delivering my paper without prompts terrified me more. Mm, my memory stick, my slides, my jokes! Still, if I could just find my way to the sports field then perhaps everything would be all right; I mean, all I had to do was follow my footprints in the snow, make my way back through the labyrinth, re-trace the way back home. Sure, there was clay on the floor and blood on the towels, but I couldn't worry about that now...

Unfortunately one brown block looked very much like another, the windows dark and the path tied up in knots. Instead of asking for help, I shuffled uncertainly toward a line of ill-marked trees, my shoes two puddles, my suit as wet as a sail. Pretty soon even the dull, brown blocks started to disappear; shapes falling into one another, distances shrinking, lines dripping into odd, unsteady dots. When I took a step away from the path it was as if some kind of crevasse were opening up beneath me; then, when I looked for a way back, the path had somehow entirely disappeared, the ground the very definition of nothingness.

"Er, hello?" I said.

Snow whipped up from the spaces on either side and there was no telling where the campus buildings began or ended. The odd pyramid shaped building was barely discernable now, coming and going through the snow.

"Hello?"

All of a sudden a large, obscure shape appeared next to me in the murk. Was it a figure or the largest snowflake I'd ever seen in my life? I blinked twice, stamped my feet, and suddenly glimpsed something brown and hairy, rolling like a boulder from the corner of my eye. What was it: ursine, lupine, other? It seemed awful close – as close as a razor and a chin. When the ball rolled back I smelled matted fur, fetid breath, a thick animally musk; then the thing rolled off again, circling back before re-appearing behind a long, black line. Yes, a circle, a blur, a ball. I peered myopically into the gloom, trying to make out its shape. Was that a nose? If so, the rest was sure to follow…

Breathing hard, I hid behind a tree and listened to the sound of heavy paws padding through the slush. Yes, the thing had mass, bulk, weight; how would my wool mix protect me against that? The snow came down and then seemed to rise upwards. There were no signs anywhere.

"Hello?"

Whatever that thing was, I wasn't going to stay there and saddle it; instead I stepped back into my own footprints, my shoes slipping and sliding, great flipper-shaped marks in the snow. Had it seen me, heard me, picked up the scent of my Boss for Men? Snow covered the ground and snow covered the sky and after a while the thing seemed to disappear too, its snuffling becoming more muffled, its nose (nose?) no bigger than a berry.

"Good boy," I whispered. "There's a good lad…"

I backed slowly away and found myself back on the walkway between blocks, midway between a petrified sign post and one of those big brown cinder blocks. The thing? Who knows. I fancied I could still hear it out there, shuffling around in the snow, snorting, coughing, sniffing at a tree.

"Shhh," I said. "Good dog…"

My cheeks were cold, my bruise ached, my hands shook; also something in my ear was weeping. Dazed, I crept past cabins, a gymnasium, some kind of dotted line, and then there I was: back at the cabin where I started. I put my key in the lock but for some reason it wouldn't go in. I tried the door but it refused to open. I jiggled my key a little, but still, no go. Ah, what now, I thought – were even my towels to be taken from me? I tried it again but the door stayed stubbornly shut. Mewing softly, I followed the clapboard wall round to a window. There were shapes inside but I couldn't say what exactly: wardrobes maybe? Trying to see better, I placed my good eye right next to the glass and that's when screaming started – for the most part female but with some manly shouts thrown in. What they were yelling about, I don't know – something about an intruder, or a pervert or suchlike. All of a sudden the cries grew louder and I sprinted for a nearby bush, rolling myself up like a ball.

"What was that?" someone asked. "Some kind of… thing?"

I crouched lower, the greenery tickling my chin.

"Where did it go? Did you see it?"

26

I jammed my head between my thighs and thought about nothing. "What *was* it?"

To be honest, with no glasses and amongst falling snow, it was very hard to see. The figures – or specks – seemed to split up, dividing themselves into vague, uncertain shadows, some going left, others turning right.

"Jerk-off Weirdo," somebody yelled. "Crazy freak!"

The blobs and specks were in a state of great excitement and I lingered a little longer, my face buried deep in the foliage.

"This way!" a gruff American baritone shouted. "He's right over here!"

"There! No, there – c'mon, he's getting away!"

Fortunately the scribble of figures seemed to be following the wrong target, and after a few minutes the sound of their yells and footfall was swallowed up by the snow.

Ah, but were they really gone? Slowly I crawled out of the mulch and felt my way around the outside of the cabin: no, this one wasn't mine, nor the next block along... It was only late afternoon but the light of the world was already going out. The sky was closed, the snow the colour of a duffle-coat. Whither the academic life, I thought, whither the life of the mind? I was cold, wet, some kind of greenery caught in my hair. Ah me: five years working on my book for *this*?

From the student block I crept awkwardly from dot to dot, slipping soundlessly in the murk. Without my glasses the world sunk into a deep, dark pool; shapes floated past, blobs came apart, spills turned into less and less distinguishable things. Walla Walla: Many Waters. The only thing that truly stood out was the totem pole and I staggered toward it almost gratefully, hanging on to it for dear life. Close up – and by this I mean the length of my nose – the faces seemed distorted, cruel, monstrous. The one closest to me had spiked hair, an evil squinty eye, some kind of horrendous lump on the side of its head. It stuck its tongue out so I stuck my tongue out too; it was only when I felt my tip make contact with the freezing trunk that I realised my terrible mistake.

"Urgggh," I said. "Plllbbb, urgggh."

My tongue wouldn't let go. Saliva dribbled from my mouth. The cold seemed to travel up along my tongue and down into my cheap suit.

"Urr…" I said.

I was, shall we say, not entirely unaware of the foolishness of my position: tongue stuck, face red, eyes flapping wildly. The beast, Ms. Levenstein, the angry mob: pff, who did I want to find me least?

In the end I was found by two Chinese guys, shyly holding hands as they walked between class. They kindly poured hot tea down my face from their thermos, the liquid strong and smoky.

"That ith moth ethtraordinarily good oth you," I said.

One was called Wai So Nao, the other Shun Ding, though, to be honest, I might have misheard; my ear was closed up like a sprout.

They seemed more concerned about my jacket than my tongue but perked up when I said I was from the UK.

"Britain? Great Britain?"

"Um…"

They looked excitedly at each other and then one of them – Shun? – rooted urgently through his bag.

"Eastenders, yes? Doctor Who?"

"I…"

"Dancing! Come dancing! Come dancing with me!"

"Thath's very kind buth…"

He emerged from his bag with a big glossy picture of Princess Di. He looked at me expectantly.

"Yes?"

"Um, yes…"

They obviously wanted something but for the life of me I couldn't work out what.

"Please, yes?"

I stared at the picture, stared at them, and then reluctantly felt in my jacket for a pen.

"Well…"

Awkwardly I scribbled my name – along with a polite best wishes – over her face and then looked back at my new friends.

"Um, thath right?"

The guys stared at the picture and then back at me. Their faces swiftly clouded over. Wai looked on the verge of tears.

"Sir, sir, what have you done?"

"Well, I hath to be going…" I said. "I hath to give a paper…"

"Paper?"

Shun looked back at my squiggle and frowned. My pen had obliterated Diana's shy smile. Uncertainly I started to back away.

"Sir, my photo…"

I looked at the picture and made some kind of meaningless gesture.

"Well, cheerio. Thankth for the tea… thelly good."

Their eyes seemed to bore into my soul.

"Um…"

Tch, why did they look so downcast? Why so sad?

"Thelly good. Thelly nice. Bye bye."

And with that I ran, sprinting off into the snow without so much as a backwards glance.


Anyway, at some point I must have left the campus behind me 'cause after a while I passed a long white wall (or snowdrift) and found myself at a busy intersection, trucks and farm vehicles spraying the sidewalk with slush. It was some kind of highway – perhaps the one I'd arrived at with Charlie, perhaps another, I couldn't really tell. The light was starting to go by now. The wheels of the trucks were very large, the space between them very small.

Bespattered and exhausted, I drifted along the road for a while and then ducked inside a nearby diner, the red, plastic seats occupied by a series of truly enormous behinds. Um, I'd never seen such acreage of jeans in my life! The guy at the counter was as wide as a hay bale and even the smallest of the diners looked like they'd been lowered into their seats by crane.

I nodded politely to the waitress (no sylph, herself) and made for the first empty booth. But no sooner had the seat of my (discounted) pants made contact with the plastic when one of the huge wide farmers turned to stare at me.

"That's Mr West's seat, mister."

"Sorry?"

"Mr West. You've seen *Batman* haven't you?"

"Ah…"

"Well, that's his seat."

"Thorry, my mithake."

I moved sideways and collapsed into the next booth along; the view wasn't as good as from Mr West's seat, but I couldn't see much anyway. When the waitress appeared the whole diner was eclipsed.

"What can I get you?"

"Mm?"

For a brief moment I couldn't work out where I was or what on earth I was doing here. Unable to think of an answer I pointed to the menu and smiled thinly.

"Patty O Link?" she snapped, brandishing her red pen aggressively.

"Thorry?"

"Patty O Link?"

"Um, no, I…"

"How do you want your dogs – patty or link?"

My smile stretched to snapping point.

"Link?"

"Link?"

"Ah, that thounth lovely…"

Steaming hot coffee appeared in a receptacle next to my hand and I squinted at the waitress through my good eye.

"Thank you, thank you, thath very kind…"

The waitress sailed off down the aisle and I stared down at the table struggling to recover my thoughts. I tried looking at my watch but I must have broken it in my fall. Had I missed the faculty meal? Was Ms. Levenstein even now combing the campus for me, her massed files blowing in the wind? Outside the last few rays of light were slipping out through the cracks, the snow falling on soft, wet clumps.

"That's some buster you took, fella."

"Mm?"

Adam West's pal, the wide-screen farmer, had slid his seat over to look at me.

"Your eye. Some lump. What happened, you kicked by a horse?"

"Ah, no, no, not theally…"

The farmer scraped his seat closer. "Where'd you get that accent, fella? You not from round these parts?"

"Um, no, no. I'm juth visiting…"

"Yeah?"

The farmer paused, expectantly. The plastic on his seat squeaked.

"England. Th'UK."

"England? You mean like Lady Di?"

"Mm, I…"

"A tragedy, a real tragedy. She was a fine-looking piece, you know?"

"Yeth," I said, staring at his jaws methodically chewing. "Yeth, he was."

"So whatcha doing in these parts, fella – buying or selling?"

He seemed to be looking for a very precise answer but I couldn't work out what it was.

"Thelling?"

He nodded as if satisfied and looked contentedly down at his meat; his neck was as wide and furrowed as a tyre.

"Everybody's buying or selling in this world; anyone says otherwise, they just haven't picked up the cheque."

"Mm…"

"You here on your own?"

For some reason I thought of Ms. Levenstein, but then realised that I had absolutely no idea where I might find her.

"Well, yeth, I gueth…"

"Got any contacts?"

"Contacth?"

"Customers?"

"Ah…"

"A man in need will always seek out the man who has. But the real trick is to convince the man who doesn't need that he's really in need of something…"

"Mm."

The farmer winked at me and then went back to his steak.

"Ah, I'm giving a paper…"

The farmer nodded but kept on chewing.

"Thith paper, ith, um…"

The guy didn't look up and I fell silent, staring intently at my truly filthy finger nails. When I looked up a second farmer had taken his place.

"Hey fella," he demanded. "Yeah, buddy, I'm talking to you…"

32

All I could make out was a ruddy face, blurry eyes, a great wide brush of a 'tache.

"Tho thorry…"

"What have you done to Mr West's chair?" he hollered. "Take a look fella…"

"Um…"

"Ed, you leave this here fella alone," said the first farmer, sliding back over. "His Princess Di has passed…"

"Princess Di?"

"I…"

"You know: the Queen of England?"

"What's the Queen of England got to do with anything? There's seven shades of shit on Mr West's chair."

"Um, fellas…"

"Ed, quit your yelling and sit. He's fresh in town and…"

"I ain't sitting till he cleans up his mess. You seen *Batman* mister?"

"Yeth, yeth, I…"

"The *real* Batman?"

"Well…"

My waitress was back, but there was no way both she and Ed were going to fit down one aisle.

"Move over Ed, I got this fella's dogs…"

"You better go and fetch a mop fella, 'cause I ain't sittin'…"

"Ed, you heard about Princess Di…"

I looked back at Mr West's booth and then noticed a great crush of blue-ish figures massing outside. But what were they doing out there, and what did they want? I peered past Ed and the blobs peered in.

"These dogs are getting cold…"

"You don't think Batman deserves some respect?"

"Ed, eat your eggs…"

One guy – a blue smear of indeterminate stature – seemed to be gesturing at the diner and repeating something to his friends. Somebody at the back jumped up and down and a third blob shook his fist theatrically.

"Um, fellath? I…"

One of the crowd seemed to be holding a baseball bat, another a rope. My insides gave a sudden spasm. Here or Delaware, I thought, here or Delaware…

"Guyth? Guyth, I…"

No, there was no doubt about it, some kind of mob was gathering – the shadows, the streaks, the bats. Was that a ball or a head? "Sweet!" somebody yelled.

"I really hath to…"

"Sweet, sweet, sweet!" echoed the chant. The window was a mess of blue. What looked like rocks were being tossed from mitt to mitt, flags and banners flapping in the wind.

"Fellath…"

All of a sudden the door of the diner flew open and I gave a tremendous jerk, my arms and legs springing up like a puppet. I don't know what happened; plates fell and condiments shattered. The first farmer tried to get up but his gut seemed wedged in place. Dogs and sauce dripped from the second farmer's 'tache.

"Um…"

I tried flicking at the farmers with my napkin, but it wasn't any use. Coffee dripped from every surface. There was some degree of bad language.

"Th'okay, th'okay, no need to get up…"

Good eye squinting and bad ear closed up, I backed slowly toward the men's room locking the door behind me. However I only had time to splash water on my face and smooth down my tie when the banging started. Whoever was there sounded kind of agitated.

The water was hot and the banging very loud.

"Juth a minute," I said. "I won't be long…"

Bruise throbbing, I placed one foot in the sink and yanked myself up to the bathroom window. The sink gave way and suddenly there was water everywhere. If anything the banging on the door sounded even louder.

"Guyth, guyth, I'd leath it a minute…" I said.

Water sprayed off the tiles, the wash unit, and out under the floor. A little concerned now, I yanked the tiny window open and squeezed my wool mix through. Behind me, the banging increased in tempo. Many waters flowed. But what did I care? I was free, free! Out in the alley the snow was blowing sideways and I realised I'd torn my pants lengthways on the latch. One shoe was taking in water and the other frothed mysteriously. Atop my skull, the bruise throbbed like an evil toad. But what to do? The alleyway was very slippery. Behind me a frozen line of washing slow-hand-clapped in the wind.

On the main drag I could see the blue-ish mob, some carrying sticks, others flags or pennants. On the head of some kind of effigy some kind of onion squatted maliciously. Backtracking, I found myself in a maze of outbuildings at the rear of Main Street, picking my way through the slush past snow covered bins and frozen gates. A strong smell of fried food came from one block, the tang of urine from another. And alongside it: what was that? Something earthy, animally, sour? Unsettled, I turned a corner and suddenly saw a whole line of posters, all displaying the same, slightly distracted looking mug. Sad eyes, lopsided face, weak chin; I tip-toed forward and inspected the features close up. Yes, it was definitely me: but what was I doing there? 'Neath the picture – two good eyes, two normal ears – the letters danced and swam, breaking up into squiggles, lines, blots. I leaned in closer – the posters were stuck to what looked to be a boarded-up drug store – and then retreated for a better view. But no matter where I stood I couldn't make out the text at all: only the face was familiar, the eyebrows, glasses, my uncertain chin.

Just then I heard a fearful commotion and saw a mass of stick figures and overweight farmers advancing menacingly, moving along the alley as if one. "Sweet, sweet!" they chanted.

I waved weakly but my blood ran cold.

"Guyth, guyth, I can explain…"

"Sweet! Sweet!"

"Um…"

I stumbled back from the kerb and glanced up just as a large blocky automobile rounded the corner, skidding to a halt mere inches in front of me. A horn blew and various blobs turned. A dash of blue appeared at the corner of the page.

"Mister?" asked the driver. "Mister, is that you?"

Some guys with bats were pointing at the cab and yelling. Farmers tumbled in the slush. Bon Jovi was playing very loud.

"Mister, I will get *you*…"

Charlie opened the door and I jumped in. My lump was throbbing, trousers flapping like a saloon door. He looked me up and down with an expression of infinite sadness.

"Oh Mister," he said, "that suit…"

# 3

Charlie took a left at the intersection, the traffic lights winking, the trucks rolling through the slush like ships. There were blue blobs everywhere and I kept my head between my knees.

"Sweets and Blue-jackets," said Charlie.

"Thorry?"

"Sweets and Blue-jackets. How sweet you is…" said Charlie, gravely.

I blinked.

"Yeth," I said. "Thath right…"

Although I felt a little better sitting in the febreezed comfort of Charlie's cab, I couldn't help noticing him gazing in his rear view mirror, anxiously sizing up the upholstery and the state of my clothes.

"Um, I had a bit oth a trip…" I said.

"Trip?"

"A thall: well, a tumble, really…."

My tongue seemed to be swelling and I had trouble squeezing the words out. Inside the dark cave of my mouth my tongue lay like a thick, black snake.

"Mister? Mister, do you want the airport?"

I shook my head and gestured hesitantly toward the campus. I didn't know where else to go. Posters were everywhere. There I was in the window of the bait and dry good store, betwixt the bear traps and the rifles: and there I was again at the grain wholesalers – same picture, same words, same expression. But what did the words say? Wanted, dangerous, lost? The shadows gave me a thick beard and a yellow bulb illuminated the odd thrust of my chin.

Charlie looked at me with a certain degree of concern.

"Mister? You cannot give somebody paper, looking like that. Who would want such paper? Your pants are torn and your ear is very red."

Charlie took another hard left and I wondered where we were going. The stores looked closed, the snow strangely blue.

"You should come with me. Tidy up. Trust me – no one would want paper from pants such as these. My home is very close. Ten minutes. I have pants and socks…" Charlie made a funny clicking sound with his teeth.

"Mm? Thmmth mmth…"

"Mister? Your ear is sticky and your fly unstitched…"

"Mthhh…"

We passed a bible warehouse, a cement works, a dairy. Oddly there didn't seem to be any cows around at all.

"Brotherth? Thmm, uhh, mmm…"

"Brother? My brother's store is a good hour from here. Golf equipment. You do not want his pants."

"Noo, mm, thmmm, mth…"

Charlie looked at me pityingly. "We're nearly there. You can wash your face and put something on that ear. Rest too…"

In the gloom I could make out great boxy looking wooden houses, as well as the occasional shack or mobile home. Some kind of mark or smear circled above us, though whether it was some kind of vulture or a small black cloud I couldn't really tell. The night rolled in like the tide. A water tower wobbled on long crutches. A cat lazily crossed the road.

"My pants are blue. A dress suit. Very nice cut…"

I didn't know what to say. Charlie's place was a plain one-storey box, with a gravel driveway and a pick-up truck parked out front on blocks.

"Luisa is at work. I'll let you clean up…"

"Mmm, th, th, th…"

"Come in, wipe your feet. No, not there – there."

Charlie's lounge was dominated by a drum kit, a huge, baggy sofa and a truly enormous flat screen TV. VHS boxes lay everywhere. On one side of the room a framed Guns N' Roses album hung next to a pale water colour of a desert; on the other, there was a startlingly realistic painting of a horse which seemed splendidly well endowed. Charlie switched on a Tiffany lamp and examined my face cautiously.

"Mister? Your face is very bad. Sit down and I'll fetch something. Don't go anywhere. There is something bad in your ear."

"Mthuu, mm, mm."

"Stay. I'll be back in a moment. Sit, sit…"

I sat. I could hear movement in some back room, but my neck and shoulders ached and I couldn't bear to turn. Instead I flicked through some magazine about American football, tossing it aside to pick up a coaster with a picture of some kind of bird I had never seen before in my life. 'So far from home,' I thought. Just about everything about me seemed to ache: my eyes, my limbs, my lump. One arm of my suit had come unstitched. My left shoe bubbled alarmingly. There was an enormous tear in my trousers at groin-level, rather as if I'd been attacked by a wild bear. Had I been attacked by a bear? The day had gone on so long I couldn't really remember…

All I could be sure about was how tired I was. I carefully eased myself back on the sofa, rested my eyes, and after a few minutes the room seemed to drift away, retreating from view like a train backing into a tunnel. In one corner of the room I glimpsed Ms. Levenstein sifting through her files in her underwear. "Logic is a crutch for the cripple, a burden for the swift of foot, and a greater burden still for the wise," she recited, her enormous ring-binder clicking shut. I tried to speak but my tongue lay in my mouth like a broken arm. The eyelids on the totem pole winked. Adam West nodded. "But what sea is this?" I asked. "Where the further shore?" Mr West smiled. "And yet – how much more infinite a sea is man?" he asked, flicking through the sports pages of a glossy magazine. "Be not so childish as to measure him from head to foot and think that you have found his borders." When he removed his mask I saw a mug strangely familiar from a wall of posters, a face swollen and distorted, a great blue onion in place of a head…

When I opened my eyes I was lying spread out on Charlie's couch, my clothes damp and my hair stuck up in a tuft. It was difficult to know how much time had gone: minutes, hours, years? The house felt like a box adrift in a sea of nothing. The window was a great black hole, the TV also. I pushed myself up and forced my legs to shuffle toward the kitchen. It was all strangely orange in there, a single mug and saucer left on the draining board, the torn flap of an Oreo packet. Of Charlie, there was no sign. There were no Native American taxi-drivers anywhere. From the kitchen I wandered into a dim utility room and then opened a door to some kind of granny flat, the door creaking a little as I pushed. Inside was a single bed, a chair, a night-table and a chest of drawers. Some kind of Indian quilt laid on the bed, and under that a tiny, wizened figure was laid out like a board, two yellow feet poking out of the opposite end. Her head was nearly bald with just a few colourless wisps clinging to the skull, cheeks sunken, eyes blank and watery, its mouth a dark sucking hole. But the worst thing about her was her skin: more yellow than pink, like a cheap candle or a plucked chicken, the spots on her cheeks like tea-stains. How old was she? Old enough to have spanked Sitting Bull when he was a little boy! The old lady didn't have lips, just a spout.

"Who is it?" she asked. "Who's there?"

I tried to answer but my tongue filled my mouth like a shoe. Instead I bent over and flapped my arms as if signally from very far away.

"Who are you? What do you want?"

I tried to say something about Charlie and my trousers and my paper, but all that came out was a strange, strangled mumble, as if my mouth were a dry river-bed, the bottom full of stones.

The mummified head nodded, some kind of cloud drifting across her two blind eyes.

"What you need is some kind of stock," she said. "Something convertible, transferable. Stock you can liquidate if you need to, then sell high and buy low. Listen to me, mister! Some kind of stock you can move around…"

"Mmmth," I managed.

"Don't waste your time worrying about storage. Why bury the cat? Keep everything on display. If a fella can't see it then he can't buy it. But if you can't shift it then swap it without a second thought. There's no such thing as a sentimental seller – make sure the tear is in the other fella's eye…"

I smiled and patted the quilt sympathetically. Her sheets smelt of camphor, her mouth like an open grave.

"That's the trick, sonny. Let the other guy lift and you provide the bag…"

The old lady's lids started to become quite agitated, though I wasn't sure she could see me; mind you, without my glasses I could barely see her either.

"First sell the hole and then sell the dirt…"

"Mm. Mmth thur mmumf…"

The old dear nodded and then lay still. We looked at each other for a few minutes but it was pretty clear the audience was over. Her eyes closed, her limbs stiffened, the quilt lay still. I straightened up, rubbed my eyes, and when I glanced back a big black turkey was standing there, looking tremendously important.

It was, it must be said, a big old bird to be standing there in an old lady's bedroom, with enormously broad legs and a truly impressive wingspan. Its pink head shone and its wattle quivered expectantly. Taking his time, the turkey slowly checked me out and then strode out the way he came, everything about him suggesting that he was engaged in a very important activity indeed.

What could I do but follow him? Patting the old lady's blanket I wandered back over to the door and stumbled after him, the turkey's tail feathers wagging and his clawed feet almost seeming to strut. When he turned round to look at me, his eyes looked like two round, black beans.

"Mmmffuh muff uh…" I suggested.

Alas, the turkey didn't look too impressed. His head twitched, his eyes blinked, and he strode out through an open door onto some kind of veranda, his claws making queer little scratching noises on the wood.

The snow seemed to have stopped, but it was still terribly cold. A few cars slid past on the nearby turnpike, and the turkey wandered up and down the veranda as if waiting for a bus. When he reached the far end of the porch a security light suddenly clicked on and I could see Charlie talking to his neighbour over by the back fence, Charlie holding a poster and the guy gripping the end of what looked from where I was standing to be the loop of a rope. The guy's hands were *enormous*. I looked at the turkey, and the turkey looked at me and we both agreed: time to go.

One eye on Charlie and one eye on his neighbour, the pair of us backed carefully away, trying to make ourselves as small as possible. When I slipped on the stairs, the turkey fanned his tail angrily, as if to say, 'What now, you idiot? Lie low!' Only when we reached the driveway did we take off in a mad tangle, slipping and sliding as we plunged awkwardly into the snow.

Charlie yelled something but I didn't hang around to listen. Instead I fled from the road and made towards a patch of waste-ground, my feet flopping awkwardly between puddles, my arms flapping like a bird. It wasn't long before the houses – and Charlie's bungalow – started to recede. The road vanished and streetlights blurred. I lost Mr Turkey by a row of half-built retail units, my left shoe in a snowdrift at the back of a 7-11. By this time Charlie and his cab were long gone – hell, Walla Walla seemed to have gone too. Lights thinned and disappeared and then there was just *this*. Whatever *this* might be…

So there I was – lump swelling, eye squinting, ear leaking. Not even my trousers wanted to play ball. First a few fat snowflakes drifted past, then a sudden fistful, finally a great white clump, blotting out the sky, the ground, me. One moment there was a fence and some kind of track, the next – not. Lines became scribbles, things mere specks, the outlines of the city no more than blobs or streaks. Footprints above me, clouds down below. Feet, shoes, socks: all gone. But if they were gone then where was I? Only my aches and pains afforded me purchase – my knees throbbing, fingers frozen, the lump sitting on my head like a hat. But why hat? There was no hat. Nor suit nor papers too…

To be honest, I didn't know where I was. Street lamps came and went. Silhouettes appeared then turned into puddles. A wall turned into a dribble, a stream, a ditch. How difficult it was to be sure of anything! My head was an overstuffed pillow, my ear – we shall not speak of my ear. Sounds seeped down into darkness. Light hid like a cat. 'Ho,' I thought, 'a man could freeze to death in this!' When I opened my mouth my tongue lay numb and lifeless, a frozen joint of meat. 'I have placed myself,' I reflected, 'out of the circle of things, out of the circle-horizon in which all the forms of nature are locked.' O such emptiness, such space! Then, just when I thought I recognised some kind of outbuilding or barn, my last shoe stumbled on an incline and I plunged headfirst into a snowdrift, sliding down into the whiteness like a drunk flopping down on a soft, fluffy bed.

O me – who could have guessed that so much white could be so dark? In an instance my mouth was covered, my eyes pressed shut. Only my lump poked free from the surface, like a beacon, like Mount Ararat, vultures circling above it, looking for a place to land. My lump, my lump, my red and throbbing hump! Otherwise the drift packed me tight like Styrofoam. Ho, I thought, how would Ms. Levenstein find me, how would anyone get to hear my paper now? And then I felt it: solid, comforting, familiar, its leatherette finish redolent of well-stocked libraries, learned discussion, the earnest life of the mind. Tch, could it be? Scarcely believing my luck I pushed awkwardly against it, running my purplish fingers along its surface. 'Oh my bag,' I wept. 'My true and trusted friend.' I rolled again, case in hand, and felt one leg push itself free. A further roll and I felt myself sliding to one side of the ditch. One more roll and I skittered down another embankment, a great avalanche of snow coming with me. 'Oh, not now,' I thought, 'not when the way out is so close…'

I rolled and rolled and when I opened my eyes I saw a kind of glow – at first just a halo or glimmer, but then a figure, a woman, her shape becoming clearer and clearer as if some kind of lens had dropped in front of my one good eye. When she brushed the snow gently from my cheek her hands felt cool, refined, ladylike. The sapphire in her engagement ring winked like an eye.

"Hello?" I whispered. "Hello, is that you?"

She smiled the same sad smile she'd smiled in a million

photographs and helped me to my feet, the very air illuminated around her, like the soft glow of a desk lamp in a cosy room. Blue dress, blue scarf, blonde fringe. Diana!

"Mth."

She placed one hand on my lips and the other on my lump; a third hand appeared as if from nowhere and ministered tenderly to my ear. O my princess! Her face rose high above me and I felt her gather me gently in her arms and carry me far from the snowdrift, up, up, toward the light. O, how soft her hands, how satiny the fabric of her dress! I wanted to ask about my lost shoe but it didn't seem right somehow – not with socks like mine. Instead I allowed her to pat and caress me, bearing me further and further from the playing fields until we were someplace high in the sky, drifting above the soft security lights of the campus itself.

"The Kretscher Hall," I whispered. "Just next to the Havstad Alumni Centre."

Diana cupped her mouth demurely; her face was small, round and pinky, her feet amazingly tiny – just dots. As we neared the maze of brown block buildings I could follow the occasional streak rolling like ink across the snowfield, the blurs and blobs forming scribbles, signs, words. Everything – the accommodation blocks, the totem pole, the labyrinth of paths – seemed to vibrate with a mysterious meaning, impossible to translate. It was as if each door opened onto another door, and beyond that another door again. And then?

Then the next door was the door to the Arts Pavilion, and I was standing on my own in a dull and charmless lobby, my chest shaking and garments torn, Diana nowhere to be seen. But this was definitely the Arts Pavilion. Posters advertised my talk, drug drop-in centres, an 80s fashion night. I advanced along the corridor, my wet trousers clinging to me, my bag the same size and weight as a dog. 'This is it,' I thought. 'My papers, my talk, my speech...' I paused, smoothed down my tie – surprisingly unaffected by my recent misfortunes – and with a certain degree of apprehension flung open the double doors before me.

And there I was, standing to attention in my cheap wet suit, and there before me was a vast and empty hall, desks, seats, a lone over-head projector, but of hungry minds – not a bean. No, really: aside from the roaring in my ear, the whole theatre was silent. No whispers, no rustling, no clearing of youthful throats: just my slow and dignified tread as I squelched my way toward the podium, my unshod foot making a sucking noise like a sponge. Stage lights illuminated a board covered in mysterious scribbles and marks – mathematical formulae or chemical symbols or maybe even words. When I reached the front the handle of my bag came off and my valise hit the ground like a stone. 'Even this,' I reflected, staring sadly at its torso. 'Finders are keepers for but a short time...'

With as much gravitas as I could muster I bent down, retrieved my papers, and spread them on the lectern in front of me. Sure, they were a little higgledy-piggledy and not necessarily in the right order, but it was too late to worry about that now. I looked back at the empty room and waited patiently. The auditorium clock showed an unreadable hour. 'Ah, yes,' I thought, 'perhaps there's still time...'

I mean, what was I worrying about? Ms. Levenstein was probably just looking for a glass of water, the faculty assembling in the common room, bright-eyed students lining up in neat and scholarly rows. For the first time in what felt like days I felt myself relax, my breath coming easier now, my chest not quite so tight. 'Ah me,' I thought. 'I can see the whole room and there's nothing in it...'

The lights flickered, the projector hummed, I listened to the roaring in my ear. And then, just when I thought that nobody would ever enter the room – not tonight, not tomorrow, not ever – a side-door opened and I saw an enormous turkey hop awkwardly down the steps, choosing his seat with great discretion. The bird looked at me and I looked at the bird. 'You again,' we thought. 'Who knew?' The turkey eyed up my suit, my ear, my lump, its eyes saying, 'and I turned out in the snow for this?' Then, no sooner had he taken his seat, a fire-exit near the far-end opened and a vulture flapped down in a most business-like fashion, followed, I was somewhat perturbed to see, by an enormous brown bear, rolling down the aisle like a vast hairy ball.

Ho, what were they doing here, the turkey, the vulture, the bear? The birds shuffled up, the bear took his seat, and the three of them gazed at me expectantly – the bear even took out a notebook, scrunching it awkwardly in one paw. My legs felt weak, my mouth dry. I heard a pencil fall from the back row and roll all the way to the front, its descent seeming to take forever. Before my eyes letters swam like pond skaters. My slides were missing. The pages were covered in khaki.

"My brothers, my brethren, my tribe," I intoned, improvising as best I could. I paused dramatically, the very hall seeming to hold its breath. The turkey looked up, the vulture nodded, the bear took notes. "My people, my tribe, my clan! If we're all here then perhaps I might begin…"

The lights went out like a gun shot.

# Two White, One Blue

After a typically frugal lunch ('Who would get fat on this? Gandhi?') Nussbaum forsook his plate and went off to find his pills, mooching to the kitchen as a prisoner to the gallows. Ach, those pills! Two white, one blue: or was it two blue, one white? Either way, Nussbaum had to take them after every meal or his heart would fold up like a map.

Nussbaum was a tall, heavy-set man set at an oblique angle, like a train rolling slowly downhill. Such gravitas! Such bulk! You might have thought that nothing would stop such a man, but when Nussbaum opened the kitchen cupboard his little tray of pills was gone, replaced by a jar of mayonnaise and a box of something *he had never before seen in his life*. Nussbaum's only reaction was to nod. 'So it's finally happened,' he thought; 'the calamity that's been waiting for years…'

"Somebody's moved my pills," said Nussbaum, an unfamiliar numbness spreading down his left side.

"What?"

"Somebody's been here and moved my pills."

"Somebody? Somebody who?"

"I'm not casting aspersions."

"No, you tell me – somebody who?"

Ach, how could he hope to explain? A dull ache pulsed between Nussbaum's eyes and for a moment he had to steady himself on the counter. Why wouldn't they be there? Listening to his wife slurp her soup he felt a gassy burp rise up inside him. Three pills to get him through the next few hours – was that too much to ask? Only then did it occur to him that he might have left them in the bathroom sometime, between the plasters and the haemorrhoid cream maybe, or betwixt the razor-blades and oil. And yet in the cabinet – nothing. How could this be? He could picture the pills, imagine the stopper, almost read the label, yet for some reason the pills stubbornly refused to fall into his lap.

"I can't find my pills," he repeated.

"Did you look in the bedroom?"

"Why would I look in the bedroom?"

"Where else – your beard?"

"I put them in the kitchen cabinet."

"The kitchen cabinet then."

"I looked in the kitchen cabinet – somebody's moved them."

"Why would anybody move them?"

"Ask *them*," he growled. "How would I know?"

Mentally Nussbaum checked his heart, stomach and lungs: blood was still sluggishly pumping through his heart, his insides were digesting his meagre meal, and his breath came and went in sudden, chesty gusts. He was still functioning then – beyond this Nussbaum had very few plans. But where were his pills? Without them, a clot the size of a grapefruit could be forming inside him, his arteries knotting around the lump, a thick wall blocking the way to his heart. And this on a bin day too!

"Robbers! Larcenists! Thieves!" he roared.

"What are you yelling?"

"A den of vipers in my own home!"

"Do you want the neighbours to hear such nonsense?"

Nussbaum shook his head disbelievingly. Without his special pills he might drop dead at any moment and yet there was his wife, still eating soup. And this after forty years of marriage?

"Nonsense?"

"Yes, nonsense. Now come and sit down."

"Mizzy – fetch my hat. I need to go and buy pills."

His wife watched him evenly, her eyes following him across her vast expanse of soup.

"Take off your coat and look in the bedroom. Have you checked the sideboard?"

"Why would I leave them on the sideboard – in plain view for any passing crook?"

"Who would *want* your pills?"

"Intruders, drug addicts, lunatics! Also, I can't find my hat."

His wife sighed and walked into the hallway, pausing only to retrieve a battered old cap from the side.

"Here's your hat."

Nussbaum's lips recoiled in a sneer.

"What's that?"

"I said 'here's your hat'."

He peered at the item as if it were something inching its way out of a dog.

"That is not my hat."

"What do you mean?"

"Where would I go in such a hat? Fetch me my other one."

"There is no other hat."

"Hush woman! The other hat!"

"Who are you, the Queen Mother? There is no other hat."

Without his pills – two blues, a red and a yellow – Nussbaum could feel the blood start to squeeze through his body like toothpaste.

"The one that isn't this one."

His wife started to say something but Nussbaum couldn't hear for the sound of his heart: thump, thump, *bump*, thump, thump, *bump.* Did it always make that sound? Nussbaum was no doctor of medicine but his internal plumbing seemed dangerously out of sorts, things either moving the wrong direction or not going anyplace at all. Such indignity! Such dishonour! And at just such a moment, his wife should fetch him a hat like this…

"Suit yourself," his wife said turning on her heels. "I'm going to finish my soup."

Nussbaum scowled – let her drown in the soup if she wants! – But he satisfied himself with yelling "fine!" And stormed out of the flat, his head as bare as the moon.

Just outside the door – indeed, within only a few inches of Nussbaum's nose – was the nose of Mrs Miskell, his neighbour. Both jumped, though perhaps Nussbaum slightly more so. 'A man can die of such things,' he thought, but Mrs Miskell seemed unperturbed, her face a child's drawing of the word 'smile'.

"Oh, Mr Nussbaum – I was just returning your *People's Friend.*"

"My what?"

"Your *Friend.* Your wife leant it to me. How is she by the way? Any better?"

'My wife?' he thought, 'what would be wrong with my wife? My wife is awash in a sea of soup.' But instead he contented himself with saying, "Fine, fine, you're very kind…" his lips as straight as a clothes line.

"And how are you coping? I mean, with your heart?"

On his guard now, Nussbaum sized up his neighbour with a practiced eye. True, she seemed to have little in common with the anorak-wearing thugs who hung around by the bus stop – but who knew? There were filchers and kleptomaniacs everywhere: the world was full of thieves.

"Aha. Yes, yes, still there…" he murmured, while all the time thinking: 'Crook! Scoundrel! And what is it to do with you?'

"Well, if there's anything you need…"

"Need?"

And that's when it came to him, settling on his head like a crow. Mrs Miskell must have crept inside his apartment – like a shadow! Like a mouse! – Swiping his pills and placing that box of *things* in their place. Nussbaum could scarcely believe her dissemblance, her duplicity. And Mrs Miskell a Rotarian too!

"A glass of water."

"I'm sorry?"

"A glass of water. I am most terribly thirsty." Nussbaum paused uncertainly. "Also, I have pains."

Mrs Miskell blinked at the Nussbaums' open door, but instead of shooing him discreetly away, murmured, "Why yes, but of course…" and ushered him across the landing, her fingers dancing from apron to necklace to hair.

"Such pains," said Nussbaum.

Mrs Miskell's flat was just like the one he lived in with his wife – same hall, same desk, same beige carpet; for Nussbaum it was like entering his apartment by mirror. The place was tremendously tidy, and finished off with what he considered to be a delicate feminine touch. *Was* there a Mr Miskell? Nussbaum felt he should know the answer to this but didn't dare enquire too deeply lest it should turn out to be him.

"Very… clean."

"Why thank you."

"Exactly the kind of place where one might find running water…"

"Well, I…"

"Fresh, clean water…"

Mrs Miskell smiled – though a little less convincingly this time – and stared down at the rings on her hands. "I'll fetch you a glass…"

"Yes," he said. "A glass…"

As soon as she'd gone, Nussbaum began to methodically sack her sitting-room, tossing aside cushions, turning over the magazine rack, slipping his hand under the fabric of the couch. But where had she hidden his pills – under the carpet, down the toilet, in her bed? 'How should I know?' thought Nussbaum; 'the mind of a criminal is a deep, dark pool…'

Beads of perspiration formed on Nussbaum's large, round head. His hands started to shake. His cardiovascular system knotted. For a moment he thought he'd found the pills stashed in a toffee tin but on closer inspection they turned out to be toffees.

"Would you like ice?" called Mrs Miskell from the kitchen.

"Yes, yes I would," replied Nussbaum from beneath her dresser. "And perhaps a biscuit too."

His jaw set, Nussbaum went back to manhandling Mrs Miskell's belongings – a line of potted plants, a neat nest of side tables, a cabinet of ugly pottery animals – and that was where he found it: a black and white photograph in an old, battered frame, a photograph showing some fella standing on a rubbish heap with a dog and a pipe, wearing *exactly* the hat Nussbaum was looking for.

Breathing hard, Nussbaum picked up the frame and tried to force it into his coat pocket; when the fabric started to rip he gave up and shoved it inside his shirt front instead. It was then that he looked up and saw Mrs Miskell staring down at him, a large glass of water in her hand.

"It is best if we do not talk of this," Nussbaum said, not blinking.

"No…"

"I will not be informing the police…"

"No…"

"Or the housing supervisor…"

"But…"

"Nor the caretaker too…"

"Mr Nussbaum, I..."

"A thief always returns to his own vomit!" he warned, and with that he was gone, stumbling down the stairwell, dog and pipe poking out from his vest.

Outside, the cool autumn wind seemed to blow the fog from Nussbaum's beard. 'It's true,' he thought – 'every man is a thief if the bough hangs low.' Every place you looked, people were pulling up manhole covers, melting down telephone wires, levering the plaques from benches – and all for what? Why, for the simple pleasure of stealing. Tch, a curse on this light-fingered island! On the radio he had heard about some intruder who had broken into a house and swiped one of everything – one shoe, one slipper, one sock. What kind of man would do such a thing? Yet here such actions were the norm. Nussbaum wanted to spit! Why had he ever come to these benighted shores? This midden, this slag-heap, this dump... you could throw a stone from any point in the country and hit somebody with his mitts in the till...

All around him leaves were falling despondently, the driveway flanked by a line of bald trees holding their hands up in the air. Perhaps his pills were here, buried beneath these wet, dirty leaves. Or perhaps they were hidden in some deep hole, amongst the mushrooms and the moles and the bones of robbed and swindled men... Either way, Nussbaum had no choice but to walk all the way into town, a walk of twenty, maybe twenty five minutes... more! And him a poor man with a broken aorta, a man living in sheltered accommodation with a soup-eating wife...

All of a sudden Nussbaum's energies seemed to sag. He listened to his heart and heard an evil voice hissing, 'Not long you old goat!' Then he looked up at the trees and they rustled, 'Not here you old fool!' Even the mulch beneath his feet seemed to murmur, 'Not likely you old dog!' Hadn't even his own doctor tried to steal his blood; 'Ah, Nussbaum, a drop of the good stuff, dearer than the price of champagne!' But what was Nussbaum to do? Without his pills they'd be tying a tag to his toes by the morning...

Rolling slowly downhill, Nussbaum passed tired-looking charity shops, cobwebby playgrounds, wet, puddle-strewn underpasses; every once in a while some passing ruffian would bump against him and all over again he had to check that the photograph was still there – one dog, one pipe, one hat – pressing the frame ever closer 'gainst his sad and desiccated heart. What kind of place was this? Snitching, swiping, grabbing... Ach, such a country! One had to have ten arms in this world, and four eyes in one's head...

But when Nussbaum thought his heart must surely burst, he finally stumbled upon the chemist's, a yellow square of light squeezed in between a betting shop and a solicitor's. The chemist was over-lit, over-stocked, over-complicated. The only other customer was a woman and her baby, its fat little arms reaching out to grab whatever it could; 'Yes, the stickiest fingers are furthest in the pot,' thought Nussbaum, shuffling uncertainly along the aisles. Why come to this place? Why bother? And yet what else was he supposed to do – without his pills his heart would snap shut like a purse.

The girl at the pharmacy was busy with something in the backroom, and Nussbaum lingered by the prophylactics, his heart in turmoil and valves gummed up with fat. Was it two white and one blue, or two blue, one white? For a moment he felt confused. Little needles pricked his skin and he thought, 'Yes, even my organs are plotting against me...' It's true! His heart, his lungs, his brain: all of these were his enemies now. Whom could one trust? His marrow was full of gall and his wife was full of soup. What was it his own doctor had said? "Those bones, Nussbaum, I could make a step ladder from such a set..."

The only thing distracting Nussbaum from his gloom was a small moulded dog sitting quietly by the weighing machine, the *Hund* yellow and plastic, a little hole by its mouth where one should introduce a coin. Good doggy, clever boy! Nussbaum felt a sudden longing to stretch out a hand, to pat or stroke or tap – though not to insert a coin, heaven forbid: who was he, Rockefeller? The dog had a little sign attached to its chest, but for some reason Nussbaum seemed to have great trouble understanding it. Why would one use a blind dog for a guide? 'Why blind?' Nussbaum thought. 'Why 'blind dog?"

Glancing round, he bent down and tentatively petted the little dog's head, whispering, "You're a fine fellow, eh? Yes, you are," and gently rapping its ears with his knuckles. The funny thing was, the more he looked at it, the more it resembled the dog in the photograph: same coat, same eyes, same faithful mien. True, the dog before him looked considerably less mobile, but still: there were real things and there were true things and this dog was incontestably one of the latter...

The girl was still busy so Nussbaum leant over and looked the animal straight in the eye.

"Why stay in this place, with these people, eh, boy? Why do it?"

The dog's eyes shone brightly.

"Tch, these people, these crooks..."

Nussbaum's voice broke gently.

"Eh, *mein kleiner Hund...*"

Then in one swift movement, Nussbaum picked up the animal and leapt to his feet. The dog was lighter than he thought, but still kind-of awkward, and as he reared back he caught a display of sanitary products, sending the boxes crashing to the floor.

"You saw nothing!" he yelled to the girl behind the counter. "There is no need to call your supervisor. I will take care of him from now."

Nussbaum's bald pate gleamed in the light and the girl stared at it, transfixed.

"No, no, I will not tell…" said Nussbaum.

For a moment his eyes seemed to cloud over.

"A thief does not plough in season!" he yelled, and with that he was gone, dog, collecting box and all.

Outside Nussbaum could feel envious eyes following him along the road, eying up his dog, his frame, his life. 'Well, let them look,' he thought. 'You can't pluck a chin with your eyes…'

Strange pains ran from his chest to the peripheries, and there was some kind of liquid beneath his tongue. 'If only I had a pipe,' Nussbaum reflected. 'And perhaps a bench on which to smoke it…' It seemed to him that some wonderful tobacconist shop was waiting just around the corner, its doors lying open, stock arranged in rows, the mellow fragrance of pipe smoke carried as if on a young child's breath. 'Ah me,' thought Nussbaum: 'My pipe! My matches! My home!' But even as he pictured himself flinging open the glass doors, his foot caught on a paving stone and he toppled violently forward, his head connecting unexpectedly with the ground.

"My pills!" he gasped, "my beautiful pills!"

When he looked up a gang of robbers and thieves were standing above him, their faces merging together into a thick cloud of villainy.

"Whoa, big fella – you trip? You okay?"

Nussbaum wanted to spit but couldn't roll himself into the right position. Why didn't his left side work? And why was somebody moving his arm? Criminals, hooligans, mountebanks, thieves!

"That was some fall, mister. You sure you can stand?"

Nussbaum tried to say something but his lips seemed gummed together. Stabbing pains spread down from his cheek to his jaw. Also, his chest was on fire.

"Amber! Amber!" he whispered to the dog. "Amber, attack!"

"Ambulance?"

"Amber!"

"You want an ambulance?"

The next thing he knew Nussbaum was being pulled to his feet and manhandled into the back seat of some conveyance, firey hands clutching inside his shirt. When he felt inside his jacket, the frame was broken, vicious shards of glass piercing his side. The picture was all bloody too.

"Are you alright back there?" asked a voice. "The hospital, is it?"

"Hospital?"

"You'll be alright – big fella like you can survive a trip, eh?"

Nussbaum's chest felt very tight. 'But this is not an ambulance,' he thought. 'This is not a bed...'

He tried to take in the driver's reflection in the rear view mirror, but could only make out a thick pair of glasses on a red, bulbous nose.

"I need pills," he said.

"Pills? Well..."

"Two blue and one white..."

"What?"

"Blue, white, round..."

"Don't you worry, I'll get you there..."

The nose put his foot down and the conveyance started to pull away. The buildings were colourless. The trees were dead. On the streets were looters, housebreakers, felons of every stripe. 'Oh, this is hell,' thought Nussbaum. 'And to face it alone, hatless, pill-less, without medication of any kind...'

The vehicle started to pick up speed but as it passed the supermarket it seemed to Nussbaum that it was carrying him ever further from where it was he wanted to go. 'This is not the way to the hospital,' he thought. 'This is not my car!'

A quick glance at the fellow's glasses only confirmed things: the *Schwein* was some kind of kidnapper, a hoodlum or 'hard-man of the streets'. Why else was he transporting Nussbaum against his will? No, the way to the hospital was to avoid the ring-road, turning right at the lights and then again by the pub...

The get-away car was moving at dangerously high speeds, paying only cursory attention to the rules of the road. Nussbaum was outraged. 'Where are the authorities, the police?' he fumed. 'Back at the station with their panda cars and whistles...' The gangster was driving at nearly thirty now. 'Ach, where will this end?' thought Nussbaum. 'What will become of me?'

"You okay there fella? You don't look so good..."

Blood was spreading across Nussbaum's good, clean shirt. "I need... my... pills..." Nussbaum snapped, but of course the villain paid him no heed. No, the fella would drive out to the rubbish dump, rob him blind, then hide his body in the ground. Such things happened all the time in this country. Decent law-abiding citizens were picked up, fleeced, planted in the earth like potatoes. Would his wife even notice? Would she even look up from her soup? "Oh Mizzy Mizzy," he whispered. "Does your heart beat faster at my name?" And all the time, like Saint Sebastian, vicious shards pierced his side...

The town was behind them now, along with any chance of rescue or escape. Instead the road turned left toward the estuary, only the occasional snack-van or burnt out car breaking up the landscape of black fields and brown clay.

Nussbaum stared at the muddy waters with distrust. 'This is it,' he reflected; 'a body hidden in such filth would remain hidden for all time.' The trees were bare. The sky was grey. The smudges above his head might have been birds or marks on the glass – it was very hard to tell. His cheek was slumped very close to the window and his breath created a kind of fog. 'Still alive then,' he thought. 'One lung still works even if that crook of a doctor removed the other.' 'This lung, Nussbaum, has been smoked like a kipper: how can I find a buyer for this?' Ho, doctors: one may as well toss oneself into a cannibal's pot. A pox upon such doctors! A pouch of pipe tobacco and a bench: that was what one needed. Pff, what were pills, tablets, suppositories? Sweeties for the hungry dead...

The car continued to hurtle at reckless speeds – forty, forty one, forty two – and Nussbaum elected to spend his last few minutes putting his affairs in order. The dog would have to go back to the chemist. His wife would have to take his things to Age Concern. Mrs Miskell would have to do without her pilfered goods. And yet, and yet... what if they weren't pilfered after all? Nussbaum looked down at where the glass had pierced his side and studied the picture mournfully. "What was I thinking?" he murmured, wiping his blood from the print. "That is not my dog. That is not my hat. This is not a pipe..." Alas, poor Nussbaum! Only the rubbish tip seemed right.

Nussbaum grimaced and felt the darkness begin to gather. When he looked up, three birds were flying low above the estuary, their graceful ticks swooping effortlessly between the banks and reeds, a faint 'v' or arrow, moving silently across the land. *Were* they birds? The more Nussbaum followed them the more their bodies seemed to blur and glow, the dots diving close to the water before flying up again, bursting into flame as if striking a match. How beautiful they seemed to him! How free! Nussbaum rubbed furiously at the glass and watched as the birds traced an elegant arc across the mudflats.

"Two white, one blue," he whispered. "Two white, one blue."

The lights skimmed low across the reed bed and then turned back on themselves, disappearing between the low-hanging trees and the sky. Nussbaum strained his neck but couldn't see beyond them. His face felt numb. Pins and needles pricked his side. The verges were full of rubbish. All of a sudden his mouth seemed to open in a terrible grimace. O Nussbaum/ O Nussbaum/ where do you go?/ Your hat full of rain/ and your shoes full of snow...

At the hospital, they mis-spelt his name with an 'm'. Nussbaum fumed: fools, charlatans, quacks! Also, his gown was too short – but, then, what did he want? What did he expect?

# Llewelling

Okay, take a look outside your window. Which window? The bathroom, the kitchen, the bedroom – who cares? So – is it raining? Of course it's raining! The sky is a dirty dish rag, the ground a puddle, great tubs of water emptying out onto the earth. But now take a closer look. Is that *really* rain – that drizzle, that mist, that spray? No. No it is not rain – pff, barely enough to wet a sparrow's hat. Now that day, two years ago, two days before Christmas – *that* was rain. Hm? How much rain? Think of a bucket of water being poured over a feather bed. Now think of a swimming pool being emptied over the same bed. What's that – what's a bed doing out in the rain? Listen, forget the bed. The bed is soaked through. You cannot get back in the bed. In fact, there is no bed. Just rain.

My wife and little girl were both ill, laid low by a sick bug. What can I say? Trouble at both ends and hollowness in between. One would start to over-heat and the other would shiver beneath the covers. Then one would come down with the shakes and the other would blaze like a candle – first Claire and then Tallulah. The worst was if both were sick at the same time. There was only one bowl, as the other was used for the washing up. Who wants to be sick on the washing-up? No one. And all the time the rain like the Gestapo at the door…

Okay, let's suppose that Claire was on the couch and Tallulah in bed: it might have been the other way round, it doesn't really matter. I was betwixt the two, mop in hand, my mien that of Heine contemplating life. Such sadness – I was supposed to finish the Christmas shopping in *this*? Outside, the sky was a well without bottom or end, the horizon a dam ready to burst. And then, just when it seemed things couldn't get any worse, Fergus leapt to his feet and began barking at the window, his tongue lolling wildly and saliva dribbling from his jaws.

Now Fergus was an old dog, his legs as stiff as bed posts: most days he had to be lifted up and slowly lowered into his dinner, his jaws opening and closing like a scoop. But that day – the day just two days before Christmas – he was up on his back legs and smearing his chops on the glass like a mad thing. I peered out into the gloom but it was impossible to see anything. "You must be mistaken," I said but when I looked down Fergus' lips were curled back like a discarded glove. For a moment he looked exactly like my Uncle Julius trying to find his slippers. "Okay, okay," I said, not wanting to wake my patients. "But it would have to be some kind of lunatic to be out on a night like this…"

Anyway I opened the door, and of course, there was nobody there – not at eye level anyway. But down by my bony knees, curled up against the rain, was a brown and yellow dog, mangy as a dish cloth, shaking and shivering in the cold. His ears were down, his tail drooped, his ribs poked out from his sides as if from some kind of string bag.

"Hello Boy," I said. "You're a sad looking fella aren't you?" Fergus was less moved. With a vehemence and alacrity previously absent from his golden years, he made a move to devour the said dog, or at least administer a vicious nip to one ear.

"What's got into you?" I yelled. "Just look at that poor thing…"

"Who's there?" croaked Claire from either the couch or the bed. "What do they want?"

"It's no one," I whispered. "Just a brown and yellow dog…"

"Yellow?"

Outside, I could hear the thing scratching at the door and whimpering. I moved to open the door and Fergus did a double take, distractedly trying to gnaw his knuckles.

"Fergus? Fergus, desist…"

By this point the Unknown Dog was digging away at the front door as if trying to tunnel its way inside. Fergus frothed and snarled. Some kind of fountain was erupting from the guttering. Cars struggled against the rapids. Outside was a whole universe of rain.

"Are you okay boy?" I said. "Good boy, good dog…"

The dog shivered and shook. But what could I do? It was Christmas, it was pouring, the animal looked like something pulled rudely from a plug hole. I inched the door open and before I knew what was going on, the hound was in, capering in mad, concentric circles around the living room, pursued by Fergus' wildly snapping teeth.

"Hey, hey, stop!" I yelled. Rain water went everywhere. Big wet paw marks circled the couch. Within seconds the whole room was in chaos.

"Fergus!" I yelled. "Fergus, let go!"

Something tore into a cushion and tried to devour it. The Christmas tree swayed, a lamp exploded, a slim volume of Modernist poetry was sat upon. And all the time water poured off the dog in a great, brown flood.

"What's going on?" yelled Claire, her voice taut as a telephone wire. "What is that thing and why is it here?"

I was at the business end of a mongrel and momentarily unable to answer. Chairs toppled, trays slipped. Two dogs were under the table, one biting, one yapping. Before I knew what was going on, the table cloth and all of my paperwork had joined them.

"Nick? Nick, what's happening?"

"It's... it's okay..." I wheezed. "The yellow one is a little wet, is all..."

By this stage the mutt was making towards the kitchen door, Fergus trying to reel him in by his tail. Claire emerged in her dressing gown, pale and drawn, her lips parted in a silent 'O'.

"S'okay, s'okay," I said, attempting to separate the pair at some cost to my trousers. "I'll put him in the garden..."

Alas as soon as the beast realised the stranger was about to return him to the deep, he started to struggle and whine all the more.

"Come... on..."

His paws back peddled wildly, but I managed to get him to the door.

"There's a pup," I said, "Have a run around out here..."

The dog gazed up at me like Rembrandt's hound. His tongue drooped helplessly and for a moment I thought he could see his heart beating between his ribs like an apple in the branches.

"Out... you... go..." I hissed and with that the dog was again on the other side of the glass, albeit now in the back garden and in dangerous proximity to our ficus. Fergus stood behind me and glared.

"What do you want?" I asked. "It's out of your hair isn't it?"

Fergus barked and Unknown Dog whined, only a thin partition of glass between them. Back in the living room Claire silently surveyed the wreckage, her lips as thin as an envelope. There was brown *everywhere*. Chairs lay hobbled on one side. The stuffing of various pillows collected in puddles. The sofa smelt of wild dog.

"But it's Christmas..." I said.

Claire nodded and fished a big tuft of wet hair from an over turned mug.

"I mean, I couldn't just leave it out there..."

Upstairs, Tallulah was crying.

"You know, Christmas…"

A low, plaintive keening carried on at the rear of the house, cutting through the endless, percussive rain. Oh, how could I abandon him to the elements, leave him to the cold and the flood? And yet there was no way that Fergus and the *Hund* could share a dinner bowl. Not to mention the fragile state of my family's digestive systems: who needed another hair in one's dish? But perhaps there was a simpler solution after all.

Squeezing past Fergus I left dry land and paddled out into the garden. "Here boy, over here," I said. The dog turned to look at me, albeit a little more sceptically this time. Dirt dripped from every hair. He looked like something pulled awkwardly from a plug. "That's it my boy, here you come…"

Around its scrawny neck a mud-spattered collar hung like a noose. On it was etched 'Llewelling' and a telephone number it took me several attempts to remember.

"Llewelling," I said softly. "Llewelling, everything is going to be okay…"

Then I raced back to the kitchen before the thing could squeeze past me and find its way back in.

Reciting the number I breathed in and rang it. No answer. I paused and re-dialled: still no answer. Taking a deep breath, I left a message. 'I have your dog in our garden and so forth… If you want to get him, then phone etc…' Only when I finished did I realise that I sounded exactly like a dog-napper. The vets was closed – likewise the animal sanctuary. Nobody answered at the council. The dog warden was probably this very moment attaching the Christmas angel to his tree. What did I expect? Meanwhile the toilet flushed and the beast howled. Rain hit the roof like cannon balls. Llewelling howled like a lost soul: now he was both drowned *and* trapped. What a night it was, a black wave crashing upon the earth. Even the darkness felt wet! Someplace a choir was singing, trumpets sounded, snow fell... but not here. Rain fell like ball bearings in a bin. When I looked outside, the dog was slumped by the back door like a coat only a madman would wear.

"Llewelling?" I whispered, "Llewelling, are you okay?"

The rag refused to look up and that's when I realised: what kind of a name was Llewelling for a dog anyway? Why, the name of an owner not a pet! I mean, what was I thinking? Who ever called their dog Llewelling? Not even somebody called Llewelling themselves.

This thought firmly in mind I returned to the telephone directory and sniffed out the letter 'L': Lewelin, Lewhellin, Llewelin, Llewellin, Llewellyn, Llewelyn, Llewheling, Llewhellin, Llewhelling: as populous as the stars in the heavens. But eventually I managed to match number and address. And what do you think? The street was barely a block away from here, almost close enough to see... so, I thought, the beast had travelled no distance at all. Ah, who'd have guessed? The address was no more than five minutes from our place, ten at top...

I tried phoning again but still got no answer. "I've still got your dog!" I shouted and slammed down the phone. Fergus' lead hung down from the coat rack like a tail. Was it worth searching for this place? I mean, sure, nobody was in and yet... who would be out on a night such as this? But how long could I keep the thing trapped out there? Outside, the tap kept running. Some kind of waterfall was coming down from the roof and the drains bubbled and spun.

Donning hat and rain coat I called to my wife, "Just going out," and, bracing myself, re-entered the deluge. Llewelling, which is to say, the dog, let me attach the lead to his collar and sniffed me philosophically. Rain fell on us like wolves. Within seconds my trousers were drenched and a cold trickle of rain water crept down my back.

"Okay," I said. "Just you and me now, boy…"

We left by the back gate and waded out into the rapids. The drains formed whirlpools, the road a vast ford: again I thought of a dam and looked up at the wall of blackness, waiting for the whole terrible thing to collapse… Llewelling meanwhile looked cheerful, walking with confidence and purpose. Did he know the way? Lights bobbed by like life buoys. Rubbish drifted erratically downstream. When I looked down the old fool was actually wagging his tail.

"Is this right? Eh, boy? Is this home? Eh boy, eh?"

Needless to say we met no one: neither pedestrian nor car nor fish. The sky was paint mixed with dish water. I blinked furiously and shook my head, something cold and black dripping from the end of my nose.

And yet, in no time at all, we were there. The house looked perfectly respectable, an unlikely kennel for a beast such as this. Neat lawn, well-maintained exterior, nicely painted fascias. Alas, there were no lights on in the house, and no car in the driveway, so presumably there wasn't anybody here after all. And then I spotted it: a window ajar next to the front doorway, a window low enough for a bored and boisterous dog to have made his escape. Surely this was the portal from which the thing had come?

I looked at the dog and the dog looked at me.

"Well, it's been nice knowing you," I said. "Compliments of the season."

I placed my arms under him and gingerly lifted him up. The dog gazed at me trustingly, one of my hands awkwardly cupping his balls.

"There we go. Home time fella…"

The lounge was all in darkness but I could make out the shadowy outlines of a sofa, some chairs, a tree: in the gloom — its branches seemed to move mysteriously. The dog whimpered but I pushed him through anyway.

"There you go. Good boy, clever dog…"

And that was that: my good deed was done. Retreating back up the drive I could hear the sound of high pitched barking. 'He's glad to be home,' I thought. 'Back in the dry…' Ah, what brings more of a glow to one's cheeks than the rewards of virtue? I imagined the gratitude of the owners, a warm phone call, perhaps some kind of yuletide gift…

When I got home minutes later, daughter, wife and dog were waiting for me in the hallway, two in dressing gowns, one staring at his lead.

"Somebody called Llewelling rang," Claire muttered, tonelessly. "They asked if you could phone them back…"

Grinning broadly, I picked up the receiver. "Was he glad to see you?" I asked. "I can imagine the kind of welcome he'd give… um, sorry, what? Llewelling. Um, the dog. Was he glad to be home? What? Home, home, was he glad to be home?"

For a moment I thought there was something wrong with the line.

"Yes, yes, that's right. I mean, I put him through the window just now…"

For the life of me, I could not conceive exactly how I got it so wrong: perhaps my finger had strayed to the wrong line in the directory; perhaps the howling had distracted me at just the wrong time. Either way, Llewelling was not home. I had delivered him to a Mrs Llewellyn's address. This was not the right Llewelling at all.

"Yes," I said. "Yes, I see…"

There was a mighty crash outside, as if some kind of foundation had come loose. With a creeping sense of despair, I suddenly understood that it would never stop raining again.

"No, no, it's no bother," I said. "I'll just go and collect him."

I put down the phone and regarded my audience.

"I'll just go and get him," I said, edging toward the door. "I won't be long…"

Fergus looked at the lead, Claire my shoes, Tallulah my hat. Rain dripped from everything.

"It's not far. I won't be long. I'm right back…"

Back outside everything had turned to wet. Puddles became pools, pools rivers, rivers seas. Of course I was used to it now: even a fish feels at home in the pot! And all the time I kept thinking that if this was some kind of heart-warming Christmas story then the dog would have been discovered by some lonely pensioner, an old dear in need of a little comfort and affection and that the two of them would now be curled up on a sofa, a tray of biscuits before them…

Anyway, it didn't take long for me to retrace my steps. The house was still in darkness, its walls a mixture of shadow and damp.

"Llewelling?" I whispered. "Llewelling, boy, are you there?"

The window was still open but I could spot neither granny nor dog. Instead all I could see were the fuzzy outlines of broken furniture, over turned chairs, and torn curtains. Something had taken a dump on the rug.

"Llewelling?"

Glancing around me I pulled myself up on to the sill and let myself in. My shoes crunched on broken glass. The Christmas tree laid prone in the middle of the room, like the murder victim in a whodunnit. I picked up a fallen bauble and held it gingerly in my hand. Who leaves a window open in the middle of a monsoon anyway?

Furnishings were soiled, cushions disembowelled, magazines devoured. I followed the trail of tears throughout the house, photographs and paintings joining the general carnage on the floor. Did one stray really do all this? Even the banisters looked gnawed.

"Hello?" I called. "Um, hello? Has anybody seen a dog?"

In the bedroom the darkness seemed to open as if on a hinge. For some reason I hesitated before switching on the light: foo, who wants to see the hangman's spots? But sensing the emptiness I counted to ten and flicked the switch. Screwed up bed clothes, turned over dresser, emptied jewellery boxes: what had happened here anyway?

'I don't believe it,' I thought, peering in to some kind of empty safe. 'Llewelling, what have you done?'

Outside, the darkness roared.

As I said to the arresting officer at the time, there had to be a reasonable explanation for all this, and, in a sense, there was. The burglars had jimmied open the window, climbed inside and ransacked the place in search of valuables and cash. All I had done (as I informed the nice police lady) was to introduce a wet and dirty dog to the crime scene... Anyway, statements were given, contact details recorded, Christmas greetings swapped. There was little else to say. After time, the rain stopped, Claire and Tallulah got better, Fergus stopped barking. And Llewelling? Well, there's the thing. Despite the fact that the dog had been handed over to the relevant authorities, a few days before New Year, photocopied posters started turning up in our neighbourhood, offering a reward for information regarding a lost dog. The name looked familiar, but as I bent down to look at the photograph, I felt a most peculiar sensation. Inexplicably, the dog on the poster didn't look like Llewelling at all: wrong nose, wrong size, wrong breed. Who was this Llewelling? Not our Llewelling. Not our Llewelling at all. But just like Llewelling, his eyes were as sad as the dusk...

# Anywhere Out of the World

# 1

At first glance there was nothing special about the envelope at all: cheap stationery, second class stamp, badly stuck down lip. The address was written in a neat but unremarkable hand, slanting a little toward the bottom: two six six, Rue de Coudray. Monsieur Urbino wiped his glasses, scratched his chin and read the envelope one more time: two six six Rue de Coudray. The thing was, there *was* no two six six Rue de Coudray. Two six four, yes – a plain, slightly disreputable looking block of flats, a broken 'For Rent' sign propped up against a tree. Two six eight, but, of course: office space, a boarded-up estate agent's downstairs and a stationery supply company up top. And across the road? Why, normality itself – Bassiak's greengrocers, a strikingly yellow café, an empty launderette. Ah, what else was left to say? A pretty chestnut tree softened the slightly melancholy air, a green metal bench half-heartedly hidden beneath it. Two six six Rue de Coudray, reflected Monsieur Urbino, thoughtfully. But why buy a glove if you don't have a hand?

Heaving his sack once more upon his back, the postman approached the flats and cautiously examined the entranceway, the door seemingly too big and too old for the block, as if rescued from flea market or skip. Alongside the entrance was a panel with six buzzers, the plastic stained and the stickers peeling off. On four of the stickers were unremarkable names: Araignée, Mouoche, Limace, Papillion. The fifth read Madame D'araingnée, Taxidermy. The sixth was blank. Monsieur Urbino re-read the envelope and checked: Monsieur Ferrand. But where was Monsieur Ferrand and where was two six six? Curtains twitched in the downstairs flat and a black cat pressed up against the window, its green eyes flashing. The cat looked at Monsieur Urbino and Monsieur Urbino looked at the cat: then the animal set to savagely biting at its foot and the postman backed off sharpish. Foo, what was he doing here anyway? Two six six was two six six: besides, the cat had a funny eye, the 'For Sale' sign was a broken crutch, the bottles were full of rain. Yes, it was a sad and mournful place. Across the road, the greengrocer held up the head of a cauliflower, looking for all the world like some kind of provincial Hamlet trying to remember his lines.

"Two six six, two six six," mumbled Monsieur Urbino, approaching the shop keeper rather awkwardly. "Monsieur, Monsieur – if I can have a moment of your time please?"

The grocer nodded, wiping his mitts upon his apron; he was a short, wiry man, as wrinkled as a date.

"Monsieur Bassiak? Monsieur Bassiak, I have a letter here for two six six, but there seems to be no such place… What is the number of your establishment, if you please…?"

For some reason Monsieur Bassiak lifted up the cauliflower like a ventriloquist's dummy, rolling its head to look at the postman. "We're two six six you old fart," said the cauliflower, and both men laughed.

"That's amazing," said Urbino, tapping the cauliflower's head with unfeigned admiration. "Wherever did you learn such a trick?"

"The real question is how do I get this clod to man the shop," said the cauliflower, and again the two men chuckled.

"And your lips didn't seem to move one bit!" Urbino blew out his cheeks. "Ah monsieur, that is a most extraordinary gift…"

The grocer winked and tickled the cauliflower under its chin.

"But look here," said Monsieur Urbino, resting his sack by his feet. "The envelope says two six six, and yet such an address cannot be found. Here, take a look!"

Monsieur Bassiak put down the cauliflower and put on his glasses.

"Ferrand, Ferrand…" said Monsieur Bassiak. "I know that name from somewhere, but I know of no two six six. A letter, yes?"

Urbino passed it over to Monsieur Bassiak who held it to his ear as if some tiny fellow were whispering inside.

"Hm… come inside and have a *patis,*" said the shop keeper, leading Monsieur Urbino past an old woman filling a straw bag with runner beans. "This is a mystery which merits further investigation…"

Inside the store displays of rather wilted looking greens gave way to a maze of coffee sacks, bags of dried herbs, and barrels smelling of chicory. Some old dear was busy shop-lifting out-of-date radishes and cucumbers, but Bassiak breezed past her, apparently unconcerned. At the rear of the establishment was a table where the day's racing gazette was granted pride of place, positioned alongside strips of brown paper, dried onions and an egg.

"Take a seat Monsieur Urbino. You have time for a drink I take it…"

"Pff… the President can wait," said Urbino modestly. The postman lowered himself down as if dropping off a particularly cumbersome parcel: what were people sending in the mail these days, heads? Then Monsieur Bassiak produced a bottle from behind a large box of aubergines and two glasses from a dusty drawer.

"Ferrand, Ferrand… yes, I remember the fellow," said the grocer, smacking his lips. "A very small man in a very large hat. Smoked a pipe. Fond of aubergines, as I remember. Worked at an insurance office but fancied himself a Sunday painter..."

"A painter?" Urbino's ears immediately pricked up. "Why monsieur, I also dabble in, ah, the fine arts..." Urbino fluttered his fingers. "Not in a professional capacity you understand, but..."

The grocer and the cauliflower both seemed to shrug. "Ho, I haven't seen Monsieur Ferrand in years – and besides he lives on the rue d'Amsterdam rather than around here..."

"The rue d'Amsterdam?" said Urbino, sniffing a fox. "That's a long way to come to buy aubergines..."

"His office is nearby. Lavialle and Duport. Do you know it? Place Painlevé."

"But of course! I used to deliver mail there all the time. How strange..."

Monsieur Bassiak cut the postman a slice of bread and smeared it thickly with sauerkraut. "A funny little man... short but with a great shock of hair – like one of his paint brushes. Always wore a very sober charcoal suit for the office but with splashes of blue from his lapel to his shoes. Wherever he went he would leave these little painted footprints like some kind of path."

"Sounds a character!" said Monsieur Urbino scratching vaguely at his wrist. "Of course, us artists..."

"A most peculiar individual – though you'd never know it from his shadow. Used turpentine for cologne. Black nails. Tested his cheese with a palette knife..."

"Oh Monsieur – you treat yourself to my head..."

Bassiak's dark eyes twinkled.

"True as a face in a puddle, monsieur: one doesn't forget a fellow like that! But wait, what am I thinking? You say you know something about draughtsmanship, eh, what? Ho, I have something to show you: stay there my friend, stay there..." And so saying the grocer disappeared through a rear door, the old fella whisked away like a cloth.

Left on his own, Urbino inched one shoe off and rubbed dreamily at his toes.

"Listen," said the cauliflower, as soon as the grocer had left the room. "The old goose knows nothing. Don't believe a word that that old fool says…"

Taken aback, Monsieur Urbino reached down and patted the cauliflower like a dog.

"What's that?"

Urbino looked around but couldn't see the grocer anywhere.

"Bassiak? His customers rob him blind. Around money he's no better than a baby. Look – fifty francs on *l'ephémère* on the 2.30 at Rennes. The man's a fool. You'd be better off talking to Madame Lacarrié at the café across the way. She knows all about Ferrand. Ask her about the blue nude…"

"Monsieur Bassiak, are you playing tricks? Were you hiding, you naughty fellow?"

Back in the shop the old dear was filling her coat with parsnips, but of the proprietor: not a sign.

"I'm telling you – forget the grocer. His head's as empty as a sack. Ask Madame Lacarriè what happened to Ferrand. After all, she… but shh, he's coming back…"

Monsieur Bassiak re-emerged carrying a small painting in a shabby wood frame. The whole canvas was scarcely bigger than a postcard, or approximately the size of M. Bassiak's apron pocket.

"Do you know, I almost forgot I had this. Once upon a time I assisted Monsieur Ferrand with a small personal matter – the merest trifle, I assure you – and to show his gratitude Ferrand made me a gift of one of his compositions. As for the degree of generosity involved… well, you can make up your own mind in that regard, Monsieur Le Poste…"

The painting was some kind of still life: peppers, or perhaps garlic bulbs, positioned by an old fashioned lamp, the whole thing, lamp, produce, table and all, painted an eerie gas-light blue. But what a strange looking thing it was! The painting looked less like the product of a talented child than the work of somebody terribly short sighted, probably holding a brush at the end of a stick.

"Hmm…" said Urbino, thoughtfully. "What colour do you think that is? Cyan?"

"The devil knows," muttered Bassiak darkly. "Monsieur Ferrand was either ahead of his time or of another time entirely. But there is something odd about the picture, naive though its technique may be…" And so saying Monsieur Bassiak turned the frame round and round in his hands: no matter which way up the picture was held, the lamp and peppers – if indeed peppers they be – remained in the same position, as if they were rolling round inside a box.

"Mm…" said Urbino, pulling at the bristles on his chin. "How peculiar! Some kind of compositional trick I suppose…"

"A trick? Or perhaps some kind of clue…"

Urbino rubbed his lips, assuming the mien of a great critic. "Yes, very different from my own humble efforts – simple water-colours, dear sir, nothing much, and yet…"

"Take it!" said the grocer, placing one hand over the cauliflower's mouth. "The thing is of little monetary or aesthetic value, but perhaps Monsieur Ferrand will be glad to be re-united with it. If, indeed, Monsieur Ferrand is to be found…"

"Really? No, no, you are far too generous monsieur…"

"Take it! Take it to aid you in your quest…"

Urbino and the grocer shook hands. "Many thanks for your help, Monsieur Bassiak, and for your hospitality too. Two six six! Surely a place cannot be so very far away…"

Back in the shop the old woman was filling her pockets with

split-peas and cress but Bassiak strode past her regardless, Czar of all the bushes…

"Good luck Stout Fellow! And give my regards to Monsieur Ferrand. Tell him the greengages are in season and the strawberry bushes bloom…"

Exposed to natural light Ferrand's painting looked, if anything, even less life-like, less a still life than something found at the bottom of one's plate. Nevertheless the postman thrust the found object into his sack and stared at the envelope one more time. Neat handwriting, inexpensive paper, an unfamiliar looking stamp: ah, how perplexing it all seemed!

Across the square a figure in overcoat and hat suddenly bolted from the block of flats and fled as if the devil himself were on his heels. Urbino tried to hail him but the figure himself disappeared behind the chestnut tree before magically re-appearing and taking off down the street.

"Monsieur? Monsieur? Two six six, if you please…"

Needless to say, the hat and coat failed to stop. Was that a splash of paint on the back of his coat? Alas, from this distance it was very hard to tell.

Shaking his head, the postman straightened his back and hid the letter inside a pocket as if slipping it into a drawer. What a puzzle, what a mystery! Ignoring a persistent itching in his arm-pits, Monsieur Urbino strode past the chestnut tree and up to the yellow café, his heavy post bag following close behind…

# 2

One approached Madame Lacarrié as one might an elaborate dessert or hand grenade: cautiously and without any sudden moves. Thin as a knife, she nevertheless filled the café from floor to ceiling, her red hair creating the impression of a burning building, black eyes still smouldering.

"Don't think you can bring that big, mucky bag in here my lad! And wipe your feet why don't you? What were you, raised by apes? And now he's scratching – how charming! Quite the gentleman! Take your paws off my counter, monsieur: decent customers have to eat here too, you know…"

Madame Lacarrié's hair might have been carefully coiffured or she might have been pulled from her bed by a policeman – it was very hard to tell. Like a doctor's signature her hair seemed both careless and yet full of mysterious significance.

"I don't normally serve manual workers at this time of day, but, well … what is it? Looking for some place to skive when you should be out giving respectable folk their post? Eh, what do you say – given your tongue to the cat? Now look here monsieur, this establishment is for the sale of quality items, not for loitering or prevaricating…"

Although a large door of a man, Monsieur Urbino hummed and hawed, nervously wringing the neck of his sack.

"Ah Madame, I, which is to say, Monsieur Bassiak…"

"Bassiak? Pff, I've no need of his cast offs! This is a respectable café for creditworthy customers, not some den of iniquity…"

Ah, how tiny her ears were! Like two tiny handles on a tiny porcelain cup.

"No, no, the thing is, Madame... I have a letter for a Monsieur Ferrand, and well..."

"Ferrand? Yes I remember *that* rascal... that rogue and his hair..."

Madame Lacarrié's lips pursed in a disapproving pout, her brows two wagging fingers – nevertheless she poured Urbino a black coffee and offered him a pastry.

"Poof! Gone like a soufflé! And owing two weeks' pay too – not to mention the damage to the rug..."

"Rug?"

"He came round one day in that chimney of his, a tiny fellow, like he'd just stepped off the top of a cake... And oh, that smell – turpentine, glue, sawdust... Always in that fancy suit he always wore which looked like something had shat all over it..."

She made a face as if blowing smoke into Urbino's eyes.

"No, don't talk to me about Monsieur Ferrand! He dances in here with a string bag of greengages, and then turns up two weeks later smelling of cleaning fluid with a root of rhubarb in his hands. What a clown! What a *plouc*! And after that he rolls in nearly everyday, that suit of his like the pavement outside the Palais Royale, all blobs and swirls and dribbles, his beautiful hair hidden under the brim of his hat..."

Madame Lacarrié's voice seemed to drift over the counter, smoothing down Urbino's collar, brushing his shoulders, blowing into his ear. And all the time she kept pouring coffee and adding sugar, a great, black sugary sea approaching him...

"So did he live here, Madame, say at ah, two six six...?"

"Who knows why he dragged that hat of his here everyday? Nobody needs that many aubergines... but finally he says to me, 'O Madame, your pain aux raisins are so flaky – are you able to let me a room, and perhaps warm something up for my breakfast?' Ah, he was a rogue and no mistake! If you were to ask me, 'Oh

Madame, who was Ferrand?' I'd have to say, 'A hat to hide a fool in…' "

"And then he moved in?"

"Only on a professional basis, you old goat! Foo, what lady could put up with a scent like his, hair or no hair? Tobacco, gouache and white spirit! And those hands of his, leaving blue handprints everywhere – this is a reputable establishment sir, using only the finest of ingredients…"

Madame Lacarrié batted her eye-lids like a fly flicking its wings.

"Anyway, so Monsieur Ferrand moved in and, oh, that stink – paint thinner, enamel, English pipe smoke – but he paid his rent and I never said a word about the banging and thumping and humphing of furniture in the middle of the night, not to mention all those dribbles on my rugs: do you know anything of the life of artists, monsieur?"

Urbino's hands fluttered like birds. "Well, I like to flatter myself that… um, simple water-colours of course, and yet…"

Her eyes flashed like flares.

"Knaves, cheats, wretches!" Her hands stalked up and down the counter as if hunting a mouse. "Ho, if he hadn't possessed such heavenly hair I wouldn't have… I mean to say… foo, the fellow was no catch, but every once in a while it feels nice to feel a tug on the line…"

For a moment Madame Lacarrié's candle seemed to dim.

"Still, even for a dauber, there was something strange about him. One day I went in there and he had a whole row of eggs lined up, all painted various shades of blue, and the fellow was tapping the top of an indigo egg, some kind of inky yolk starting to spill out…"

"Mm, most strange…"

"Another time he was boiling up some red cabbage, purple beetroot and green kale, all in big pots of what looked like glue, and when I asked him what he was doing he said 'Why, looking for the missing shade, of course…'"

"Hm… now in my own landscapes, I…"

"I ask you, what kind of a gentleman does a thing like that? Not to mention the cost to my pans…"

"Yes, yes," said Urbino, "but what happened to him, where did he go?"

"Pff – out the back and round the bend! One day he was there – spattered suit, billowing pipe, beautiful hair – and the next he was gone, taking his hair with him. Tiny little fella: probably slipped between the teeth of his comb. And the funny thing was, he had a decent job too, respectable employment in an esteemed occupation, yet all he wanted to do was paint eggs and dip vegetables in who knows what. A lady has to be on her guard with a lunatic like that….such a fellow doesn't care where he puts his inky mitts…"

Urbino nodded and cleaned his plate. From where he was sitting Madame Lacarrié's lips were painted to look *exactly* like a padlock.

"But of course my own work is…"

"Perhaps some tart?"

Urbino took a slice and blew what looked like ash from the top. Ah, perhaps the cauliflower was wrong. Perhaps Madame Lacarrié knew nothing…

"Madame, would it be possible to view his room? That is if some other tenant hasn't, ah, placed his luggage on the rack?"

Madame Lacarrié glanced behind the counter and ruffled her fire-damaged hair.

"Oh, Monsieur… well, for a representative of the postal service, I suppose… but wipe your feet why don't you, traipsing around the streets all day and stepping in heaven knows what…"

A swing door led to a yellow papered corridor and thence to an exceptionally narrow staircase where Urbino had to squeeze himself between the walls like an awkward and unwieldy fridge.

"Is that bag heavy, monsieur? I would tell you to leave it at the bottom but who knows what dirt and diseases might…"

"No, no, Madame, 'tis fine…"

"I mean, sanitation is my watchword…"

"Yes, yes, but of course…"

Madame Lacarrié reached the top of the stairs and stopped before a surprisingly low and narrow door, more like a slot than a portal.

"Well, here it is: but remember, my lad, this is a salubrious establishment, and not one in which unhygienic acts are in anyway condoned…"

As Madame Lacarrié opened the door an enormous moth blew out, flying straight into Urbino's face. Urbino tried to swat the thing but it seemed to dance around him, trying to impale itself on his bristly chin.

Behind the door was a nondescript room with a single bed, a sagging wardrobe (actually smaller than Urbino), a chest of drawers and a large stained rug. The rather gloomy room lacked even the smallest of windows; the only thing to look at was a picture in a broken frame nailed crookedly above the bed.

"Hmm…" pondered Monsieur Urbino, modelling himself on the investigator Dupin, whilst trying to keep the moth from flying into his eyes. "And this painting, Madame? Is this a work by Monsieur Ferrand himself?"

"That? Oh, well, yes, though there's nothing much to see…"

"May I?"

"With those paws? Well, yes, I suppose…"

The nude was painted in a style which might charitably have been described as primitivist, although other, more stringent terms were available. A blue, under stuffed pillow sat atop an elongated blob on which two balloons awkwardly reclined. The face resembled some kind of balaclava, or perhaps a snowman beginning to melt.

"Quite a beauty," whistled Urbino, winking at Madame Lacarrié as he leaned in closer. "You wouldn't happen to know who the model might be by any chance?"

"Oh monsieur: such an insinuation! And I'll ask you to keep your sweaty hams away from my canvas too…"

The moth swirled around Urbino's chin and re-doubled its efforts to reach his eyes. What a pest! The postman reached out to grab it but it cannily evaded his reach.

"Yes, yes, quite the work of art…" said Urbino, staring hard. As with Monsieur Bassiak's still life, the paint had been applied in crude daubs, perhaps with fingers rather than a brush. The lady's legs seemed awfully small for her body, her knees bent most uncomfortably. Everything – her body, the bed, the room behind – was made of the same viscous material, more like oil than flesh or cloth or wood. As for the shade of blue: turquoise? Azure? Lapis lazuli? Urbino had never seen such a colour before in his life.

"Well, don't let that painting be putting ideas in your pocket, my lad – this is an establishment of sound virtue, whose levels of cleanliness and hygiene are second to none…"

As Urbino leant in closer he felt as if, with just a little effort, he might somehow peer over the shoulder of the naked model and magically enter the room, pushing his way past Madame Lacarrié's bare torso to climb into the painting itself. Foo, what a peculiar feeling the painting gave him! By squeezing behind the naked figure and following the line of vision, Urbino pushed past the nude and entered the rear of the bedroom. But how odd the space, and how strangely lit! When Urbino looked up he saw a window previously masked by the thick oils of the nude, a window which didn't seem to have any kind of corollary in the real room in which he stood. Outside, illuminated by a blue street light, was a blue house, floating in an otherwise perfectly black space. Urbino blinked and tried to roll his eyes toward it: a blue house lit by a blue light, its façade whorled like a finger print. And inside the blue house – a figure?

"Pff! Such a man – I'd rather have a pound of pork. And there were even spills and drips on that hat of his: what had he been doing, painting on the ceiling? Listen, I said to him, you don't ask a waiter for the menu by pointing to his jacket..."

Urbino blinked, coughed, and looked at the corner of the room. No window, no door, no opening of any kind. So why had that fool of an artist painted one? If, of course, this was the same room after all. When Urbino turned back round Madame Lacarrié was as close to his ear as a breath.

"A most insalubrious gentlemen... and I told him, I keep my premises clean, I thank you to remember, there isn't a speck on the counter and my linens are as sanitary as any hospital... banging around all hours of the night, chairs scraping, beds creaking, not to mention that strange stain..."

Mme. Lacarrié's lips were very close: but just as Urbino started to close his eyes, the moth flew straight at him, causing him to take a great leap backwards.

"Monsieur?"

"O Madame, um, it's nothing... I thought I... no, no, 'tis nothing. Well, thank you Madame for taking the time to assist, but..."

Mme. Lacarrié was still very close – as close as death and the old. Blushing, Urbino backed carefully out of the room, casting one last glance at the blue nude hiding the secret window from the world. Madame Lacarrié hurried after him.

"Come back and see me, monsieur! Come tonight for dinner – I think you'll be surprised by the piquancy of the sauce...but make sure you wash sir, and perhaps run a razor across that chin..."

The postman headed back down the stairs, his sack banging against the banisters all the way down.

"Shall we say seven? As long as your nails are clean monsieur, as pink and scrubbed as a surgeon…"

As Urbino retreated back through the café the knuckles on his hands started to itch crazily.

"Thank you Madame… alas, the postal service awaits and I have my deliveries to make… oh my dear, if only my sack was not so heavy…"

The rings on her fingers clicked like castanets.

"Ox tongue à la polonaise – don't forget Monsieur: but wear some cologne, you smell like a dog…"

# 3

Thick, dusty cobwebs covered the drums in the deserted laundrette, thrown like sheets from basket to tub to drier. By the door a great nest of unopened mail lay in a vast untidy pile: menus, bills, and what seemed (at least to Urbino's eyes) to be a surprising quantity of personal mail, all sent in the same kind of envelope, written in a neat but unremarkable hand, slanting a little toward the bottom. Two six six Rue de Coudray... Yes, reflected Urbino, there had to be a clue here somewhere...

The postman knitted his brows and surveyed the land. Now, if there had been an upstairs window in Madame Lacarrié's apartment, just as Ferrand had painted it – and if that window had looked out onto a blue house lit by the glow of a blue lamp... Urbino scanned the horizon... then that house would be... just... there. Except that the space indicated was an alleyway between the two blocks, a grubby hole squeezed in between the offices and the disreputable block of flats. 'No,' thought Urbino, 'such a view was surely no more than the feverish brushstrokes of a Sunday painter...' And yet for all that the postman felt a strange compulsion to take one more peek at the grocer's painting – just to check on technique or perhaps Monsieur Ferrand's use of space. Scowling, Urbino squinted at the picture and rolled the shapes this way and that: yes, yes, a truly extraordinary piece of work. It certainly made the postman's own amateur efforts seem rather green in comparison...

At that very moment the communal entrance to the flats flew open and a fashionably dressed young lady burst out, almost colliding with Urbino before toppling awkwardly onto one heel, her parcel skidding crazily across the pavement and landing in the gutter.

"Oh, Mademoiselle, excuse me…"

How distraught the pedestrian seemed: pale, drawn, blue shadows beneath her eyes. She stared angrily at Urbino and then groped around for her package, which was lying upturned in the dirt.

"Where is it? What have you done?"

"Um, well…"

"Where's it gone? Have you snatched it?"

"Ah…"

"There!" she screamed. "No, there…"

She snatched something tiny from the cobblestones in front of her and then examined it in her palm. From where Urbino was standing she seemed to be cradling what looked for all the world to be a tiny, curled up spider.

"Um, is that…?"

"Shut up! You oaf! You ape! You better not have broken it… you, you…"

The woman's chin was like a clenched fist, her mouth an ugly gash. Although well dressed, her coat looked curiously stained, as if she'd been leaning up against some newly painted lamp post. With one last glance at the postman she closed her fist carefully around its occupant and started to slowly back away.

"Mademoiselle! Is everything alright?"

The postman made a move as if to help her, but with that the woman turned and ran, her one heel tapping erratically along the pavement.

"Mademoiselle! Mademoiselle!"

Urbino picked up the empty box and examined it. The box was filled with old newspaper, and loosely tied with string.

"Mademoiselle, wait!"

The bluish stain disappeared behind the chestnut tree and then was gone. Urbino looked at the box, the broken heel, and then back at the alley. 'Foo, what can I do?' he thought. 'I don't turn the handle. I just feed the bear...'

Behind him a lonesome melody fell from the upstairs window of the nearby stationery supply store, the record crackling and jumping as if the needle were about to come loose. In the alley-way black bin bags were piled up against the remains of a half-built wall, next to which several sheets of tarpaulin were left abandoned in a pile. The whole alley smelt obscurely of pineapple.

A little distracted, the postman poked his way warily amongst the bags, his foot skidding on something wet and oily. 'This two six six?' he thought, whilst all the time soft, dissonant chords fell from the sky, chasing each other in lazy, repetitive patterns, stopping and starting as if by chance. Urbino gazed up at the open window from which the music spiralled down: was *this* the window from which Ferrand had painted his strange blue house?

His head aching, the postman picked his way back past the bins and cautiously ascended the dim stairwell to the stationer's on the first floor. As he climbed, the lonely, sentimental music seemed to circle down to meet him, constantly repeating itself yet somehow never quite the same.

"Ah, hello?" called Urbino. "Hello, is there anybody there? Monsieur? Madame? Just a moment of your time, if you please..."

The notes spiralled down like sycamore seeds, falling and falling, yet never quite reaching the earth...

"Hello? Hello, is there anybody at home?"

The office supply store seemed to be in a state of advanced disorder. Boxes of paper and card lay everywhere, alongside great cartons of pencils, pens, correcting fluid and the like. The air was thick with dust, the powder gathering on files, binders and gramophone alike. Next to it a bald, portly man lay on the floor as if in ecstasy, his eyes closed, toes twitching in time to the sweet, sad music.

"Monsieur?" coughed Urbino. "Monsieur, I am sorry to interrupt, but…"

The music played and the fella rocked, rolling from side to side like a pencil in a box.

"Umm that is to say…"

What was that smell? Something fruity?

"Ah, if you could spare a moment…"

The man beamed, his expression that of an aging cherub. When he spoke his voice was surprisingly high.

"I'm sorry my friend, but the office is closed – closed forever, my sweet prince…"

Urbino smiled, scratching at his great hairy chin. "Closed? No, no, monsieur, I am not a man in need of stationery…"

Stepping carefully, the postman made his way between the towers of paper, planting his feet in the strange white dust.

"… um, I have here a letter. Two six six Rue de Coudray…"

"Two six six? But this is two six five, my dear… There is no two six six Rue de Coudray… should there be?"

Urbino watched the fat fellow's feet sway rhythmically to the record, his toes wriggling a little with sheer delight.

"No two six six?" said Urbino, uncertainly. "No monsieur, that can't be the case. Tell me, has this place been here long? Perhaps before you…"

"Foo – I set up this store nearly twenty years ago, back when I had teeth in my mouth and hairs on my head. But everything has gone now, my angel, my sweet. My quiff, my gnashers, the store: boof – all gone!"

"Gone?" Urbino rested his post-bag by a pile of papers and looked around the room. Citadels of paper toppled over. Boxes lay in odd piles. There were pencils everywhere. "Ah, just so…" he said.

The man beamed, music fell, dust covered everything. "But, if you don't mind my asking," said Urbino, scratching at his pits, "what happened here, what became of all this … stuff?"

"What happened?" The fellow's lips twisted into a rueful smile. "Why – the bugs."

The fellow's voice was very high and for a moment Urbino feared he had misheard.

"Mugs? My dear fellow, I…"

"Bugs, monsieur, bugs! Where they came from I do not know: from under Vauvert's floorboards for all I know. First they got into my desk, then my chair, the envelope cupboard, the filing cards – oh, such a thing! Then, before I knew it, there were bites in the notebooks, holes in the graph paper, tunnels through the coloured card. An infestation, monsieur, a plague! And all the time this strange white dust rising up from the shelves… O my roudoudou, you simply can't imagine…"

"Bugs, you say?" said the postman, considering the dust. "Like weevils or eerie-wigs, you mean?"

"Ah, who knows?" said the proprietor, his eyes tight shut. "The things themselves were too small to see, just this invisible nibbling and gnawing, eating away at everything… within weeks the work of a lifetime was gone… devoured, my dove, consumed! I frothed and raged, my hair fell out, my teeth went black, and meanwhile the bugs went on eating my livelihood, gobbling up my store. O my *nounours*! I had stored up my treasures where moth and vermin destroy, and thieves break in and steal: What a goose, what a fool… No, no, all is folly: the locusts will eat it all…"

"Ah, yes, I see…"

Urbino stared out of the window and gazed down at the alley. Bin bags, rubbish, the unmade wall: but just for a moment he thought he could see a blue chimney atop a blue house, some kind of smudgy thumb print, the glow of a blue lamp… yet when he blinked the ugly alley was still there, and behind everything an insidious chewing, munching, a universal digestion…

"Yes, everything was taken from me: my livelihood, my savings, my stock! But fortunately there are things which even the beetles cannot eat. Beauty remains, my pearl, even though one cannot weigh or measure it…"

"Beetles, eh? Well, I too am in my own way an artist, a mere scumbler, 'tis true, and yet…"

"Yes, yes," said the stationer, not listening. "The world will pass, its goods will perish, all will fall prey to the bugs and the worms, but beauty, ah, beauty my friend, that will go on forever…"

"Hm, yes, beauty, yes indeed," said Urbino, embarrassed. The notes seemed to chase each other round and round, like a squirrel chasing its own tail.

"And what is the essence of beauty?" asked the funny, round man, his arms flapping as if conducting an invisible orchestra. "Why that which repudiates this sad world, which is to say, what lies beyond the veil of the seen, as imperceptible as the missing shade of blue…"

"Blue?" asked Urbino. "Like the sky you mean?"

"Blue as the colour not of the muddy earth, but of the higher spheres, that which is sequestered beyond one's eyes or head…"

Urbino squinted at the man as if he'd quite forgotten what he'd been talking about.

"But why write a letter to a place that isn't there?" asked the postman. "Ho, it doesn't make any sense…"

The record jumped and Urbino stared at the gramophone: there too tiny holes perforated the teak finishing.

"Um, monsieur, your record-player, ah, it…"

Woodworm had obviously infected the mechanism too, but Urbino felt too embarrassed to mention it: besides, the fellow wasn't listening. 'Ah, what do I know of the higher spheres?' thought the postman. 'All I seek is a door and a slot…'

The fellow smiled his nut-like smile and Urbino folded up the letter, shrugging his shoulders as if to say 'Ah, what can I do? Every letter has a destination, every bug a stone…'

The man started to open his mouth again, but Urbino backed slowly away from him.

"Well, thank you monsieur. I won't detain you any longer…"

The needle jumped, the record wobbled, and the achingly sad chords started all over again.

"No need to get up," said the postman. "I'll let myself out. Well, farewell monsieur. I'll leave you to your ears…"

"Blue, that colour of non-being…"

"Mm, yes, well…"

"Light as the absence of form…"

"Indeed, indeed…"

And with that the postman retrieved his sack and tip-toed sheepishly from the room, the music following him back down the stairwell, the notes lowered down one by one behind him, somehow heavy and weightless, all at the same time.

# 4

As the postman emerged from the building he was almost knocked from his boots by another furtive stranger, eyes lowered, face down, the man as square as a pillar-box. The guy – exactly the same size as Urbino, yet with remarkably long arms – pushed past him, clutching some kind of cigarette box; for some reason the fingers of the fellow's gloves were stained blue, but before Urbino could speak, the figure ran off behind the chestnut tree as if pursued by the cops.

Across the way the communal entrance way now lay open, a dark, gloomy threshold, framed by an ancient, over-sized door. Before he knew what he was doing Urbino's nose was inside and sniffing the dank air, the rest of him wheeled in as if on runners. Ho, what was he playing at? There seemed no concierge, no light switch, no lift: instead the postman made his way up the stairs by touch, doing his best to ignore the wet clammy feel of the walls and the strange sandpapery feel of the balustrade.

"Hello?" he called out. "Hello? I am the post!"

As if in answer to some silent summons, Urbino dragged his mail sack up each steep floor, the staircase a well of shadows, the gloom almost tangible.

"Hello? Hello?"

The staircase seemed to grow beneath him, as if he were on some kind of extending ladder; only when he reached the open door at the very top of the building, stepping into the yellowish light, did he realize that his right hand and mail bag were stained blue from where they'd brushed up against the damp wall.

"Monsieur Vercel?" called out a woman's voice. "Monsieur Vercel?

Please take a seat, monsieur; I'll be with you in a minute..."

This, the taxidermy? Urbino expected some kind of alchemist's laboratory or witch's cottage, but the flat resembled some kind of functional office or supply depot, with a long counter, a plastic seat, large clock, and small ticket machine. Urbino took a ticket and sat. What kind of place was this? Either it was high noon or the clock only had one hand.

After an indeterminate wait, a middle aged woman in a tabard appeared carrying a clip board and a large, brown box.

"Monsieur Vercel? If you'd just like to sign here..."

Urbino looked at the box and shook his head.

"Ah, Madame, no, no, I'm not..."

"Then here, here... and... here," said the woman, blinking at him behind her thick bottle-top glasses. "Thank you, monsieur. If you'd just like to attach your claw..."

"Madame D'araignée?" inquired Urbino. "Ah, I'm here looking for..."

"Madame D'araignée cannot be disturbed," replied the woman airily. "The office is working at full stretch and we don't have time to answer specific queries or requests. Who do you think we are monsieur? This is skilled work, not some kind of factory floor..."

Urbino picked up the wooden box and examined it.

"But Madame, I am looking for a Monsieur Ferrand, not Vernal. And I assure you that I am in no need of any stuffed animals at all..."

The woman stared at him sniffily.

"Animals, monsieur? As I'm sure you well know, Madame D'araignée works only with insects, arachnids and worms. We are speaking of art not some wadding of badgers..."

"Oh Madame!" said Urbino, grinning. "You are pulling my hair! Who would want a cootie filled? Foo, Madame, I'm not..."

The woman glared at Urbino and then bent over and opened the box. Inside was a slightly smaller one and inside that a smaller one still. When it seemed as if the whole counter might be lined with boxes, the receptionist handed over a tiny matchbox to Urbino and said icily, "Your order, Monsieur Vernal, if you please…"

Urbino slid it open, but could see nothing inside at all.

"What? Oh Madame, is this all some jest? No, no, you don't catch my nose that easily…"

Blinking angrily the woman leant over the counter, handed Urbino her glasses and took one step back; when he looked again, this time through her wide, thick lenses, he could make out a tiny tower of fleas or bed bugs, each louse carefully arranged in an undeniably dramatic pose.

"Ah," he exclaimed. "Well, that is to say…"

"A-huh." The woman snatched back her glasses and said coldly, "Sign here, here and here…"

"But how is such a thing possible?" asked Urbino. "Why to work on such a scale with so miniscule a subject…"

The woman tapped her pen and then handed it over. "Here, here and here – you simply cannot imagine the number of orders we have to honour…"

"And that strange, quizzical expression…"

"A-huh…"

"Not to mention those tiny clothes…"

"Monsieur, please…"

"What? Oh yes, but of course…"

Without fully thinking about what he was doing Urbino signed for the package and stared back at the box, squinting.

"D'you know, in my own time, I too am an artist of sorts. Foo, I mean just water colours and the like, but…"

"Indeed, monsieur. Good day, monsieur…"

"But I understand the need for realism, for detail, ah, if you see…"

"Good day…"

"Yes, yes, of course…"

And with that Urbino took up his sack, descended the stairs and, still staring at his tiny pack of bugs, climbed distractedly onto a waiting bus, not even looking at the line of customers loitering nervously outside the tenement door.

# 5

"Remarkable craftsmanship," said the nattily dressed gentleman sitting next to Urbino on the bus, squinting at the creatures through his *pince-nez*. "Why, it even looks as if the wee beasties are wearing clothes... ah, what work!" The fellow stared into Urbino's box with unrestrained enthusiasm. "Madam, that flea which crept between your breast/ I envied that there he should make his rest – eh, postmaster, what do you say?"

"Well..."

The passenger stared at the box like a starving man at a chicken.

"Of course," said a small bearded chap with a beret behind them, "these dots are not always so benign. As we all well know, the Black Rat Flea transmitted the Black Death in the mid fourteenth century, thus causing the death of..."

"Death? No, no, you've got it all wrong," said the first man, his voice full of indignation. "When my parents were married in Rouen a tiny flea bride and groom were placed atop the cake – mere specks yet in full morning suit and gown. Aye, the humble flea is always associated with the act of love: and no wonder! The male flea's member is five times the size of his body whilst the female lays eggs at the rate of thirty to forty a day... what better symbol of fertility and procreation, eh? What symbolism! What poetry!"

"A strange metaphor for life," said the second man. "After all, these creatures exist by feeding on the blood of their hosts: indeed, the female flea consumes fifteen times her own body weight in blood daily... one cannot even consider such a thing without a shudder..."

The be-suited gent turned on his interlocutor with some vehemence.

"No, no, monsieur: you are failing to grasp the meaning of the whole thing: we are talking of Eros, monsieur, not death! Imagine: during the act of love making, the male must cling on to his love with two large plungers, so powerful is the act of copulation…"

"And then he dies my friend! No, no, the flea is an agent of ruination and demise…" The fellow in the beret mopped his brow. "Honestly, one might as well become aroused by a corpse…"

As a Frenchman, Urbino tried to think of something to say, but for some reason his head seemed filled with soup.

"It seems to me," said the female conductor, ably navigating the aisle and clipping Urbino's ticket with some aplomb, "that as literary fellows you two are both some distance from the mark. Why, from an objectively scientific – which is to say, evolutionary – point of view the status of the *pulex* is most remarkable. Consider, gentlemen: the flea is wingless, possesses no ears and is virtually blind, and yet it has persisted for over one hundred million years…"

"Once again I am misunderstood," said the first gentleman, handing over his stub. "I speak of the human meaning of the humble flea, its symbolic dimension and meaning, which tends, despite my learned friend's impassioned objections, toward the art of love. As I'm sure the erudite gentleman knows, the term 'a flea in your ear' derives from one of the most lewd of all Medieval poems, the flea in the young lady's ear provoking desire and arousal…" Obviously excited, the fella's voice started to rise. "Did you know that in Borneo a man can be fined for picking fleas from the head of a married woman? And in parts of the Belgian Congo…"

Meanwhile the guy in the beret was practically bouncing out of his seat.

"Ho: tell that to the two hundred million dead! *Yersinia pestis* was first manifested in boils as large as an apple or as curved as an egg, usually in the groin or arm pit. From there black spots and livid rashes mark the progress of the infection, followed by acute fever and the vomiting of blood. Once these mortal freckles start to appear the conclusion is inevitable…"

Urbino tentatively raised his hand but then placed it back in his lap again.

"You are obviously a historian, sir," said the conductress, "a fine calling which does you much credit. And yet for all the horror of this terrible period, man and some two thousand species of *pulex* have co-existed throughout time. And there are still so many phenomena we have yet to explain: why does a flea reverse direction with every jump? Why do its larvae flee the light? Even those plungers to which your fellow passenger applies such carnal meaning are in truth far more enigmatic and mysterious…"

"Excuse me," said a passenger carrying a step-ladder sitting opposite, "I could not help overhearing your scholarly debate, and I wondered whether any of you might have come across the work of Jean de Venette, a Parisian friar from the late 1340s?"

The various parties looked at each other blankly. Urbino opened and closed his mouth uncertainly.

"Wait, hold on a moment, madame, please hold this…"

And passing the conductress his step ladder, the gentleman fished a large leather bound tome from out of his rucksack, and began to read.

"In the month of August 1348, straight after Vespers, when the sun was beginning to set, a very bright star appeared above Paris," he intoned. "It did not seem, as stars usually do, to be very high above our hemisphere but rather very near."

The fellow paused as if this might be significant and then buried his face in the book once more.

"As the sunset and night came on, this star did not seem to me to move. At length, when night had come, this star, to the amazement of all who were watching, broke into different rays of colour. Then, just as it shed these rays over Paris, the light turned blue and the star was completely annihilated. Whether it was a comet or not, I leave to the decision of astronomers."

The fellow nodded as if in agreement.

"It is, however, possible that it was an omen of the pestilence to come, which, in fact, followed very shortly in Paris and throughout Europe. So high was the mortality at the Hotel-Dieu that for a time, more than five hundred dead were carried daily in carts to the Cemetery of the Holy Innocents for burial. Many believed that the plague arose from contaminated water and as a result the Jews were suddenly and violently charged with infecting wells. Throughout Europe many thousands were…"

At this point in the fellow's monologue the bus suddenly lurched to the left, and for a moment it seemed as if Urbino's box were about to leap from his hands.

"Yes, yes, all very tragic," said the first interlocutor, dismissing the man with a cough. "And yet such facts are again irrelevant to the thrust of my thesis: which is to say, the erotic symbolism of the flea, and its poetic significance." The man's face was in alarming proximity to Urbino's own, and for some reason the postman felt his cheeks begin to flush.

"Ah…"

"The traditional box containing the nineteenth century flea circus was called a bridal bed, the red silk cushion – the symbolism of which will not be lost on a gentleman such as yourself monsieur – a Dutch wife…"

Retreating from the poet's ripe breath, Urbino accidentally bumped his head against the window and suddenly realised where he was. Remarkably the bus had come to a stop directly outside the insurance firm of Lavialle and Duport on the Place Painlevé, which is to say, Monsieur Ferrand's very place of work.

"No, no, your facts are all wrong," stated the fellow in the beret. "The box was originally called a *sargen*, from the German for coffin…"

"Aye, coffins indeed," said the guy with the step-ladder. "Nearly a quarter of the world's population died during the spread of *Yersinis Psetstis*… except for strangely, an area surrounding the Polish capital of Krakow, spared it seems, by the exceptional moral purity of King Casimir the third…"

"Foo!" hissed the conductress. "One would be better off tracing the pattern of trade routes from the East, the host rats being regular passengers on ships from the Mediterranean…"

"Yes, just so, but the symbolism of the fur…"

Without thinking Monsieur Urbino grabbed his box, scooped up his sack, and pushed his way past the colloquia of scholars, the nattily dressed poet, the bearded man in the beret and the conductress still squabbling and pontificating.

"Consider the witticism, 'Adam Had 'em'…"

"In August 1349, the Jewish communities of Mainz and Cologne were virtually driven out. In February of that same year, the citizens of Strasburg murdered two thousand Jews…"

"The medical faculty in Paris blamed a conjunction of three planets causing a great pestilence in the air…"

"*Siphonaptera* can jump some thirty thousand times without stopping!"

But by this time Urbino had leapt from the bus and was gone.

# 6

No, Monsieur. Ferrand was no longer employed by the firm. Nor had he been seen for several months now. Unfortunately, the firm was unable to accept personal mail. The receptionist knew nothing of stuffed daddy long legs or other such mites. Two six six, Rue de Coudray, monsieur? Non.

Urbino blew through his lips, placed his meaty arms on the counter, and sighed like a suitor.

"O Mademoiselle," said the postman, his hands scampering plaintively up and down the woodwork, "I am sure that you possess a sensitive soul, easily moved by the beauty's breath. Now when it comes to matters of the brush, I am no more than a beginner, a bungler in the graphic arts…"

The woman regarded him through dark, heavy-lidded eyes, the very light seeming to slink beneath the counter.

"Ah, but the thing is," said Urbino, momentarily losing his thread. "Monsieur Ferrand, he, ah, borrowed certain, um, art materials, palettes, oils, brushes and the like…"

The receptionist's expression was a dark bank of cloud, its arrival presaging heavy rain.

"And, ah, certain canvases which I, um, allowed Monsieur Ferrand to borrow, that is, to study in order to, ah, learn of sfumato, and the like…"

Urbino adjusted his face to try to make it as sympathetic as possible, all the time massaging the back of his hairy neck.

"Sfumato coming from the Italian 'sfumare', 'to evaporate like smoke'…"

The receptionist's voice was as cold as sleet.

"Monsieur: do you mean to say that you're here to collect his shit?"

"Um…"

"Wait here, monsieur…"

Moments later the receptionist returned carrying what seemed to be a dilapidated wooden drawer. "Monsieur," she said, her face as closed as the door.

"Mademoiselle…"

"Monsieur."


The day was long, the drawer was cumbersome, and before long the postman found himself pleasantly ensconced in a sleepy park, watching the world and his wife float aimlessly by. T'was early to shave the dog, yet too late to beat the cat – besides one place was as good as another to take stock.

Glancing cautiously around, the postman laid out the contents on a bench as if constructing some kind of private still-life. Two paint-encrusted brushes (blue); one paraffin stained rag; a necklace of paper clips; some kind of rotting fruit (an apple?), a broken pencil, crumbling eraser, a small bottle of dust. Everything seemed terribly distressed.

'Oh, Monsieur Ferrand,' thought Urbino. 'What kind of a last will and testament is this?'

On the top of a great ream of crimpled and browning graph paper the postman flicked through a series of crude sketches, finger paintings almost, showing some kind of oblong on sticks approaching a blue house. By flicking the pad of graph paper with his thumb, the postman could animate the scene and let the figure open the door: indeed, the illusion of movement was so great that the figure seemed even to hesitate on the threshold, turning from left to right, before rotating the knob to enter.

'Very odd,' thought Urbino. 'And look at the way the funny

fellow scratches!'

'Twas the same blue light, same blue wall, same blue door. But as the postman turned the graph paper round and round the figure seemed to both approach the door and descend a series of graph paper stairs – and this without flicking the page at all.

'Extraordinary!' breathed Urbino, watching the little stick legs sink deeper into the page. "But what is this labyrinth and whither is it going?" The floor seemed to come up to his knees now, almost as if he were entering some kind of well, or lake. Remarkable!

Around him office workers drifted past, young mothers with prams, old men with bottles, the occasional yellow dog, and all the time Urbino lay there like an abandoned piece of furniture, staring deeper and deeper into the depths of the page. Birds sang, pedestrians floated by, and Urbino felt as if he too might drift away, untethered from the world… Each of the pedestrians seemed to carry a small cardboard box under their arm, a white disposable carton, like a tiny coffin, and though many stumbled and tripped, all held fast to their container, clutching it to their chests as if it were a child or a pet… Urbino stared with unease at his own paper-thin package: just how many customers of Madame D'araingnée were there? And for a moment it seemed as if the whole park roared with the din of chomping and mashing, a great and terrible feast…

# 7

By the time Urbino returned to his apartment the day had disappeared into its footsteps, the shadows long and crooked. Somehow the postman had failed to deliver any of his mail, locate the missing painter, or dispose of this box of fleas: instead he had spent the afternoon nursing a small coffee in a *tabac* on *rue Narboni*, leafing through the sports section of *Le Télégramme*, and dozing intermittently throughout.

Crossing the communal courtyard, Urbino was detained by the trenchant gaze of his formidable landlady, Mme. Auffay.

"Monsieur Urbino! Monsieur Urbino, a moment if you please…"

Unable to escape, Urbino slunk toward Mme. Auffay like a cornered cat, a guilty smile fixed upon his mug.

"Ah, Mme. Auffay! How beautiful that house dress looks! And clean, too…"

"Monsieur Urbino: you have received six urgent calls, all of which I have noted down in my best book…"

"Really?" A guilty expression raced across Urbino's face. "Oh, Mme. Auffay, how worn your pencil must be…"

"Three calls from Monsieur Melnik of the postal service, enquiring as to your whereabouts…"

"Foo, a misunderstanding…"

"One from a Monsieur Vercel enquiring as to whether you may have picked up a certain package by mistake…"

"I see…"

"One from a Mme. Lacarrié to say that she has something cooking on the stove…"

"Oh Mme. Auffay…"

"And one from a Monsieur Ferrand…"

"Ferrand?" Urbino felt as if some vital pump inside his body had suddenly stopped. "Ferrand, you say? Are you sure?"

"Yes, yes… Ferrand." The landlady paused, rolling her tongue as if she held an onion in her cheek. "He said that he would come to see you tonight – at midnight."

"Midnight?"

"Indeed…"

"I see," said Urbino, fingering the dimple in his chin. "Thank you Mme. Auffay, I, um…"

"An awful lot of messages monsieur: I assure you that I have better things to do than act as your personal stenographer…"

"I am forever in your debt Madame…"

"And this on laundry day too… Fee, is that your post-bag with you, Monsieur Urbino? Monsieur? Monsieur!"

The postman climbed the stairs to his apartment, rubbing his neck as if measuring it for a noose. How on earth had Ferrand found him – especially when Ferrand himself had fallen into his own shadow? And what of the letter: were its contents so significant that the recipient had been forced to return to this world just to read them?

Unlocking the door, Urbino stared into his dark and terribly cramped apartment, the main features of which were the canvasses and torn pages left leaning against care-worn furniture and unwashed dishes. Urbino looked at his sack and the sack looked at Urbino: what was to be done? The postman carefully opened his box of bugs and placed the tiny figures on a table. If he only he possessed some kind of magnifying device in order to truly examine them: when he looked at them now they looked more like tiny specks of ash, one of them sticking awkwardly to his thumb.

Well, there was nothing else to do: he broiled some chicken, cooked some potatoes and rubbed his chin as if applying a lathe to a plank. Night spilled across the floor. The sky was the colour of black bread. The chicken tasted of glue.

Nu, why hadn't he ignored his conscience and dumped the whole lot in the Seine – or Monsieur Ferrand's missive, at the very least. Misappropriating mail was a felony, punishable by jail – tch, what if the police burst in now and discovered a whole bag of undelivered mail? Or what if Monsieur Vercel lodged an official complaint in regard to his purloined parcel? And how did Vercel know who had taken his precious *Yersina Pestis* anyway?

Urbino drew his chair closer to the fire and softly broke wind. Yes, this was a fine fix right enough – yet perhaps there was still one last way out. Fishing in his pocket he retrieved Ferrand's by now rather crumpled letter: cheap stationery, second class stamp, badly stuck down lip. The address was written in a neat but unremarkable hand, slanting slightly toward the bottom: two six six, Rue de Coudray. The stamp was unfamiliar, the franking office illegible. The weight of the thing suggested a single sheet of paper, nothing more. For some reason the envelope smelt vaguely of pineapple.

'What if I open it?' thought Urbino. 'Perhaps the answer to the whole mess lies within…'

But what kind of answer could it be? A love letter from Mme. Lacarrié? Some kind of bill or receipt relating to Ferrand's strange artistic investigations? A map or – still better – instructions?

The letter was evidence, that was clear enough, but evidence of what? Of some great secret, or simply the absence of Monsieur Ferrand from the world? And yet the more the postman stared at the slip of paper, the more he felt that the letter was really meant for him, and not for Monsieur Ferrand at all. Yes, that was the only explanation which made sense: why else would things have conspired to take place according to such a strange and unbelievable pattern? There was only a single set of footprints in the snow, and the postman's boots seemed to match them...

Without even realising it the postman had torn open the envelope and pulled out the sheet of paper within. Ho, what a peculiar colour: blue and yet not blue: indigo perhaps. Why, what did the fella say was blue after all? The colour of everything that was not... The paper was thin, almost transparent, without markings of any kind. No words, no pictures, no clues: what then did it mean? Three glasses of cognac later, the paper remained closed, an empty window looking out onto nothing. By the fifth glass the blue seemed closer to purple, the colour of plums and aubergines...

Urbino awoke at precisely five minutes to twelve, a spider trying to drop off a heavy package inside his skull. His picture of the Parc des Buttes-Chaumont had fallen from the wall, the brandy bottle was tipped over, and Ferrand's letter lay screwed up at his feet. Why did he feel so awful? His head felt feverish and a fierce itching radiated from his chest to all stations south. Stumbling to his feet, Urbino noticed the shoe box from Madame D'araignée lying upside down by the remains of the chicken, its contents scattered. Urbino shone his torch inside but to no avail: its miniature occupants were gone.

A little unsteady now, Urbino threw the box across the room and warily stalked about the room. The mail bag looked at him slanderously, the portrait of Monsieur Szzcygiel was crooked, the Canal St. Martin was full of paint. Worse still, between his ears he could hear a terrible gnawing sound, a constant nibbling as if something were chewing away at his skull. 'Twas as if his very head were made of timber; something was worrying away at its foundations, grinding, champing, tearing – the sound was quite intolerable.

Everywhere ticks were tucking into his furniture, the walls, between his ears. It was as if Urbino's apartment were one enormous canteen, the table and chairs transformed from furnishings into the very banquet itself. Worse still he imagined his own head as the first course, jiggers feasting on his eyes, boring into his ears, uprooting his teeth. But the worst thing of all was the sound… the biting, the munching, the swallowing: when would it ever end? And then, with a series of loud knocks on Urbino's door, it did.

Midnight.

"Hello?" the postman called out uncertainly. "Hello, who is that, please?"

No answer. Then the banging started again, like some kind of heavy stick had been swung violently against the door.

"Hello?"

No answer.

"Hello? Monsieur?" Urbino placed his ear against the woodwork. "Monsieur is that you?"

"Where is it?" yelled a deep, male voice. "What have you done with it, you dog?"

"I…"

"Don't prevaricate with me, you swine! I have with me an officer of the law and suggest you open this door immediately…"

Urbino blinked foolishly, his fingers across his chest as if playing the harp. "Monsieur? Ah, 'tis but a misunderstanding my friend, a simple mistake…"

"Mistake?" The voice was more like a roar. "We'll see what the law has to say about that! Open this door, monsieur! I demand that you hand back that which you so callously stole…"

"Stole? Ah, I…"

"My box, monsieur!" yelled the voice. "Stolen from Madame D'araignée. No use in protesting your innocence you swine: I know all about the likes of you…"

"Box?" Urbino cast an uncertain glance back toward the fireplace, where the afore-mentioned item lay upside down under a large standing-lamp. "I fear you have the wrong address, my friend. Come back in the morning – I'm sure we'll be able to clear this up…"

"Pig! Dog! Pig Dog!"

Urbino backed away from the door, but could hear a second voice speaking to the first in somewhat more subdued tones. Immediately an altogether more professional and regimented knocking started up.

"Monsieur Urbino! This is Inspector Rispal, monsieur. We wish to talk with you in regard to a missing delivery of mail. Monsieur, monsieur, are you there? Open up, monsieur! You are only making things harder on yourself…"

"I know of no Urbino," said Urbino, not altogether convincingly. "There must have been some kind of mix up in your files. Urbino is not here…"

"Monsieur Urbino, I have spoken with the post master and the chief of delivery services. Monsieur, I insist that you open this door…"

"Foo, it's so late," said Urbino, hands all a-flutter. "Let's settle everything in the morning like civilised men…"

"Civilised!" snorted Mme. Lacarrié. "Why he comes into my establishment with his mucky boots, spreading his germs like the lord of the manor… then, when a lady makes him a perfectly respectable culinary offer, does he so much as darken her door? He does not! And him with my brioche crumbs still sticking to his stubble…"

"O Madame, I feel that you must have misunderstood me," mumbled Urbino, "why I never meant to, um, which is to say…"

"These artists: all the same. Pop your clothes on the chair and no thought as to germs or hygiene or sanitation of any kind…"

"Ho, I never, well…"

"Here!" cried Madame Auffay's voice in triumph. "Regard – the key!"

More muffled conversation followed, accompanied by some kind of scuffle.

"O, I'll be glad to be shut of him, monsieur," confirmed Madame Auffay to a third party. "Telephone calls and visitors all hours of the day and night – not to mention the wear and tear of my pencil. Here, let me through, No, not that one, this one. O, give it here, Inspector…"

The postman heard Mr Key being introduced to Mr Lock, and fled back into his bedroom, his rash burning like a match.

'If I can just reach the letter,' thought the postman. 'If I can find the letter then everything will be all right…'

Tearing at the envelope, the thin blue rectangle again fell into Urbino's paws. Holding it up to the window the postman's apartment seemed suddenly bathed in a strange and unfamiliar shade of blue, as if some kind of curtain had been pulled shut against the world. Indeed, by placing the sheet against the glass the very window seemed to disappear, replaced by a perfectly fitted canvas. But how could this be? The usual view from his apartment – the back of a Kosher butcher's, a small yard, Mme. Audibetti's garden – vanished, replaced by a series of crude blue blocks, steps maybe, or perhaps a ladder, leading to some kind of opening. Beyond, the blue house, lined like a thumb print, flickered uncertainly in an otherwise black space, the stick of a light attached to it like a lollipop. And inside the blue house – who knows?

Behind him the postman could hear the sound of a great scrum, as if a whole swarm of angry strangers had burst into his flat. There were whistles, yells, cries, and with that the postman took a deep breath and plunged through the paper as if through an escape hatch

– or perhaps a trap door some ingenious architect had succeeded in miraculously installing against the wall.

Amazingly the postman found he could wriggle directly from his apartment into the street below, his bottom waggling provocatively at his pursuers. Everything was blue here: the street, the walls, the lamp post, the light. And everything seemed made of the same elastic material, somehow springy and tacky all at the same time.

Yes, this was it, he was here: two six six Rue de Coudray, the house almost invisible against the enigmatic blue light. But what shade was it: sapphire, indigo, cyan? The blue seemed to seep over the edge of the lines and the square mysteriously folded in on itself, like some kind of paper toy.

"Monsieur Ferrand! Monsieur Ferrand, is that you?"

Gentle, endlessly recurring music played somewhere, the melancholy notes chasing each other up and down an endless flight of stairs. Behind the postman, a pretty chestnut tree was painted to look like a hand, the crude lines of a bench scribbled half-heartedly beneath it.

"Monsieur Ferrand, open up! It is I, The Post!"

Urbino could hear various shouts and yells coming from the direction of his apartment, as well as that endless tune, rising and falling, drifting up and down the stairs as if it had forgotten its key.

"Monsieur Ferrand!"

The postman moved across the tacky surface as if some kind of dribble or clot, his blob drawn moth-like to the lamp. But was he outside the scene or already within?

"Monsieur Ferrand, I have your note…"

How beautiful the blue was, how transparent! The postman rolled across the road and reached out a stub toward the door.

"Monsieur Ferrand! Monsieur Ferrand! I have found the key…"

The door opened and for a moment the space of the canvas

seemed to concertina, folding in on itself in a curious, unfamiliar shape. Hesitating slightly, Urbino turned the handle left to right, his shape now no more than a finger print.

"Monsieur Ferrand?"

The blue deepened, the paper turned, and the postman entered the house as if opening the lip of an envelope...

# 8

Inspector Rispal arrived at Monsieur Bassiak's greengrocers the next morning, police notebook and crumpled envelope in hand. Two six six, Rue de Coudray: the address was written in a neat but unremarkable hand, slanting slightly toward the bottom. Rispal read it, nodded curtly, and approached the rear of the shop with a vaguely military gait. Inside an old woman was busy filling a bag with pickles, whilst two skinny kids lined their trousers with apples: nobody turned to look at him.

Bassiak emerged carrying a small glass of Turkish coffee and a cauliflower, the latter tucked under his arm like the head of a ghost.

"Inspector!" said Bassiak, smiling. "However may I be of assistance?"

Rispal nodded and brandished the envelope.

"Monsieur I have a letter here for number two six six but there seems to be no such place… What is the number of your establishment, if you please…?"

Bassiak glanced at the cauliflower and the cauliflower glanced at him.

"Two six six? How peculiar! I'm afraid that there must be some mistake Inspector: there is no two six six, Rue de Coudray. Here, let me take a look at that in the light…"

The inspector accompanied Bassiak to the lamp at the rear of the shop and both stared at the slip of paper. Monsieur Urbino, two six six, Rue de Coudray. Cheap stationery, second class stamp, badly stuck down lip; no, there was nothing special about the envelope at all.

Bassiak shook his head and wiped his sticky hands on his apron.

"No, I'm afraid not Inspector…"

"And what of Monsieur Urbino, the postman? Have you seen him recently? Ho – even yesterday, perhaps?"

"Urbino? A most charming man – and a highly conscientious representative of The Post. But I don't believe I've seen him for a few days, maybe more…" Bassiak smiled. "Ah, a great wardrobe of a man! Tremendously kind eyes – like a puppy or some kind of mule…"

"Monsieur Urbino is a fugitive from the law!" snorted Inspector Rispal. "It is my duty to drag him back to the light…"

"I see," said Bassiak, "how awful, how awful. Here, let me see."

Monsieur Bassiak turned the envelope this way and that as if the postman might fall out at any moment.

"Hmm, how curious: Monsieur Urbino doesn't live here but someplace in Belleville. No, there must be some kind of mistake…"

Rispal snatched the envelope back.

"A second address, a hide-away. Two six six, Rue de Coudray is the place that I seek…"

"And the contents of the letter, Inspector?"

"Nothing for you to concern yourself with, monsieur. Unless you know more about this case than you're letting on?"

"Case, Inspector?" Bassiak shrugged and even the cauliflower seemed to assume an innocent expression. "Alas I know nothing of any case… although I am sure that Monsieur Urbino remains absolutely innocent of any harm…"

"That, monsieur, remains very much to be seen." Terminating the interview, Rispal clicked his heels, smoothed down his hair, and nodded like a duck. "Well, good day then, monsieur. I'll try the café across the way, perhaps – you will of course let me know if your wardrobe rolls back in…"

"Of course, Inspector, of course…"

The grocer and the cauliflower watched as the policeman marched out across the street, the fellow pausing by the green metal bench half-hidden beneath the pretty chestnut tree. There he flipped open his pad and began to sketch a rough map of the neighbourhood, noting down the location of the café, the launderette, the boarded-up estate agent's and with the office supply store up top. Sketching the alleyway the inspector paused for a moment, squinting at something just out of sight – a blue blur, perhaps, or a house.

"Do you think he can see it?" Bassiak asked, stroking the cauliflower's leaves almost tenderly. "The door, the opening, I mean…"

The cauliflower rolled to one side.

"Zip it, Bassiak, don't you dare!"

The grocer made as if to wave. "But what if he too received…"

"Not one word," said the cauliflower. "Not one word."

Above them a cabbage white fluttered uncertainly, its wings the colour of bone.

# The Pool at Wiene Street

The first thing I want to say is don't go to the swimming pool on Niblo street. The showers are cold, the vending machine eats your money and the lockers don't lock. The second thing is that don't go thinking the baths at Mamoulian are any better. Not a bit of it! The pool stinks of chemicals and you'll notice a yellowish tinge to your skin for days afterwards. Trust me, such a tinge is not good for your health. So why go there? But the third thing I'd like to say is that the pool on Wiene Street is the worst of all.

I used to go there as a kid. As soon as our school bus would start to pull up my insides would feel as though they were being wrung out like a towel. Just thinking about it brings it all back – my ears go fuzzy, my scalp starts to itch, I sweat all over. True, I've never been a confident swimmer. 'That boy could drown in a tea-spoon of water,' (my dad). But at school what could you do? I joined my schoolmates and helped form a disorderly line. The entrance stank of small boys' sweat. Dark stairs led down to the changing rooms. 'This is it!' I thought as I descended into the depths. I fingered my wristband and squeezed hard on the locker key.

And then, many, many years later, I found myself standing there again. 'What are you doing here?' I thought: seven years of misery not enough? But lately I'd felt myself growing slightly less trim. My waist had expanded, my limbs grown flabby. I'd had to let out my trousers to permit extra parking. There was no getting around the fact; I was no longer as svelte as I had been. Looking down I could no longer tell if my shoelaces were tied. Climbing stairs, I sounded like a balloon losing air. 'This can't go on!' I said, fixing myself another bowl of waffles. Most exercise however, was out. Strict moral and aesthetic strictures forbade me from the wearing of shorts or T-shirts. I had heard of gyms, but never actually seen one. The idea of running didn't do anything for me – what's more pleasurable to do standing up than sitting down, or better yet, lying prone? At least when swimming, the water does half the work. True, when fully immersed I tended to flounder like a man trying to attract a passing plane, but what did I have to lose? Maybe the water wouldn't give way this time.

And so, against my best instincts, I went back. As my grandmother said, 'a fool hits his thumb three times.' From the outside, the baths were just the same as I remembered them: a concrete lump that from the back could have been a prison block, a rendering plant or an abattoir. Black smoke was billowing from a chimney. In the car park there was broken glass everywhere.

But the worst thing was the smell. As soon as I pushed open the door I smelt it: a potent combination of sulphur, chlorine and dread. I mean, I suppose there were chairs, posters, a desk, but all I could think was: the smell! I was seven years old again, half a pound of nothing, skinny as the stroke of one.

Strangely though, the girl behind the desk looked at me as if I were a long lost relative. She flashed me a dazzling smile and her big black eyes opened wide as a sunflower.

"Hiya old timer," she said, cradling her face in her hands. "Couldn't stay away, huh?"

"That's right…." I said, keeping one eye on the door. The girl's head was propped up on the desk like a vase, her eyes as dark as tar.

"So how's the fitness regime going? Shedding those pounds?"

"Well, you know me…" I said. "A slave to physical perfection."

"Mm, so I see," she laughed. Her big black eyes seemed to draw me in like a bee.

"It's true," I said. "The weight is just falling off me. From the side I'm just a shadow."

The gal eyed up my ample belly and smiled. "Mm, from this angle I can barely see you." Then she sighed, stretched and handed me a ticket. "Well, there you go. Don't drown in the foot-wash."

I smiled weakly and shuffled past. My face felt hot as a bowl of soup. I rushed down the dark stairs but tripped on the last three.

The changing room was the colour of a smoker's lung, and awash with dirty water and sweet wrappers. Some school class must just have finished 'cause a whole bunch of squawking kids were running around, flicking each other with towels and 'getting up to high-doh,' (my mother). I waited until they'd gone before removing my clothes. Everything inside me, physical and spiritual, seemed to shrivel. Stepping in a puddle, I noticed a sticking plaster sticking to my foot. But what could one do? I stripped off, donned my voluminous trunks, and placed my clothes in the highest of a line of stained, rusty lockers. In my hand was a small, gold key.

But where, I ask you, is a man supposed to put such a key? In his beard? I possessed neither pin nor armband nor pocket. The changing-rooms seemed to be unmanned. I stared at the key and sighed: 'there's no point in asking a naked man for change,' (my grandfather). So I carefully placed the key in the waistband of my trunks. The light was very poor. Without my glasses on all I could see were vague blobs and shapes.

The showers seemed to be full of naked old men chattering away, but luckily I couldn't see too much. They were skinny as a copse of ash-trees. As I tiptoed past them my feet seemed to flap and stick. Nobody looked up though and I made my way past the petrified figures as unobtrusively as possible.

Past the showers was another set of dark stairs and then there was the pool itself. Ach, what a sight! The pool seemed to be in some kind of draughty, badly lit bunker. Black waves lapped the surface but there was absolutely no one about, neither bathers nor spectators nor attendants. I edged my way to the side. The water looked cold and black. Best not go too far from the shallow end, I thought. Even my goose bumps had goose bumps (Bob Hope). A rusted metal ladder led down to the lower depths. I lowered myself in up to my ankle and – ah, me! – it was like dipping your toe in cold tea. Nevertheless, I allowed my extremities to edge south; when the icy waters made contact with my thighs I had to bite hard on my arm. And this, the shallow end? I tried splashing water on my arms and bobbing up and down, but nothing seemed to help. 'Well, that's enough for a first attempt,' I thought, hauling myself back out. Strange shadows jumped on the walls and smeary blobs bobbed in the water. 'Best not over-do it before lunch.' And so saying I retreated back up the stairs, my feet still flapping and sticking as I went.

I was still breathing heavily from my exertions when I got back to the lockers. Ah me, I thought, dry land at last. But what about the key? I looked down in my trunks: nothing. Feigning non-chalance, I looked down at the floor instead: nothing also. What was I supposed to do? I couldn't go back past the girl undressed. In this state I looked no great prize: my gut seemed to cover my trunks like an avalanche. Well, there was nothing to do but push open an access door and leave the back way, by the bins. 'This is what comes of such foolishness,' I thought. 'Man is not a duck.' I pushed open the doors and felt the cold wind buffet my belly. By the dual carriageway, it was even worse. Drivers blew their horns and pedestrians stopped and pointed. I shall not speak of what I had to plod through with my two bare feet. Tch, what a pitiful figure I must have cut! A round, bare man, hobbling along the side of the road. After a while it started to spit with rain and the sky made an angry face. My skin seemed to be powder blue. My teeth chattered like they were about to fall out. What a fool I'd been, what a goose! When I got back home and found a neighbour to let me in, I vowed never to set foot in a swimming pool again. What were these places anyway? Sink holes for the unwary. From now on I'd keep my feet on solid ground. And I'd have to go to the shops and buy a new set of clothes too.

Anyhow, months went by, and it's fair to say that I might have put on a few extra pounds. In bed at night I felt as if there were an anvil on my chest. My knees and I were now on only a nodding acquaintance. Still, I thought, I have learned my lesson; physical activity and I do not mix. 'A beaten dog recognises the stick,' (my Uncle Tibor). Nevertheless, a few days later I had to go on a business trip to a nearby town, and found that I'd been booked into a very swanky hotel indeed. Honestly, it was enough to make your eyes water: liveried flunkies, mints on your pillow, gold trolleys, the whole shebang. "Ah yes," I said, "a man can get accustomed to such luxury." Sitting there in my bathrobe, watching wide-screen TV, fluffy white slippers on my nippers, 'I was grander than Solomon in all his splendour,' (St. Matthew). And it was just then, as I was flicking through the hotel's glossy brochure, that I noticed that the place also had a private pool. 'Just look at the size of that TV', I thought to myself: 'how bad can the swimming pool be?' And so saying, I plodded down from the top floor, room key in my pocket, and went to look for the spa and relaxation pool. Out in the corridor my slippers made funny little smacking noises on the woodwork.

And oh my friends, the reception was like a dream – soft lights, perfumed towels, pot-pourri by the bucket load. Yes, this was a different kind of establishment entirely. But then I suddenly clapped eyes on the girl behind the desk. Tch, I couldn't believe it! It was the gal from Wiene Street, only now in a white smock with her hair pulled back from her face. She didn't seem to recognise me though. Her eyes looked red from crying, and she handed me my trunks and towels without so much as a by your leave.

"Miss, miss?" I asked. "Are you alright? What is it, what's wrong?"

Her expression was tragic, her button nose as red as a cherry on a bun.

"Oh, fella," she said. "What are you doing here? Why did you come back?"

"Me? But miss…"

Her face was crumpled as a tissue.

"Oh fella, don't you see? There's nothing left to do. It's finished now…"

My mouth opened and shut but nothing came out. Even the girl's ears looked red.

"Just take it, will you?" she said, handing over a gold locker key. "We both know it's too late now. Why torment each other any longer?"

"But miss…"

"How did it happen?" she asked. "How did we let it slip away?"

Ach, what could I do? I looked down at my wee bundle and then retreated down a dark stairway. As I turned back to see if I could still see her I stumbled and slipped down the last three steps.

Down below, I couldn't believe it. The changing room was the colour of dentures and absolutely packed with school kids. What were they doing here anyway? They climbed on all the benches, chucked bars of soap at each other, and tried to whack each other with towels. 'Aye, even here,' I thought, as a missile went ricocheting off my head. I placed my clothes in a wee cubby hole and tried to ignore them. 'Nothing changes in this world,' I thought. 'The school gates never close.' I started pushing my way through to the steps but they kept grabbing at my bathrobe and trying to pull my trunks down. What a pack of monkeys! Just as I walked past them a sudden shove sent me stumbling into the naked old men in the showers. Close up, the old sticks were as shrivelled and wrinkly as papyrus. "'Scuze me," I said, "coming through," and with that fled down the second dark stairwell, down to the pool itself.

The pool seemed to be in some kind of draughty, badly lit cave. Black waves lapped the surface but there was absolutely no one about, neither bathers nor spectators nor attendants. I edged my way to the side. The water looked cold and black. It was like jumping into an inkwell. I tried extending one exploratory toe. Cold as a penguin's lunch. I placed my whole foot in. The pool was just unbelievably icy. There wasn't even a shallow end here, not even a ladder. Just a sudden drop, just me and the pool. Then I must have slipped, 'cause the next thing I knew my mouth was full of foul-smelling water and I was splashing about for my life. Fortunately though, one foot found a slippery tile and after a while, so did its mate. Coughing and spluttering, I hauled myself out and flopped down on the side. Oh, the taste! Like the smell, only a hundred times worse. What was I thinking of, coming to this place? As my mother used to say, 'never put anything on your plate that you wouldn't put in your mouth'. Shaking, I pushed myself back to the stairs. Clumps of hair lay all around me. When I pushed my hair back from my eyes a whole kink came off in my hands. Feeling kind of wobbly, I didn't even bother to look for my locker key, but just ran back up to my room. When I got there I couldn't find my hotel key. My hair was coming out in tufts.

By the time the concierge let me in, I felt awful. I couldn't eat, couldn't sleep. My flesh seemed to sag like an over-stretched bag.

By the time the trip was over, I'd lost nearly a stone. The weight kept sliding off and I was bald as a sausage. I could still smell the pool, though. Chlorine, sulphur, cleaning fluids. The devil's soup.

Ach, after a fortnight I had no choice. An ambulance took me to hospital. The doctors were baffled. I weighed no more than a shadow's suit. My hair refused to grow back. My skin was as wrinkled as a turtle's chin.

Strangely, all the doctors in the hospital seemed really short and really young. Indeed, several of them looked hardly old enough to be wearing long trousers. Instead of examining me, they seemed to just prod and poke, and kept telling me to take down my trousers. Finally, after being ferried between cardio-vascular, ears, nose & throat, and gastro-enterology, I was packed off to hydrotherapy. When I got there a little doctor winked and stuck out his tongue. A few minutes later a nurse came to get me ready. I was put in a hospital gown and given a small gold key.

"Don't lose that," said the nurse, rather severely. She reminded me of a teacher I used to know, from my old school. Her breath smelt of Fisherman's Friends.

"Tell me, sister," I whispered. "What is it with this place? Why are all the doctors so little and so young?"

She glared at me through her glasses. "Hm, well, and what about you? Why are you so old and so wrinkled?" and I have to admit, I didn't have an answer to that. Then, with a whole line of shrunken old fellas, I was led along a dimly-lit corridor and into a side building, my feet flapping and smacking on the lino. As soon as they opened the door I smelt it. Well, what did you expect, I thought? *'Après la dernière marche, la grande chute,'* (Voltaire).

The girl behind the desk looked at my file impassively. She didn't even seem to recognize me. Just one strand of golden hair escaped from under her nurse's cap.

"So how are we today?" she asked, flicking through my file. She looked younger than ever, whilst in the last few weeks I had shrivelled up like a punctured balloon.

"Oh Missy, I haven't been so well," I said, my tongue sticking to the top of my mouth. My ears felt fuzzy and my insides felt twisted like a dishtowel. "But oh, my dear, do you remember me at all? Do you remember how I once looked? Ah, Miss what happened to the two of us? How did it go by so fast?"

The girl looked at me strangely.

"Let me take your robe," she said. "That's it; off you go, down those dark stairs. Mm, just there, that's right. Take care not to slip on the last three."

The pool seemed to occupy a kind of draughty, badly-lit hole in the ground. Black waves lapped the surface but there was absolutely no one about, neither bathers nor spectators nor attendants. The waters were as black as night. Somewhere above I could hear the junior doctors laughing and playing. But where else was I supposed to go than down? With the other stick figures I entered the pool. The slope was surprisingly severe and pretty soon I was up to my neck. What could a naked man do? 'No one digs a hole from the ground to the sky,' (my mother). The smell was pretty bad. After a few minutes I started to lose feeling in my arms and legs. 'This is it,' I thought, 'the deep end at last.' I was calmer than expected, though. I felt numb rather than cold. When I looked down I couldn't even see myself. My belly, my trunk, the little gold key – all had gone. Darkness seemed to surround me. Yet, though my eyesight was fading fast, I could just about make out a sign on the wall next to me. No petting, no bombing, no splashing. Aye, that's right, I thought: no petting, no bombing, no nothing. And then the waters claimed me.

# This Neck of the Woods

For a time it seemed as if the posters were everywhere. Dogs, cats, pets of all kinds – yanked by the scruff of the neck and carried off in the night. O those posters – you couldn't pass a lamp post without spotting one: so heartbreaking, and yet so badly printed too! I mean, would it kill people to invest in some kind of laminator? The print smeared, the ink ran, and after a while all you could make out was a grey daub and a black pair of lips, like the Cheshire cat, but worse. Loitering by the traffic lights, I tore off a sheet and examined the blobs: this tail and that the head? Or perhaps it was the other way round? It looked more like a paw print than an animal, as if Mr Raggles had been finger-printed and booked. By my feet, Fergus pissed blithely: a dog this old and slow one couldn't steal in a hurry.

The worst place was the park. There, the posters hung to the trees like tinsel, shredded and shrivelled. How sad they made me feel! I moved amongst them like the survivor of a hurricane checking for relatives. The lines of text ran in to one another, the typeface turning to squiggles: unless, of course, everything was written in another language. The type shrunk and the picture blurred. When the wind blew, the paper seemed to clap.

Progress was modest. These days Fergus was so slow it seemed as if the earth had stopped turning. What was he doing over by the rubbish bin – sniffing or having a stroke? When he walked strange snuffling noises came out from his nose: sometimes the other end also. His knees rubbed together like two dry sticks, his hips grinding like the wrong key in the lock. Where were the rabbits of yesteryear? Fergus walked as if testing whether the earth would take his weight. His limp was turning from a verb into a noun: he was *all* limp. Increasingly I looked on him as a hairy piece of luggage which needed to be carried and then stowed.

Unfortunately I had been nominated as the designated walker. Claire was busy at work with some kind of hub-based re-alignment or administrative re-calibration or something like that: either way her Productivity Flags depended on it. Tallulah was too little – crossing the road with Fergus was like fording a river whilst lashed to a stone. Besides, she wanted a pup – what should she do with a geriatric pet? Fergus snored, he slobbered, he stank: hair clung to the carpet as if to a balding skull. No, Fergus ticked none of his boxes. Only his sad, brown eyes seemed to say 'who would have thought life would have come to this?' So, when I got back from work, I walked. Fergus walked too, but only in the loosest sense of the word. Never mind whether dark or raining or Fergus' rear end slumped in the leaves: we walked. More than a lead lashed us together.

It was on just such a night – a month or so after the lost pets posters started to appear, January clinging on like a head cold – that we ran into the crazy woman. A half-hearted darkness had descended. The clouds couldn't decide whether to rain or not but pointed at passers-by, awaiting further orders. The old dear was hopping about near the park like a crow, without dog or bag or torch. Instead she clutched a piece of paper like a petitioner at the gates, a prisoner's wife gone to beg the king for pardon.

As soon as she spotted me, she started to skip over. What could I do? With Fergus one might as well make a getaway tied to a cart. I eyed the old dear warily.

"Nussbaum," she croaked, pointing to the slip of paper. "Nussbaum!"

"I'm sorry?"

"Nussbaum, Nussbaum…" After this her words turned into unknowable vowels and clicks. She stopped talking but her lips continued to move.

"Nussbaum…"

"Must?"

"Nuss…"

The little mother reached up to my cheek and caressed it. Then she brought her pinkie down to the scrap of paper, smoothing it down for me to read.

"Nyeim, Nuss, Nuss…"

What was that accent? German? Czech? Somewhere further East? A string bag of consonants clustered together, forming unfamiliar sounds – maybe letters too.

I didn't know what to make of her. Despite her odd, jerky movements, the woman didn't look like a lunatic. Of course she was wearing black – what Central European granny wasn't? – but her coat was substantial, her clothes neat, dyed black hair tied up in a tight bun. Two things worried me: the old lady wasn't carrying a handbag and she was wearing only one shoe. When I looked down I saw long nails poking out like chicken claws.

"Um, English? Ah, *sprechen sie*, um, English?"

The woman pressed the sheet of paper upon me and then tapped my chest. The paper looked just like all those strips snagged on the branches: badly copied, off centre, illegible text. Instead of some kind of animal though, the photo was of an old man: a little out of focus, true, but definitely no spaniel. Bald of pate and severe of gaze, the old man glared at me defiantly: you expect this *trottel* to help?

"Um, he's lost? You've lost him?"

The old woman took me by the sleeve and insistently started to tug. Fergus, who had slumped to the ground like a blanket, stared at the two of us unblinkingly.

"But I don't…"

The woman pulled and I followed, Fergus dragged behind like a scarf. Someone painted the night in with quick brushstrokes. Streetlights threw up their arms. The light was the colour of a mouse.

"Um…"

The old woman set off up a steep hill, one arm on the railings, the other on me. Fergus regarded the ascent with alarm: with these knees? He made as if to squirt on a bag, but there was no time to pause; the three of us were connected as if by rope.

I tried to gain some perspective. There the twenty-four hour convenience store (closed), Liquor-Save, a Gentleman's Barbers, the latter festooned with posters advertising the lost. Ah, where was the old biddy going? Behind drawn curtains, suburban houses watched on, their cozy lights seeming to say 'Don't even *think* about ringing my bell', the cats in the windows slowly shaking their heads.

By now Fergus, the woman and I had left the park far behind, seeming to drift in ever wider circles along ever narrower streets, three black specks in the gloom. Fergus began to whimper and I took him in my arms; the poor dog was beat. Alas he was by no means a miniature hound, and I felt my knees buckle and strain. Fergus trembled and I groaned: only the old woman seemed as full of life as ever. Her beak like nose cut through the night like an ice-breaker, the claws on her one bare foot tapping like a cane. "Nussbaum, Nussbaum, Nu…" she whispered, alongside words unfound in any dictionary…

I could not recall ever having walked down any of these streets before; they seemed diminished somehow, as if lacking some vital dimension. The colours seemed faded, the ink worn out, as if copied over and over again. I passed a street sign yet couldn't make out a word. The words above a garage had turned into squiggles. Strange runic symbols topped Liquor-Save.

But for all that, this was no alien land. Same terraces, same shops, same tower blocks. When they passed the squat cubes of assisted housing, my heart began to quicken: surely this was where the old dear lived…

There had to be some kind of superintendent around – probably like the old guy in the picture, balding, with a pipe, some old duffer who would be able to take the old girl off my hands. Not before time, too. Fergus nestled in to my chest like a baby, his sides shaking – mine also. The sky was washed out, the houses badly printed. Even the horizon had vanished, replaced by a wavy black line.

Just as the old dear turned in to a dark little square – more a fold, really – Fergus began to growl.

"What is it boy?" I asked, feeling Fergus' lips part right next to my throat. "Eh, what's up?"

Behind us, the shadow of some kind – perhaps a pedestrian, perhaps a dog, perhaps a bear, it was hard to tell – followed us reluctantly, hanging back a little by the bins. It shuffled rather than stalked, seemingly embarrassed about the whole thing; upright it hunched its shoulders awkwardly, on all four it looked even worse. What was this thing? On the wall by the barriers, its hairy shadow seemed like no more than a stain, a trick of the light – and yet for all of that it followed like bad news, sniffing the air once in a while whilst gingerly scratching its arse.

Fergus howled ferociously, flecks of saliva dotting his chops.

"Shhh," I said, "Fergus, desist…"

The shadow stretched out its arms, a cartoon monster.

"Fergus," I hissed.

The thing seemed to shrug, stretching a little as if its shadow didn't quite fit. Fergus started to whimper.

"Fergus?"

Before I knew what was going on, the woman let go of my arm and hopped away into the darkness. Like a bird she ducked through a small gap and I squeezed after her, the three of us emerging in an oddly proportioned, strangely blue square. Dull looking apartment buildings looked down all around, whilst a pretty chestnut tree softened the slightly melancholy air, a metal bench hidden half-heartedly beneath it. Fergus was still whimpering.

"Shh boy, stop, stop…"

I expected lights to click on in the apartments, but everything stayed frozen, like a painting. Where was this place? It felt foreign somehow, far from home. The rooftops said Paris, the light said midnight – but where was the sheltered housing, and where was the precinct? Still cradling Fergus, I stumbled closer. The tree was gnarled, old and expansive, like a well-thumbed gothic novel. Somebody had carved deep letters and shapes into the bark but I couldn't read them. Somebody had also spray painted the bench but I couldn't read that either.

"Um, this place…" I said.

The woman was hopping around the tree, one leg higher than the other. She stared up at the branches, clicking in her incomprehensible tongue. Then, as the shadow shuffled in after them, she disappeared entirely, seeming to fly to the top.

"Mrs Nussbaum," I cried. "Mrs Nussbaum, I…"

Fergus flopped from my arms and rolled off like a carpet. Black turned to blue. The shadows rubbed its paws. Of Mrs Nussbaum, nothing more could be said.

Following Fergus, I squeezed myself back through the fissure.

Here things felt more substantial, less blue. The blocks of the assisted housing complex were reassuringly ugly. Somebody had dumped a Chinese takeaway by the bushes. In one of the apartments an alarm blinked noiselessly.

It was nearly an hour before I got Fergus home, the dog as immobile as a couch. Tallulah was in bed. The carbonara was over-cooked. Fergus lay in his bed as if in the grave. What to tell Claire? I mentioned the old woman, her missing husband, assisted housing. But hairy shadows, blue squares, mysterious letters? None of this she wanted to hear.

Outside blobs replaced buildings, dots displaced doorways, a great stain hung over the town hall. Yes, the day was passing. And where did it leave things? Poorer, balder, older. As he dreamed, Fergus' paws ran like a puppy's.

# The Bridge to Mitte Kuskil

The paperwork pertaining to the bridge at Mitte Kuskil was unearthed by Timokhin, the Tsar's assistant auditor, a man of small stature but enormous bureaucratic vigour. Timokhin, it seems, was searching for blueprints of the Perm sewage system – blocked since before the Russian New Year – when he accidentally knocked over a large stack of official certificates and came across a sheath of stained and rotting documents stuffed higgledy-piggledy into what seemed, for all the world, to be a large cow-skin bag. Though many of the records had, alas, become watermarked and illegible over time, the diligent and ambitious Timokhin nevertheless determined both that work on the bridge had been ongoing for a considerable length of time (the specific dates were unreadable) and that the total cost ran into the tens, or even hundreds of thousands of roubles. The Emperor's loyal and prudent subject could not believe his eyes: how had such a situation evaded the Imperial gaze for so long? Henceforth, and without undue delay, the matter was brought to the attention of Shliapnikov, the Tsar's Chief Auditor, Teodorovich, the Keeper of the Imperial Purse, Obolensky-Osinsky, His Majesty's Stationer, and then finally Frunze, the Holy Russian Empire's First Engineer. Chins were stroked, hairs were plucked, and a year later, Laptev, His Imperial Majesty's allotted surveyor for the region, was despatched to investigate. Alas the good people of Perm remained red-faced and constipated but what can you do? Even his Imperial Majesty in all his munificence cannot be in two places at once…

Most of the estates under Laptev's direct supervision lay well to the east of the troublesome bridge, and, as his carriage left pretty Viljandi for the boggy and little travelled land round Kaugeltki, Laptev had cause not only to reflect that he had never made this journey before, but also that he had brought with him completely the wrong maps. In truth, Laptev had few qualifications pertinent to his current undertaking; he was a merry and generous soul, a convivial talker and drinker, but an impractical and dissolute subject of the crown. Not only was Laptev barely conversant with the practicalities of his trade, but the sublime emptiness of nature suited him not one whit. No, Laptev much preferred the towns and cities of the Livionian region, where he could squint at a building, fiddle with a spirit-level, and then say 'Ah, yes, good, carry on...' before retiring with a sympathetic architect to a nearby tavern. True, the life of a building surveyor had its recompenses: but land, fields, charts – no, they were somewhat less to his taste.

Alas, in this case there was nothing he could do. The Tsar's Chief Auditor required a full and detailed response to the interminable delays afflicting the bridge, and this report had to be delivered back to St Petersburg within the month. Hence Laptev's haste, and hence also his uncharacteristic ill mood. Indeed, as the surveyor and his assistant neared the desolate locale bordering Mitte Kuskil, the rain fell and the roads became ever more difficult and disagreeable. Dense forests, frog-infested swamps, verst after verst of dreary nothingness: what kind of harvest could be gleaned from this? The mud was as thick as the local accent, the people's Russian virtually incomprehensible. What was a gregarious and companionable land surveyor to do? Interminable games of *durak* with his assistant Yelisey provided Laptev with his only relief and he was some thirty roubles up when the axle of the carriage gave way with a crack and the land surveyor's carriage limped sideways into a ditch.

'Doom!' thought Laptev. 'Starvation, ruination, death!'

Fortuitously, salvation came scant minutes later, in the form of a heavy wagon from the local quarry laboriously making its way through the muck behind them. Though Laptev had been operating under the assumption that he was journeying through some God-forsaken land, unknown to map-makers or even the basic markers of civilization, it turned out that the road was, in fact, a fairly busy thoroughfare, employed by both a local lumber mill and a nearby quarry, both enterprises intimately involved with the construction of the enigmatic and exorbitant bridge. Yes, confirmed Tiit, the quarry-owner, the stone-works existed purely to serve the construction of the nearby span; by God's grace, he intoned, this construction had kept the quarry in operation since long before Tiit had arrived (some twenty years ago last spring) and would continue for his children and his children's children too.

Twenty years? Laptev took a sharp intake of breath. Even by his own dilatory and slothful standards, twenty years spent working on the erection of a single span sounded less a matter of delay than some kind of swindle or (worse!) deliberate plucking of the Imperial chin. And yet, Tiit confirmed, both his boys had grown up under the shadow of the bridge, and both had gone on to find gainful employment in its completion. Even without them the quarry still employed nearly twenty peasant-labourers, the excavation by far the oldest and deepest in the region.

"Where would we be without the bridge?" Tiit enquired. "Nowhere!"

Laptev nodded and sipped his *medovhuka* thoughtfully. The locals had their mitts in the Imperial purse and didn't even have the decency to hide it. Still, that was no reason not to benefit from their hospitality. Tiit served the travellers some kind of pigeon stew whilst a crooked, hairless man silently repaired their wheel.

Several hours later the surveyors bade farewell to the quarry, as Kalmykov, their driver, urged the horses over a squat wooden bridge toward the local mill. All around, large expanses of forest had been cleared, vast quarries gouged out of the black and stony earth. It was inconceivable that all this activity had been directed toward the fabrication of a single bridge, and yet Laptev could see no other sign of industry. Great tracks led in to the silent and lifeless forest, the mud freshly churned up and a fierce tang of resin lingering in the air.

The mill was a large and fine looking construction, its lower storey built of stone, the upper of wood under a freshly thatched roof. The huge wheels – several fathoms in diameter – churned the water ceaselessly, and a number of wagons waited alongside it in a lazy and somewhat disorganised line. The foreman, Klaasan, greeted the Imperial delegation cheerfully, and invited them to his office for a bottle or two against the cold autumn air. Klaasan, a tall, ruddy man with blue, guileless eyes and a pock-marked face, had only been in post since the spring, but he happily confirmed that the mill had been in operation at least as long as the quarry, and that there had been a smaller, less efficient mill on this site a good twenty years before that. Laptev nodded, performing a series of swift mental calculations inside his skull. Forty years of wages, raw materials, running costs, subsidiary construction: ho, what kind of fabrication – or racket – was in operation here?

Although the bridge was no more than two hours' ride from the mill, the delegation saw little reason to hurry: the rain was heavy, the woods dismal, the vodka surprisingly strong. Between bottles, Laptev inquired as to whether any official records were kept at the mill, and Klaasan, himself a little stewed, agreed to dig them up. Swaying as if out to sea, Klaasan opened up the safe in his office and handed over the paperwork, great long scrolls, as long as a peddler's beard. His eyes struggling to focus, Laptev picked his way through the long, archaic calculations, his brain straining to make sense of the spidery, faded print. The mill seemed to have been in operation for much longer than Klaasan had suggested; perhaps all the way back to Peter himself. But how could this be? Or – and given his inebriated state this was certainly a possibility – was Laptev simply getting mixed up with his sums? No thought Laptev, better to sleep it off, to wait for a clearer head. Nobody ever caught a bird at night! When he got back to Klaasan's room, Yelisey had lost his britches and Klaasan was lying with his face in the soup.

The regional surveyor awoke the next day with a bear in his head and no sign of the books. In no condition to lace his boots, never mind examine the mill's accountancy, he elected to travel straight to the bridge instead, trusting the chill morning air to clear his head. Yelisey had to be carried on board but the driver, Kalmykov, seemed unusually awake and twitchy.

"Sir?" he said to Laptev after loading Yelisey into the back. "Sir, if you want my opinion, no good can come of this. Something isn't right here. Let's be shot of this place and go…"

Laptev was astonished. Kalmykov had rarely finished a sentence before now, and such garrulous chatter was very much out of character.

"Are you suggesting that I fabricate my report?" whispered Laptev as if the Tsar himself were listening. "Just go back to the emperor and make it all up?"

Kalmykov stared at him evenly, only his mouth seeming to twitch.

Laptev shook his head and smiled. "No, no, let's go see this famous bridge, eh? I mean, after a hundred years it must be a sight to see…"

Kalmykov spat, cursed, and took the reins, whilst Laptev was thinking, 'Yes, it's a cosy little deal these Estonians have going here; surely worth a bribe or two…'

A damp curtain of mist hung over the dark and bird-less forest, the dew sticking to the trunks like cobwebs. The path was narrow here and the trees tightly packed, as close together as a thing and its shadow. The horses seemed uneasy and Kalmykov refused to look Laptev in the eye.

Eventually sounds of human progress penetrated the gloom and the surveyor's carriage came upon a quarry wagon making slow but steady progress through the murk. Beyond lay the first few huts and supply sheds, surrounded by idle teams of packhorses and oxcarts; then the vista opened up and a small village of labourers and stone masons appeared, flat islands of earth scattered amongst great furrows of black mud, yellowish smoke rising from the chimneys of the scattered kilns. Huge chunks of stone – like plinths from which the statues had been surreptitiously filched – lay marooned along the road side, mud-coated peasants staring at them impassively. Laptev shook his head: what kind of farce was this? Kalmykov directed their carriage toward long, but somewhat ramshackle, stables, the stalls almost indistinguishable from the broken-down scaffolding surrounding them.

The foreman was a large and florid Estonian called Rücker, plainly distressed to read Laptev's letter of introduction and exceedingly reluctant to allow any kind of inspection.

"With those boots?" he asked Laptev. "Tch, sir, you would not want to dirty such boots with mud such as ours…"

For his own part Laptev was happy to linger in Rücker's lean-to, sipping some kind of juniper liqueur and stealthily taking the measure of the man and his enterprise. Somehow Rücker seemed both terrified and only half awake: his eyelids drooped, his hands shook, and his rounded figure leant like an ill-fitting post. Come to think of it, most of the labourers engaged here also seemed grotesquely crooked and bent, hobbling back and forth as if they'd transported those blocks on their own sagging backs. Mm, no need to over-do it thought Laptev; not even Alexander himself would be taken in by such an act...

Obviously none too keen to allow the Imperial designation to inspect the bridge itself, Rücker opened up another bottle and from somewhere rustled up a basket of freshly baked cinnamon buns. His Majesty's representative was more than happy to remove his boots, but as the snifter of vodka slowly brought Yelisey back to life, Laptev felt it prudent to at least take a peek at the mysterious erection.

"Yes, yes, all very good," he said, his mouth full of crumbs. "But let us see the fruits of your labour eh? The bridge to Mitte Kuskil of which I have heard so much..."

Bowing and scraping, Rücker reluctantly led the inspectors through the small hamlet of craftsmen, past the camp fires and the lines of drying sheepskin, the broken timber and sagging supports, until they arrived at the very mouth of the estuary itself. Rücker stared at his feet, Yelisey gesticulated wildly and Laptev struggled not to laugh: why, work on the bridge had barely even begun! True, the mist hid anything more than ten feet away, but after all this time all that could be seen were the foundations of the first arch and a rough wooden walkway, itself half fallen away. Huge blocks of stone lay abandoned in the slime, around them the splintered remains of joists and beams, hacked to pieces as if by some marauding army of vandals.

"But how can this be?" spluttered Yelisey. "What manner of trickery is this?"

"Now then young man," replied Laptev, calmly. "Let us see Master Rücker's handiwork close up…"

So saying Laptev hopped from stone to stone until he was at the construction's furthest point, from where he could see a few more stones upended in the foul and miry water, along with the accumulated rubbish and debris of month after month of continuous habitation.

"Yes, yes, I see…" he said, gazing out at the mist as if from the bow of some doomed and shipwrecked schooner. "Well, there seems little else to say…"

Then, just as he was about to hop back, he saw it half cemented on the shore-line: the deformed head of an enormous statue of Peter the Great, the skull caved in, the nose chiselled off, its body abandoned like a corpse amongst the hungry, endless mud. Even Laptev was shaken.

"Well," he mumbled, "Well, that is to say…"

He nearly stumbled on his way back, and only Yelisey's firm grip prevented him from taking a dive into the muck. Yelisey spluttered, Laptev wheezed, and Rücker gazed at the mud as if burying himself head first were his dearest wish.

"I fear we need to discuss your progress Mister Rücker," intoned Laptev, trying not to think of Peter's mangled brow. "Yelisey! Perhaps you could take some measurements here whilst Master Rücker and I discuss matters over a little *sült*…"

Yelisey reluctantly set to work positioning his sticks and measuring rope whilst Laptev and the foreman made their way back toward the camp. If anything the mist seemed to be getting even thicker, a great woollen sack placed over the earth.

Only when back in his tent did Rücker seem able to find the courage to address his Majesty's representative eye to eye.

"Master Laptev," he began, struggling not to swallow his words.

"I fear I can offer you neither explanation nor confession." At this he paused and carefully licked his lips. "I have worked on the bridge my entire adult life, as did my father before me and my grandfather before that. I grew up in this encampment and in all my years have travelled no further than the nearby mill – well, except once, when my father fell ill and I travelled to Aksi in search of supplies. I have given the bridge – and his Holy Emperor – the best years of my industry and strength. What you have seen today is the result of three generations of labour, and though you may find the resulting span in some way lacking or disappointing," (Laptev couldn't prevent one brow from assuming an ironic angle), "I can swear on the name of my family and this land, that no man could have given more…"

Laptev spread his hands wide as if to say 'well, yes, dear fellow, but of course…' but Rücker couldn't seem to stop.

"Each morn I gaze across that cursed span, and each day we begin anew. The men here are hard workers, sir, willing to toil from daybreak to dark, and if the bridge has not progressed as punctually as his Holy Majesty might have wished, I can only offer my head and say that no man can offer more…"

Laptev was plainly enjoying the performance, though he felt that perhaps the last gesture was over-doing it a bit. Besides, beheading Peter the Great was a tad much, even here, in the arse end of the Livonian states…

"My dear chap," said Laptev, smiling broadly, "there's no need to distress yourself. I am sure that you and your, ah, skilled artisans, have performed to the best of your abilities, and that any degree of sluggishness can only have arisen as a result of unforeseen events. So, wipe that crease from your brow, sir! I am sure that I can draft a report which will prove satisfactory to all parties involved. If you could provide accommodation for myself and my men then I will retire and give the matter some thought. And perhaps at the same time you could check your finances and see if there is perhaps any sum of which you might have overlooked…"

Laptev toyed with his gloves playfully but Rücker barely raised his head. 'These Estonians,' thought Laptev. 'You have to poke them with a stick just to check they're not dead…'

One of Rücker's assistants led Laptev away to a warm, comfy shed, someplace close to the stables.

"Could you tell my coachman that we're staying the night?" Laptev asked the fellow. "Our horses will need feeding and perhaps someone could check our back axle too…"

The hunched and round-shouldered peasant stared at Laptev blankly.

"He's already gone," he sighed in that weird local accent. "He drove away almost as soon as you arrived – you want a stall keeping for him, sir?"

The smile on Laptev's face was thin as a paper cut.

"Well, yes, yes, I'm sure… no, no, that's fine my good man, don't you worry about a thing…"

Nodding, the bespattered hunchback hobbled off, his bare feet leaving funny wee duck marks in the mud. Laptev looked once at the shed and then gazed back at the dark and silent forest. 'No, he'll be back,' he thought. 'Kalmykov knows that he can't wriggle out of the emperor's grip…'

Over at the shoreline Yelisey struggled to get his staves to stand up straight, sliding this way and that in the muck. Next to him the shell of the bridge pointed at the fog with its skeletal fingers: who knew what hidden meaning it pointed out, or what obscenity it was trying to gesture? Laptev sniffed the air and spat. Why would anyone build a bridge here anyway? On one side nothing, on the other, less. Workers transported timber along narrow gangplanks whilst Yelisey fiddled with the position of his gauges, their figures mere silhouettes against the fog. Laptev shook his head and retreated back inside his shack: Rücker's pockets had better be deep as a well, his arms as long as a bell rope…

In his dream enormous stone heads were being slowly rolled through the mire, their features becoming increasingly indistinguishable as they wound their way through the mud and slowly down to the sea. Was that Frunze, the Empire's First Engineer, or Tiit, the old man from the quarry? Laptev pushed his own kisser deep into the dirty pillow, only to be disturbed by a strange sound midway between the keening of the autumn wind and the complaints of an angry and disappointed woman. His face pale and deathly, Laptev climbed from his heavy blankets and moved over to the ratty curtain to take a look. Outside the mist seemed to roll like a strange and spectral sea; Laptev could hear the familiar sounds of sawing and banging but could scarcely credit the notion that the site's labour was continuing deep into the night. Ho, what were those fraudsters up to now?

Laptev turned to look for Yelisey's familiar lump but could see only bed clothes: tch, had Yelisey abandoned him too? Head pounding and beard a-quiver, the surveyor reluctantly threw on his jacket and stepped out into the mist. The scene which met him was madness, chaos: on one side of him a team of workers feverishly dismantled the stable block, on the other, sombre and crooked figures systematically hacked away at the supply sheds with axes, their tools moving up and down like the jaws of some terrible beast. Inexplicably the peasants toiled with their eyes tight shut, their movements frenzied and random, blindly destroying whatever work had been undertaken the day before. 'What new devilment is this?' thought Laptev, 'what do those fools think they're up to?'

Peasants overturned yardsticks, splintered scaffolding, trampled building blocks deeper in to the mud. Down by the wagons Laptev spotted Rücker struggling to dislodge a wheel with his bare hands, his face contorted with the effort.

"Rücker!" Laptev yelled. "My good man, what on earth d'you think you're doing?"

Sweat poured down his face, Rücker worrying away at the wheel.

"Rücker? Please desist. That wagon is imperial property…"

Rücker ground his teeth.

"Rücker? Rücker? What good can come of this?"

The foreman ignored him and continued to work in the bolt; his eyes were closed and his mouth pulled down at one side.

Unsettled, Laptev retreated and awkwardly groped his way through the mist and toward the shoreline. The wind sang and labourers rolled and thrashed. 'I know that tune,' thought Laptev, 'I've heard it sung someplace before…'

Down by the shoreline a great mob busied themselves in attempting to tear down the stone bridge supports, attacking them with hammers, chisels, broken fingers, all the time the mist lapping at their feet like milk. What were they: fools, vandals, maniacs? And amongst them – little mother, could it be…?

Yelisey had somehow hung himself on the wire between two measuring posts, his body twisting on the wire like a flag. Next to him bodies lay face down in the murk, workers using them as stepping stones in their haste to attack the very foundations of the bridge. Occasionally a club would crack a balding head rather than a tack line or underpinning, but nobody seemed to care. Wrenches gouged and chisels stabbed. And all the time the night was pouring something sweet and honeyed into Laptev's ear, a half-remembered song, 'You Have All Your Life to Come'…

Terrified, the surveyor turned his eyes from Yelisey's corpse and raced back toward the camp. Figures had upturned his shack so instead he ran blindly toward the trees, mud caking his legs and boots, splinters of bridge in his hair and beard. Drawing on reserves of energy previously spent on the upkeep of his plentiful locks, Laptev forced stubbornly himself on, stumbling through the warped and contorted trees until the song seemed no more than a distant refrain. 'You have all your life to come/before the work is done...'

It was nearly dawn by the time Laptev came upon the outskirts of an unknown and somewhat destitute-looking village, really little more than a few peasant huts hunched alongside a stream. His face whipped by low hanging branches and his clothes painted with mud and clay, Laptev cut a sorry and bewildering figure, the locals unable to make sense of his garbled Russian or his fevered German. Kross the dairyman, took him in, and after getting his wife to attend his face, allotted Laptev room next to his prize cow, covering him with some kind of cow-skin bag. The surveyor thrashed from side to side and ground his teeth, humming some kind of meaningless tune whilst crushing his face into the dirt. 'He has the beard of a gentleman but the mien of a maniac,' reflected Kross, suspiciously. 'What good can come of this?'

Hours later Laptev awoke from his slumbers a changed man. His beard was white, his brow lined, the right side of his face displayed a pronounced droop. The man looked as if he'd chewed his way out of the grave, and yet the first thing he did 'pon wakening was to call forth for paper and pen (Kross having to borrow these from a neighbour), whereby he began to compose a long and detailed account of all the strange events pertaining to the bridge at Mitte Kuskil, scribbling on the parchments as if a man possessed.

With an alacrity and diligence distinctly absent from his previous book-keeping, Laptev conscientiously set forth all he had gleaned from the quarry, the water mill, and, of course, the terrifying events surrounding the bridge itself, writing everything down in the most detailed manner imaginable. With a feverish glint in his eyes and despite a strange numbness on his right side, he filled page after page with calculations, diagrams, transcripts of interviews, and metaphysical ruminations regarding the nature of both the tune and its lyrics, carefully noting down everything pertinent to the case. When his report was finally complete, Laptev stretched his fingers and sighed; he then drank a whole quart of milk, ate the remains of the Kross' evening meal, and immediately fell back into a deep trance, his manuscript sleeping peacefully by his side.

In his dream Laptev was back at the bridge, but this time the fog had disappeared, and the bridge appeared inexplicably, monumentally complete. Instead of a few wooden supports and the keystone of the first arch, a mighty span reached out over the water, the bridge flanked by great stone statues forming a line of petrified figures, starting with Peter, but leading far into the future, their clothing and countenances becoming stranger with every step. 'What is the meaning of this,' asked Laptev, 'and where does it lead?' Climbing higher and higher, his surveyor's tools lying heavily on his back, Laptev gazed upward at the bridge, his heart pounding, time rushing in his ears. Only when he paused for breath did he happen to glance out over the side and stare down at the waters below; there, amongst the hundreds, maybe thousands, of bodies bobbing gently against the arch supports he could make out Rücker, Tiit, Klaasan, Yelisey, even Kalmykov, the coachman's face bloated and huge. 'You too, eh?' thought Laptev. 'Well, I can't say I'm surprised…' The surveyor stopped and put down his tools. "Well, 'praps it's best to stop here, after all," he said. "Why traipse all the way to the other side? Let the future line its own pockets. The view is always the most beautiful in the middle..." Laptev stopped, tears running down his face. "Tch, nobody ever built a bridge without getting their feet wet! How does the song go? You have all your life to come/ like the beating of a drum..." And with that, like the first leaves of autumn, his whiskers started to fall from his chin...

In the village, the peasants closed their shutters and barred their doors against the weird and unnatural wind. Only the door to Kross' new grain barn remained open: within Laptev tossed and turned, rolling around the floor like a bug struggling to escape its cocoon. Eventually one eye popped open, followed by another, and the surveyor leapt smartly to his feet, retrieving his paperwork and spreading the pages out on the barnyard floor as if presenting them to the Tsar himself. He then paused, cocked an ear, and conscientiously began to score out every word, scribbling away at the text until every last character was obliterated. When finished, he tore up the ink-spattered pages and laboriously began to eat them. What's that? What tune was he was singing to himself? Ah, I cannot say: what kind of witness could be found? Nikita the cow looked at him, lowed, and kicked over her trough. All that night she bellowed and moaned and by the morning she had trampled every last morsel of her feed into the dirty and foul-smelling ground.

# Execution of an Orchestra

**After Andrey Voznesensky's Ballad of the Year 1941**

The cello was the first to be beheaded: tch, with its long neck and plaintive tone, what did it expect? One of the soldiers – the one with the greasy cap – took hold by the throat and slashed at its strings with his knife. When he was sure all the wires had been cut, he tossed the thing to the ground and put his foot through the base. Only then did he undo the buttons on his jacket and start to wipe the sweat from his brow. There were splinters everywhere. The cello was just firewood now.

After the cello it was the harp's turn: it was harder for the larger, bulkier instruments to hang back. The harp trembled as the guy with the red 'tache plucked it violently, yanking at the wires with his long, bony fingers. When they failed to snap, he went to fetch his axe. For a long time the only sound was the soldier's vigorous chopping. He built up a steady rhythm but it still seemed to take forever. He was still swinging when they carried over the drum. The drum looked at the harp and the harp looked at the drum: it should come to *this*? The harp's strings lay on the ground like hair. And the drum? Don't ask about the drum. He had a big tear on one side. Most of his stitching had come loose. His sticks? Believe me, his sticks were long gone.

It was around then that somebody started passing round a bottle and the whole messy business gained in tempo. The first violin – a rare and dignified soul who had been with the orchestra since the very beginning – was dashed against a rock. Three guys in jackboots stamped hard upon the tuba. The violas had their necks rung like a brace of rabbits.

The other instruments looked on mutely. The horn section edged gently backwards. The glockenspiel looked shifty.

"Whatever you do, keep *schtum*," whispered the first clarinet. "If they ask about Dolgushov, act mute."

Some – like the lickspittle whistles – would have been happy to talk but they hadn't even made it to the quarry; they'd been melted down days ago, along with the triangle and the gong. Nobody had seen the grand piano but it was hard to imagine it had somehow gotten away: I mean, with *that* stool? The flugelhorn had nearly made it, but at the last minute it had stumbled on its side: what a shemozzle! As for the rest of the gang, they'd all gone the same way: clangs, clatters, clashes. And now here they all were – trapped at the bottom of the pit.

"If the strings want to make a big production, then let them. But you – don't be a *nudnik*. If the chef serves poison, why open your mouth?"

When they'd first been taken from the concert hall, there'd been a lot of loose talk about inventories, repair jobs, being taken into storage – I mean, covered in wood chips, stuffed in a darkened box, that didn't sound so bad. It was bumpy in the back of the truck, but not terrible. The sacking was a bit dirty, but that was okay. The quarry though had thrown them. Did they mean for them to rehearse here, in a place like this? Where were the lights, the instrument stands, the seating? What kind of audience would *schlep* out to a trench? Then they saw the soldiers.

Their frock coats were covered in dust, their jackboots filthy. The commissar was a tall, bald fella in a peaked cap; nobody – not even the trumpets – made a move in his vicinity. His eyes were red and sore. His cap was the colour of blood. What kind of a devil was he? When the bottle was passed round, he didn't drink but loudly spat on the ground.

Most of the others simply lay around, though whether from boredom or inebriation, it was hard to tell. It was hot in the quarry and the ones doing the sawing were mostly bare-chested and sweating. A fella with a thick, fleshy neck sliced the bassoon in half with a sword. Rocks were jammed into the trombone till it burst. The double bass was already on fire.

Aside from the grunting, chopping and smashing there were few other sounds – the acoustics here were awful. But what were the instruments to do? The violins had all been plucked. The bows were broken. The strings were piled up in what looked like suspiciously like a pyre.

"Dolgushov…" whispered the second clarinet.

"Shhh! You want to be matchwood, too?"

And all the time the instruments kept asking themselves the same questions. What were they doing here? What did the soldiers want from them – information, a confession, a tune? What kind of crime could a provincial orchestra commit?

A little further up the track a grey, tired donkey was dragging a concert grand slowly along the path, a great cloud of dust following behind it like a fist. The piano's legs had been sawed off so the donkey had to pull the thing on its belly, the thing crashing and straining with every stone. What a sight! What a shame! Its innards were hanging out, its stumps splintered, its head bowed – nu, the donkey looked little better. Every few steps the pair had to stop for breath, the donkey panting heavily, the piano stranded like a great, black fish. After a while a peasant with a wild yellow beard would urge the donkey on and the two of them would start moving again, dislodging more stones and earth as they went.

When they got to the bottom the peasant stood next to his animal and gently stroked its neck. The piano's keys were terribly crooked and there were exposed wires poking from out of its back. A strange humming sound came from inside the box, like a maddened bee. One stump was worn smooth. 'So,' thought the other instruments: 'the Czar didn't escape after all.'

The commissar brusquely dismissed the peasant, but the donkey seemed too exhausted to move, swaying uneasily as the commissar circled the stricken piano, drawing circles with his crop. The commissar's stubbled face was inscrutable. He might have been a maestro about to deliver a famous performance or a hooligan taking a dump. Who knew what went on under a cap like that? When the commissar touched a key it fell on the ground, like a tooth. O, what kind of thing was this? A whale, a wardrobe, a box into which one might climb?

"Korotkov! Grishchuk!" he yelled. His adjuncts left the fire and looked around for something to prop up the torso, as well as some kind of stool for the commissar to sit on. Trunov waited with a strange expression on his face, running his hands along the keyboard bar uncertainly. His riding-switch shook. His cap looked as if it were about to fall from his head.

After a bit of toing-and-froing the piano was leant up against the corpse of a smouldering double bass and the commissar took his seat. The other soldiers stopped what they were doing and stared: what the devil was Trunov doing? The fella breathed in deeply, lifted up his hands – and then the lid dropped down, the commissar toppled forward and the piano seemed to swallow him whole.

There was instant consternation. The keys crashed and the bottom of the thing started to sag. Yells and curses issued from the soldiers.

Seeing their comrade fall, they attacked it with axes and chisels but the thing refused to give up its meal; if anything it seemed to be pulling him in further. A foul stream of abuse rained down upon it. The insides of the piano crunched and contracted, its mouth quivering with anticipation. Above the maw, the commissar's boots thrashed about farcically. The racket was appalling.

Taking advantage of the confusion, the drum slowly rolled away from the truck and bounced away down the hill, trying to keep as great a distance between its shell and the soldiers as possible. Nobody looked at it: everybody was gazing at the concert grand instead. Every time the drum hit a stone he let off a comical 'bong', but what could it do? Its rounded tum flew high in the air. The quarry went on and on.

Meanwhile two of the soldiers had wrestled the piano to the floor. Tsyrkin laid in with his sledge hammer and administered a series of thunderous blows. Inexplicably, blood began to flow. The hacking and the splintering stopped. The soldiers gazed at the piano and the piano gazed back. The thing's back was hewn in two. There were teeth all over the place. Grishchuk reached down and picked up the commissar's cap; parts of the commissar were still inside it. Someplace, far away down the quarry, the drum was still rolling. You wouldn't believe how far it went. 'Bang' went the drum.

"Shhh," said the clarinet. "Not a word!"

# The Alphabet's Shadow

Fergus had died a few weeks earlier, the lump on his tail growing from a pea to a nut to a ball. Four inches in diameter, yet who could measure the death within? I wept like a baby, Claire like a mother, the vet like a Russian. "Fergus, Fergus," we cried, "where goest thou now?" We scattered his ashes by the skip near the playing fields, each telling the other that we'd never go back. Why go? Leaves fell, dogs pissed, yet Fergus would never know. What could the silent trees tell them of the passage of the hours? Branches broke, wood rotted, the jetty fell into the pond – and all the while Time, that old bastard, hunched nonchalantly by the fire-damaged shelter, slowly winding his watch…

How long was it before I went back: two weeks, three weeks, more? It was autumn, gusty, clouds unravelling like old wool, but there I was, sitting on Fergus' bench, my hat damp, trousers green, the ghosts of old biscuits lining my pockets. What was I thinking about? Nothing, I was thinking about nothing. My lips were dry, my nose gummed, my head a bucket from which all thought had drained. And yet, oddly, it was just when I was thinking of nothing that I saw it, scampering about in the half-light, both a squirrel and not a squirrel – the remains of a squirrel, perhaps. "Hello little fella," I said. The thing looked flattened, mangy, like a hairpiece left out in the rain. Its nose was squashed, its eyes all yellow and yolky. "Hello," I said. "Hello wee man."

What was it – puppet, road kill, pet? It scampered to and fro amongst the trees, flicking its tail and clicking erratically. Then, just as I started to lose all interest, the thing pointed at me with its little black gloves, gesturing for me to come hither. What to do? Half of me – my legs, feet, knees – started to get up, but the other half – head, shoulders and torso – stayed rigid: I was like two people, one awake and one asleep, a mechanical toy where the top and bottom don't fit. So you can imagine my surprise when I found myself traipsing off into the darkness, my feet two heavy clods of earth, legs as stiff as fence posts. What did I think I was doing? Why was I following this thing? The squirrel (squirrel?) led the way and I followed, its tail coming and going like a hand up a sleeve.

The copse was bigger than it looked: black leaves, black torsos, black bark. I mean, would it kill the council to put up some lights? Out of breath I rested my palm against a wet and darksome tree, my fingers stinging as they rubbed against the great black shape. Gingerly, I reached out and felt whorls, flourishes, a rigid and ageless sea. But what was this: some kind of a pattern or key? All of a sudden my fingers started to grip harder, burrowing deep into the tree's soft, rotten heart. I felt my nails clawing, digits tearing. When I pulled my hand away, my fingers were as earthworms, pale and long and jointless. The skin at the end was torn. Something black and painful had splintered inside one nail. 'Oh, what has become of me?' I thought. The squirrel had departed. Nuts rained down from the sky.

When I got home, I locked myself in the bathroom and guiltily scrubbed my nails. The cuticles were green, the tips black, my digits like ten runner beans. The fingers of a gardener or a corpse? A grave-digger, maybe. Anxiously I switched off the light and ate lasagne with my wife and child.

It was pretty dark by the time I finished work, so I parked up on the waste ground near the playing fields and made straight for the bench, tip-toeing my way through the mud as furtive as a crow. The park was colourless and silent – even the starlings had quit complaining. Out in the darkness, the trees held each other up like drunks, their roots as tangled as string.

"Hello?" I said. "Hello, wee man?"

No brush, no paw, no little yellow eyes; instead, the gloom went on forever. But why then had it beckoned me here – just to rub my nose in the void? I reached out one hand toward the column of trees and then pulled it back. The trunk was rutted and gnarled, lined with deep furrows. Was that an arrow: and inscribed next to it – some kind of cross? And that's when I saw it, stooped over as if looking for its glasses, the ruin of a once great tree. Swiftly I produced my papers and peeled back my crayon, rubbing as hard as I could. The paper crumpled and the crayon slipped, but that didn't stop me – I rubbed and rubbed till the whole sheet was filled. But what did the strange, frenzied frottage mean? I don't know. It was too dark to see. In the half-light there were squirrels *everywhere.*

Only back in the car, by the light of the dashboard, did everything start to become clear. The rubbing had produced a rough kind of map, or at least some kind of sketch, the dark, scribbled marks held together by long thin strings of black. Here the shelter and there the poo-bin; next to it the playing field, the vandalised posts inscribed. And yet somehow, I couldn't quite read it. I turned the chart upside down, twisted it this way and that, screwed up my eyes and squinted, but all to no avail; it was both the park and yet not the park – the park's shadow perhaps. When I looked up an inky shape rolled past my line of vision and disappeared behind the car.

"Man or squirrel?" I yelled. "Man or squirrel?"

I switched on the headlights but if anything the outside only became darker. Disappointed, I slid the paper into the glove compartment and drove the long way home.

"I thought about going back to the park today," Claire said, stirring the beans thoughtfully.

"Really?"

"Mm. You know, to his place."

"Ah…"

"Just to… I don't know."

For a long moment I held my breath.

"Did you go?"

"Go?"

"Back, I mean."

"No… I… I just wanted to… to…"

"Shh, come here…"

"It's not that, it's just…"

"Shhh, it's okay…"

I held her and felt a painful black splinter pressing in under my nail. Every time I touched it, I felt pain. The whole finger looked strange. "Shh," I said. "Why cry? No, really. Why?"

Stuck in traffic I slid the sheath of papers out of the glove compartment and spread them out on my lap. Lines, shapes, patterns: but what did they mean? 'Twas a chart without landmarks, a language without a dictionary. This a strawberry and that a grave? There a boat and next a breast? Then the lights changed, and these too, were gone.

Just imagine: a world folded, encrypted, a sign post without arms. Over lunch, I photocopied the markings again and again, seeking out arrangements, symbols, pictures. Was that a nose or a fountain?

An eye or a hole? If I folded flap A over side B, creased side 1 over page 1.2, would it all start to make sense? I spent the best part of the day moving pieces of paper back and forth across my desk, but alas, 'twas not to be: this was a door I could not budge. I mean, what if the squirrel had lied – what if there were no anagrams, no hieroglyphics, no key at all? What if I was wrong about everything? Between my eyes, the dots and the page, something refused to meet. A tome without a title, without letters of any kind: what kind of bookmark could keep my page?

That night, after dinner, I snuck off to the kitchen to unfurl the Dead Sea scrolls, something about insects on the TV. Tracing the lines and rounding the hills, I started to feel more optimistic: wasn't this the bridal-path and that the latch-gate, behind it the big hill on the rise above the car-park? But then the typography started to fade and the shapes once more turned into smears and shadows. Squiggle or road? Mark or tear? I could not tell. These were instructions in another language, signals from a sinking ship. Claire was upstairs crying and I binned the papers in disgust. Where to go, what to do? I cupped my ear to the night, but the night wasn't talking. When I went upstairs, my wife wasn't talking too.

Later that night, I was awoken by a powerful need to urinate, an urge which dragged me out of bed, across the hall, and off to the bathroom at the end. Even my piss looked green. 'Diabetes!' I thought, shaking my head in sorrow. Ah, how terrible I felt! My tongue was dry, skin bad, nails foul.

Bleary-eyed, I padded down to the kitchen, my hand hurting as if someone had driven a needle deep below the nail. As I approached the fridge the back door rattled and the security light came on. Blinking, I wandered over to the window, peering out at the gloom: first a blur, then a shadow, finally a thing, four legged and shaggy, hobbling past the tool shed and shuffling toward the bins. The thing moved awkwardly, limping on its two good legs, its back-end sloping as if struggling uphill. But what was it – fox, dog, beast? The thing was closer now, half way between nothingness and the house. My eyes throbbed, my fingers ached. I needed to pass water again, and perhaps the other too. Finally the fox (fox?) knocked over the bags by the garage and started to root inside, pulling one of the bags out into the centre of the lawn and lying there, jaws methodically clacking. What a sight! The animal was all wet and matted, two yellow eyes leaking onto its snout. It was only when I saw it cough up a ball of paper that I realised why it had come: as a messenger, a sign, a communiqué from the other side!

The moment I went outside the fox (fox?) vanished, its shadow no more than a smudge or smear. Outside, there was stuff everywhere: wrappers, crisp packets, sanitary towels. The wad of paper lay on the grass, like a ball or a poo. But then, looking at the garden again, it was as if somebody had slipped a pair of glasses invisibly over my eyes. There the park, here the lake, yonder the bog garden to the east. And there, right at the side of the gardeners' hut, a cross, an 'x', the universal sign for 'dig here'.

Breathlessly, I dressed and retrieved my spade from the shed. Claire was sleeping, Tallulah likewise. I was still in my slippers, but why worry? I climbed into my car and drove away, the need to pee coming and going in bursts. Fortunately the park had no gate, no security. It was dark, but there were still a few street lights. It was cold but not terribly so; if anything I seemed to be running a fever, sharp pains radiating from my groin and advancing on my chest in waves. First I buttoned my coat, then I checked the chart, and finally I started to dig. The ground was soft and inviting, the digging hardly taking any effort at all. No sooner had the spade entered the ground than a great clod of earth lay by its side. Another step down and a second great clod appeared. Ho, why sweat? I dug and dug and pretty soon the thing was done. My trousers were muddied, fingers black, slippers ruined, but what did I care? There they lay on the ground before me: a plastic shopping bag, a twisted spoon, a dog lead, string. Yes, it was all starting to make sense now, the next step on the bridge...

It was only after I'd cleared up that I noticed a figure watching me, though whether man or woman, young or old, I couldn't really tell. Still, let them watch, take notes, tell! The figure was scribbling in a notebook, his (his?) face obscured by the night's inky thumb. I got home about three. Greenish darkness covered my arms right up to my elbows. My slippers? We will not speak of my slippers. After kissing my wife I climbed under the covers and immediately fell into a deep and bottomless sleep.

The next morning I put the sheets in the washing machine, poured myself a drink, and went off to find the bag. No point going to the office today: no time! Instead I opened the plastic carrier and arranged the objects in neat little rows, setting out the objects in terms of size and symbolic significance. Each of the items obviously referred to a different section of the park: the spoon, the café, closed down years ago, the bag, the Spa, haunt of glue-sniffers and alcoholics, folk buying lighter fluid late at night. And the dog lead? This seemed less certain. Bag dispensers, benches, trees? The string formed a noose and I hid it beneath my desk.

The next step was to spread the items out on the carpet, cushions for hills, a wash bowl the lake, a line of pens for footpaths. But what if it were the shape or the texture which was the clue rather than the thing itself, what if the answer were engrained in the very texture of things? My skin itched and my nails throbbed. And then it came to me: the waste-ground, the skip, Fergu – tch, where else should it be? Yes, the dots joined to form a circle, a hole. But on the other side: what?

The park was a good deal busier than I'd imagined. Middle-aged men carried rucksacks and notebooks, scruffy-looking guys sketched the lake, old women wandered about with pens. But what were they all looking for, why the crafty look in their eyes, their feverish steps? For a moment I thought I saw that old woman from the night long ago, the foreign dame with the missing shoe; but no, this woman was fully shod, her hair grey as a cobweb. Lost, I turned right round. Some skinny guy in a hat eyed up his charts. A bearded gentleman holding his schnauzer nodded in my direction. Two school kids, bunking off class, compared notes. All was a puzzle, a cryptogram, a work-sheet…Pinned to a tree was one of those old signs for lost dogs, the writing spidery, the page half torn. Even the dog seemed just a blur, its shape an inky smear of fur. Only its yellow eyes looked real.

And at the bottom? Yes, a phone number. Somebody answered on the second ring.

"Hello?"

The line clicked and whirred but I could hear no voice.

"Hello? Um, I'm calling about the dog…"

Nothing. No answer. The winds of time.

"Ah, is there anybody there? Because…"

More clicking.

"Hello?"

There was a shuffling sound and all of a sudden I felt embarrassed. If someone were to answer, what should I say? I didn't have the dog, hadn't seen it, didn't have a clue. What was I doing on the phone at all?

"Ah, well, the dog, it…"

The line clicked again and then went dead.

When I phoned back there was more clicking, perhaps some breathing too.

"Hello?"

The last time the thing had gone to answer-phone.

"Fergus! Fergus! Old friend, are you there?"

Maybe the number wasn't the clue. Maybe it was the handwriting or the paper used, or the shape of the animal's head. Fingers tingling, I settled down on a half-vandalised bench, examining the graffiti and the rust marks, the place where somebody had tried to set fire to the slats. Some hooligan had written 'Dave Hays Wears His Ma's Pants' in permanent marker: heaven knows the reason why.

Across the way some guy in a tie and business suit marked up a preliminary report on the rain shelter, noting down the lines and angles. Two waiters argued over their sketch of the council toilets, a woman dressed in black studied an enormous clip file as if slowly taking in the rules of the game. Yes, all was a game, some kind of scheme or text. But how many players and to what end?

All I knew was that the contestants were *everywhere*; the guy in the wheelchair, the birdwatcher with his binoculars, the mathematician and her set-square, all of them noting, drafting, setting down. One studied the lines in the flagstones, another the contours of the hill, whilst a third counted the number of rubbish bins, his mate grubbing around inside them, examining, measuring, recording. And if all this information were laid end to end? Why, such paper would form a pathway, a passage, a ladder from one place to the next...

Next to such encyclopaedic efforts, my own poor investigations seemed awfully small. What did I have? The gestures of a squirrel and the ball of a fox. And all the time my fingers angrily throbbed and grew. One nail was loose, another had fallen away entirely; even holding a pen felt increasingly difficult. How then was I supposed to compete? Down by the boating lake some woman ticked off the number of railings in her pad, touching each bar with her glove before staring off into space. For some reason she seemed awfully familiar but for a moment I couldn't place her. And then it occurred to me: my wife! But why wasn't Claire at work – my scrupulous, conscientious, work-driven wife? I watched her checking and rechecking her numbers, comparing the number of railings with the number of ducks on the island. Was it Claire? Someone in her coat? Then some joker drifted in front of me and she was gone. Eighteen railings, seven ducks, one moor-hen, but of wives: none. Swiftly I pulled out my phone and punched in her number.

"Hello?"

The line clicked, but that was it.

"Hello? Um, I'm calling from the park…"

Nothing. No answer. The winds of time.

"Um, is there anybody there? Because…"

More clicking.

"Hello?"

There was a shuffling sound and all of a sudden I felt embarrassed. If she were to answer, what should I say? What was I doing on the phone at all?

"Um, you see…"

The line clicked again and then went dead.

When I phoned back there was more clicking, and perhaps some breathing too.

"Hello?"

Next time the thing had gone to answer-phone.

"Claire? Claire, are you there?"

The trees waved their arms in alarm.

"Claire?"

Come to think of it, the blurred shape on the flyer looked a little like Claire too - the shape of her hair, the angle of her chin, the funny little scar above one eye. But it also looked liked the ring-road around the perimeter, the traffic lights and roundabout, a map of the principality. Upside down one could see roots, trunks, arms, a copse of fist-shaking sycamore. And if one squinted *just right* the very grains of the paper produced inky pools, dark smears, lost tributaries. But which clue was correct? The last four digits were 2355: half a hair to midnight – or some other code or rune? Whatever it was, I shredded the paper before one of my opponents could discover it.

By now it was a little after six but I didn't feel like going back home. What if Claire were there? What if she'd figured things out? I wasn't hungry but I forced myself to go and eat a pasty and chips, carefully counting each chip, pushing the peas this way and that on my plate. Seventeen chips, thirty one peas. On one side of my plate, the peas formed a river; on the other, the ketchup formed the shape of an owl. It was as if the very edge of reality were peeling back like an envelope. What if everything – the tables, the chairs, the stains on the waitress' apron – were a clue? Everything meant something, but anything could also be another thing entirely. Ho, even the tiles on the floor contained secret sequences and arrangements. The world was a newspaper in which I could not read a single word. When I closed my eyes I saw blobs. When I opened them again the blobs formed shapes: but what kind of shapes – and why such tiny print? Fortunately my car wasn't too far away. Locking the door I gripped the wheel hard. My fingers looked like ten black tubers starting to sprout. Even turning the ignition felt hard: I was supposed to hold a pen with these?

As soon as I got away from the city centre and coasted along the long, looping dual-carriageway, my mind started to cool down, my thoughts again becoming my own. Slowly the two halves of my brain started to knit, my lips moving to the music, my numb, greenish fingers drumming along to the beat. How long did I drive for? I didn't know. Long enough for the light to slip between the cracks…

At 21.19 I stopped at Crossley services. There was a guy filling in a puzzle book, and another finishing a crossword, but as for other players, that was about it. I had a cup of tea. My pee was still a little green.

At 22.33 I pulled into a lay-by because my fingers were so terribly sore. How ugly they were! Without print or ring or nail. I felt terribly embarrassed but couldn't seem to be able to find my gloves anywhere. My fingers were awfully long, the tips strangely old and fermented.

At 22.56 I headed back into the city, passing the industrial estate and out of town shopping centre. I drove round and round the same six streets very slowly. The pavements were empty, the traffic very light. It was as if a series of black shutters were coming down, one after the other. Yes, it was pretty late. A dead pigeon lay by the side of the road, its broken body pointing crookedly toward the park.

When I got there, there wasn't a parking space *anywhere*. Car-parks, pull-ins, side-roads: all jammed. I ended up parking nearly four blocks away, walking slowly along back alleys and shuttered garages, purposefully avoiding the graffiti and the cats.

Even the air felt filled in somehow, big blocks of scribbled black. And yet, despite the number of vehicles – four by fours, people carriers, Land Rovers, saloons, even a mini bus or two – there didn't seem to be anybody about. The cars were parked half on and half off the pavements, in places two deep, but I couldn't see a single pedestrian, not so much as a single bum. Where was everybody?

Street lights formed fuzzy circles, iron railings leaned against each other, the post-box licked its lips. Yes, I thought, this must be the place. I picked up a stick and tapped the ground though in truth there was plenty of light, at least if one kept to the path. Elsewhere thick barrels of nothingness oozed out over the grass, the autumn night gulping shadows. Was I scared? No, not really. Only my hands worried me, my long, green fingers itching from the inside.

The gates to the park were open, rubbish blowing across from an upturned bin. Take away wrappers, crisp packets, newspapers, plastic bags: so, I thought, more clues! A green mitten was hung on a railing. A puddle formed the letter 's'. Somebody had moved the benches so they formed a kind of circle. Yes, yes, this was it; I followed the path between two great banks of darkness, smelling mulch, piss, November. The darkness was a great mouth but I didn't let it worry me. What I feared was a gravestone marked: He Sought But Did Not Find…

Cracks formed messages on the path. Stones made full stops. A broken umbrella looked like an exclamation mark. And what of the other readers? Had they turned the page? I thought about the parked cars but still couldn't understand it. There were shadows, but not the things which cast shadows. Or had I got it the wrong way round? What if it were the shadows which cast things after all?

At 23.55 the phone rang.

"Nick?" asked my wife. "Nick, where are you?"

I didn't answer.

"Listen, I've been home. What happened? Are you okay? Nick, what is it?"

The wind blew and the trees shook.

"Nick?"

"Shh," I said. "Why cry? No, really, why?"

I lifted one foot from the path and strode out into the void, the lights behind me fading until they were less than the size of a pea. Were there stars? No, there were no stars. No sky, no up, no down. And yet even here my eyes started to adjust, blurs forming bushes, holes, hands…

The dog (dog?) was waiting for me at the edge of the trees, panting softly, its yellow eyes dripping.

"Fergus?" I said. "Fergus, is that you?"

Its mouth clacked open and shut rather woodenly.

"Fergus?"

I walked the last part of the way blind, caring not for mud nor shit nor roots; instead I followed the eyes as I would a lantern, entering into a wood far larger than found on any map.

In here, the trees looked old and tired. Some of them bent down to tie up their roots, while others pointed uncertainly toward the heavens above. How ancient they seemed! When I touched them it was touching the skin of an old dead animal – an elephant, perhaps. The bark contained valleys, inlets, channels; when I pressed down I felt a kind of hinge, a pivot on which the whole of the world seemed to turn. What was this place? Above me the leaves formed letters, lines, words, a whole alphabet silhouetted against the sky. When I looked down, my feet were covered in mud, two great roots planted in the earth. My torso was a great gnarled trunk, my arms black boughs, fingers twigs ending in vowels and consonants and commas. What had happened to me? What did it mean? Near the top branch a crow watched on with cruel yellow eyes.

"What does it mean?" I yelled. "Why can't I read?"

The crow pecked at my buds and winked. The wind blew the trees. Letters tumbled all around me.

"Read?" it said.

Its wings snapped shut like a book.

# Letting Charlie Go

For some reason, it was decided that the redundancy board should be held on a patch of waste ground, just beyond the new Halfords. Malcolm drove there with Charlie in the boot. When they arrived there were no other cars, just abandoned bin bags, broken bottles, the charred remains of some kind of crate.

"Now then," said Malcolm, opening up the boot. "You're probably wondering why I've brought you here today…"

Charlie gazed up at him with trusting eyes. His nose was running and he was panting heavily. Even his tie and ID badge looked a tad skew-whiff.

"It's just that I've been looking through some of your key performance indicators and some of the boxes seem a little unticked… eh, old fella? What d'you say?"

To show there were no hard feelings, Malcolm helped Charlie out of the boot and affectionately patted his head. Charlie's eyes were as round and as clear as the world. Although his trousers were a little scuffed, at least the pens in his shirt pocket were lined up in terms of size and colour.

"I mean, we're all aware of how the slowdown has impacted our quotas, but some of the feedback we've been getting… well, between you and me old fella, it's not been all together positive."

Charlie stretched and started sniffing at a clump of weeds.

"I mean in terms of productivity, efficiency, key performance indicators – the spreadsheets all flag up a series of negatives. Charlie?

Charlie, are you listening?"

Malcolm watched him piss on a pile of old tyres and shook his head sadly: ah the folly of the lower grades!

"You see, I've had a word with resources about how we can action this situation, and, well, there doesn't seem any choice... Charlie? Charlie? I'm afraid we're going to have to let you go."

At this Charlie halted and came trotting over. He smoothed down his tie and his mouth fell open in a foolish grin. Malcolm sighed and looked toward the west. The light was fading now, the long day passing.

"Now I know this will come as something of a surprise but... eh boy? What is it? What's that?"

Charlie's glasses were pointing at something down by Malcolm's feet. His eyes expressed a yearning as old as time.

"No boy, s'no use... it's just that... eh boy? What's that? Good boy, give it here..."

Malcolm threw the stick and made as if to run after it. As Charlie bolted for the trees, Malcolm took a few tentative steps back toward the car but inevitably Charlie was there before him.

"That's a good boy," he said, "clever lad..."

Charlie bounced around in circles, his shirt coming untucked from his trews.

"Yes, yes, very clever..."

Malcolm hoyed the stick over and over again. The light faded, shadows grew, birds sang. When the stick landed close to a copse of trees Charlie was just a tiny smudge of nothing.

"You're a clever boy, oh yes you are..."

Without another word, Malcolm turned on his heels and flung open the car door. Before he knew what was happening, he was turning the key, slipping the Corsa into gear and pulling away at high speed.

"That's it, good boy," he mouthed.

When he came to, Malcolm was driving fast on the dual carriageway, his mouth dry and his hands strangely clammy. But the job was done; he had finally succeeded in letting Charlie go. And yet, and yet... had Malcolm had been too hasty in apportioning negative feedback? True, Charlie had pissed on Malcolm's rug (not a metaphor) but at the same time his consumption ratio was stable, his team-building score good, positivity positive. For the first time in his professional career, Malcolm wavered. He was driving past Aldi at speed but still fancied he could hear Charlie calling out in the night.

The more he thought about it the more Malcolm began to think that he might just have made the worst mistake of his life. Mentally he recalculated the spreadsheets, the percentiles, the scores in Charlie's debit column: besides, who else would he play with at break times? Unbidden, a vision of Charlie's waggy arse appeared before him, turning round and round in an eternal arc. 'You idiot,' he thought: 'what have you done?'

By the time he'd turned the car around, the waste ground was some ten miles away and a vast gloom had fallen upon the earth. Malcolm tried to think of the shortest route back but for some reason couldn't seem to find it. I mean, would Charlie even be there? Malcolm imagined him lost, limping, drifting ever further from the flattened earth. If he listened hard he almost fancied he could hear the trees sighing, the wind blowing, Charlie's breath coming in shallow little gasps...

When Malcolm drove back to the waste ground it was almost entirely dark. There were blobs and shadows rather than things. The crate had vanished. Charlie was nowhere to be seen.

"Charlie!" Malcolm yelled. "Charlie, are you there?"

Both sky and ground seemed dipped in the same viscous ink,

indistinguishable in the gloom.

"Charlie? Charlie, this was just a test... an exercise. Charlie, I'm giving you feedback here... Charlie? Charlie, you can come back now..."

Malcolm tried sounding the car horn and flicking the lights on and off but it was no use: the space was as empty as a pit. Breathing hard, Malcolm stumbled out into the tar, two pale hands held up in front of him.

"Charlie?"

Beyond the waste ground a little copse of trees ran down to a hidden, marshy brook. It was pretty hard to see though and pretty soon his shoes were coated in mud. Besides, was this really the direction he'd gone in? As Malcolm pushed his way between the trees a branch swiped the glasses from his nose.

"Charlie!" he shouted. "Charlie!"

He felt around for his glasses but couldn't seem to find them. The darkness was terrible, the mud very thick. Disorientated, Malcolm tried climbing up out of the mire but kept slipping in the slime and muck. Eventually he found a thick twisted root and hauled himself up. But how had it come to this? It was like crawling around in a deep dark sack. Malcolm tried scouring the undergrowth, but there were no tracks, no prints – not even his own. He walked headfirst into a trunk and all at once the gloom seemed to close in all around him. His legs, his feet, his arms – even his hands disappeared.

"Charlie!" he yelled. "Charlie, where are you?"

Oh my friends, it's true! Malcolm had stumbled into a terrifying and darksome wood, a place beyond the reach of spreadsheets, appraisals, percentage points...

What's that? What became of him? Ah, perhaps he's still there, wandering lost and bewildered through the endless night, his clothes torn, his beard unkempt. And in the meantime his desk is clogged with departmental minutes, progress reports, read-outs, his computer with spam and e-mails, his phone with special offers and unread texts. Oh, who will read them now? Who will action his to-do list? Who, dear reader? Who?

# Flea Theatre

The first package appeared a few weeks after Nick's disappearance: a plain brown matchbox, addressed to Nick in a neat but unremarkable hand, the writing slanting a little toward the bottom. When Claire opened it up it seemed empty – some kind of mix-up, she thought. But then a second appeared, and a third and a fourth. What else could they be but clues, signs, knocks from the other side? Everyone knows that if something happens more than once it has to mean *something*. Wishes, daughters, bears – like buses, they always come in line.

The dainty little boxes were wrapped in brown packaging, filled with tissue paper, lacking card, receipt or letter. Barcode or tracking details? Foo – Claire couldn't even recognise the stamp. Hidden amongst all the paper was a tiny corpse, no bigger than a speck. A looking glass was needed to see it as it really was: an infinitesimal flea, dressed in human clothing, and posed mid-shrug, as if looking for its slippers or sniffing at its socks. Most amazing of all, the thing seemed to be stuffed, miniscule wadding protruding from its bottom. But why would anyone do such a thing? Who had the time or the tools?

If one had to choose an artistic style then one would have said: realism – right down to the buttons and the laces on their tiny little feet. Admittedly, differences in anatomy necessitated certain wardrobe alterations, but still – such detail! The overall effect was of lice going about their business, the domestic life of the flea. One seemed a little stooped, another had knee problems, whilst a third squinted uneasily through miniscule spectacles. Everything about them seeming to say: what, we don't have problems too?

And yet for all this minutia, there was still no clue as to who was sending them or why. Caught examining them on the kitchen table, Claire told Tallulah that the boxes were presents from Daddy. Tally looked down the lens and made a face. Bugs? Why bugs? Claire didn't know. Nick had been gone for nearly a month now, vanishing without word or explanation or lead. Claire had come home to find rubbish strewn across the living room and a bed full of mud. When he still hadn't returned by late evening she'd called and called but couldn't get through. Only just before midnight did he finally pick up. "Why cry?" he'd said. "No, really, why?" After that just the bellyaching of the wind, the sound of something heavy falling over.

And now fleas – who would take out a subscription to such a thing? The computer provided no clues, the post office neither. The police didn't see the fleas as relevant: they were busy searching the park with dogs. Finally the boxes stopped, and then the dogs quit too. Claire collected up the flea-people and their packaging and placed them in a shoebox. Once in a while Tallulah would line up the cast on the teeth of a comb, but she soon lost interest. When one fell between the cracks in the floorboards, nobody cried. There were other things to cry about anyway.

The following spring the fair came around. It set up shop on some waste ground, just behind the new Halfords, the usual rides and bouncy castles, a little rough at night, after all the children had gone. Tallulah liked the bumper cars and the tea-cups, but the hall of mirrors terrified her: what had happened to her head? Claire took her to the food kiosk. The chips were very long and very hot.

"Like Mrs Foster's fingers," said Tallulah. Mrs Foster was her teacher.

"Mm."

"Her hands are very pointy," said Tallulah.

"That's nice…"

"Jack Whistle says she sharpens them with the pencil sharpener."

"Well…"

"Then pokes them in her ear…"

"What's that over there? Some kind of show?"

At the back of the kiosk a set of garden chairs had been arranged in front of a box cloaked in a faded red curtain. The box was on a trestle table, one leg of the trestle table on a book. A reading lamp provided illumination. A small black hat, upturned like a tortoise, had been left for tokens of appreciation. Next to it, a sign read 'Laptev's Insect Theatre', the text slanting a little toward the left. The curtain was dappled with mildew and there were plenty of free seats.

"Do you want to watch? See what's going to happen?"

Tallulah nodded, her lips sticky from the ketchup.

As they took their seats, the curtain rose to display a painted backdrop suggestive of the Russian steppe. In front of it tiny dots hauled small stones towards what seemed to be some kind of half-made bridge, the whole thing no more than six inches top to bottom. Gold wire attached speck and stone, the tiny workers struggling as if transporting vast boulders. To one side some kind of inspector-flea watched them from a small trampoline, whilst other fleas had hidden beneath a small cart, seemingly trying to turn it over. To be honest, it was hard to work out what was really going on.

Tallulah watched the lice struggle and toil and then turned to Mummy.

"Like Daddy…"

"Mm?"

"Daddy's bugs…"

In front of the stage a minikin flea orchestra, yae big, played microscopic instruments, jumping up and down with the rhythm; in truth the enclosure was heated by a bare bulb and they were trying to escape.

"Is this what Daddy does? With his bugs?"

"Daddy? No, no, I…"

"Daddy and his bugs…"

"Tally, don't grab…"

On one side mites kicked miniature balls at one another, whilst on the other some kind of Ferris wheel had been set up, though many of the flecks seemed reluctant to board. What all this had to do with the bridge was hard to say. Alongside the construction work one could make out miniature cranes and joists and tiny little bonfires. The supports jutted out over a small black puddle, and the bodies of several of the performers could be glimpsed face down within it. And this for kids? The title card for the performance was in Cyrillic.

And yet for all that, you had to admire the animation. The labourers pulled, the inspector jumped, and smoke from the bonfires asphyxiated some of the footballers. Staring at the bugs, Claire thought the same thing as when she'd opened the boxes: such attention to detail! Lilliputian tools, ropes, scaffolding equipment: there were even two fleas having a crafty fag round the back. But what did all this have to do with Nick? "Daddy's bugs, Daddy's bugs!" yelled Tallulah and Claire nodded as if thinking the same thing.

All of a sudden though, the bridge still unfinished and the toil never ending, the curtain came down and the show was over. Claire and Tallulah stared at each other excitedly. Everybody else had gone.

"Let's see the man," said Claire, peering round the table. "Ask if we can see the bugs…"

A sallow-faced guy in a red cap was carefully picking up the stage and breaking it back up into pieces. Most of the bugs seemed to be relaxing on a saucer. The orchestra he tipped in to a bag.

"Um, hi," said Claire, "these fleas, well…"

The guy looked up with his one good eye and made a strange gesture.

"No English."

"No, well…"

"No English Missus," he repeated, pulling apart the bridge supports piece by piece. Tallulah had picked up a petite statue of some Russian guy and the fella in the cap practically snatched it from her hand.

"No, no, no…"

The guy collected up his stuff and Claire followed him as he started to make his way out of the kiosk.

"But I've also got… I mean, somebody sent me, Nick, my husband…"

The guy squinched up his working eye and examined Claire suspiciously. He then gazed down at his box and made an odd noise – bleh, or something similar.

"Did somebody send these to you? Do you know where…?"

The guy – Laptev, or was that just the sign? – spat and pushed past her, carrying his act away to the other side of the fair. Claire would have gone after him, but Tallulah was crying and holding her hand.

"What is it darling, what's wrong?"

"Mummy, Mummy…"

Between her fingers was the head of Peter the Great.


At work Claire stared at the endless scrolls of spreadsheets with absolute indifference. What were they to her now? In her drawer was a shoebox containing all the packages along with their midget inhabitants.

"Claire? Claire, are you there?"

"Mm?"

"Claire, um, you're dribbling…"

It was Malcolm her line manager, his tie flamingo-pink. Malcolm peered out of his shirt like a periscope, his eyes as kind as a cow's.

"Any word about Nick?"

"Nick?"

"Um, the police, have they…"

"Malcolm, can I go on my break now? It's nearly lunch and…"

"Claire, it's half past nine…"

"Malcolm, please? There's something I have to sort out…"

"Claire, you know full well…" But she had already swiped the box from her drawer, and was heading off toward the lift.

"O-okay, but your report, it…"

As she passed Jamie in IT, Claire collided with a tray of lattes, her parcel skidding crazily across the aisle as she went down on one knee.

"Claire, I'm sorry, are you…"

Claire stared angrily at Jamie and then groped around for her package, the box lying upturned by the photocopier.

"Where is it? What have you done?"

"Um, well…"

"Where's it gone? Have you snatched it?"

"Ah…"

"There!" she screamed. "No, there…"

She snatched something tiny from the carpet in front of her and examined it in her palm. From where Jamie was standing she seemed to be cradling a screwed up scrap of paper.

"Um, is that…?"

"Shut up! You oaf! You ape! You better not have broken it… you, you…"

Claire's chin was like a clenched fist, her mouth an ugly gash.

With one last glance at the IT guy, she closed her fist carefully and started to back away. Behind her, Malcolm came lumbering up.

"Claire! Is everything alright?" Malcolm moved as if to help her, but with that Claire turned and ran, one shoe left upturned by the photocopier. "Claire?"

Then the lift opened and Claire, her box and its occupants, were gone.

She made legs down the high street, glancing neither left nor right, unaware of anything except for the shoebox 'neath her arms. Not even the absence of a shoe slowed her down.

Even at this time of the morning the streets were clogged with shoppers, students, and the lost, all of them drifting aimlessly from side to side, getting in her way, threatening to snatch her box. To avoid the scrum, Claire ducked down an alleyway by the Hearing Centre, emerging onto a quieter, shabbier road running parallel to the main drag. The walls were tea-coloured here, the doors gloomy gaps. Claire entered an underpass she'd never noticed before, emerging between a charity shop and a burnt-out florist. But what was she doing here? There was a strange munching sound coming from the box and the lid kept slipping from the top.

From time to time office workers drifted past, young mothers with prams, old men with bottles, the occasional stray dog. Claire felt lost and uneasy, a trespasser in somebody else's book. Each of the pedestrians seemed to carry a small cardboard box under their arm, like a tiny coffin: who knew what slept within? Though one might stumble or trip, passers-by held fast to their containers, clutching them to their chests as if they were an only child or a beloved pet... Claire glanced down at her own plain white package. Just how many customers had been shipped ticks in the post? For a moment it seemed as if the whole city roared with the din of chomping and mashing, a great and terrible feast…

Just behind her was some kind of corner shop, a chemist perhaps or medical supplies: it was terribly gloomy in there and kind of hard to see. A pale fella with a bald head was shuffling around in the back, the air heavy with a medicinal scent. What was she doing here, I mean, really? The place reeked of disinfectant and the light was sickly and yellow. Then the fella with the bald head met her gaze and beckoned her in.

For a moment the world shifted as if turning on a pivot. Before she knew what was happening, Claire found herself stumbling awkwardly across the road and fleeing in the opposite direction, the walls sloping alarmingly and the pavement full of holes. When she found a skip filled with odd bits of building material she paused and threw the boxes inside, the tissue paper pale and naked, without shelter or lights or stage. For a moment she felt strangely sorry: what would happen to their accessories and tiny things now? But then she heard a voice from a near-by window yell "Hey!" and without thinking she removed her other shoe and legged it as fast as she could. Let the new bugs eat the old bugs: she had to get home.

Squeezing back between the buildings, Claire caught sight of the Spar, the travel agent's, the dull concrete façade of her office. Her feet were red, and sore, cut betwixt ball and sole. 'Nick, Nick, where are you?' she thought. He seemed both far away and close, as if the two of them were separated by a single page.

That night Tallulah was busy playing school, filling in page after page of her new pink pad. There was a nature programme on TV, but Claire didn't want to watch it. Outside something dark and hairy was sniffing around by the bins, pawing at the lid uncertainly. The night closed – bang! – like a door.

# Filling

In all his years of dentistry, Lessing had never seen anything quite like it. Right at the back of the throat – behind the uvula, at the very rear of the gullet – were a series of tiny letters, each no larger than a pin. 'There,' thought Lessing, staring into the darkness. 'No, not there – *there*.' Right by the oropharynx, as distinctly as if they'd been typed: a whole row of letters, printed in gothic script. Lessing took off his glasses and squinted. A 'h' then an 'e', then an 'l', then a 'p'.

'Help?' thought Lessing. 'Help who?'

The dentist regarded his patient's mouth philosophically. Jacobson was a small, slight, elderly man with an abraded canine and a forced inclusion on his upper seventh. Why would such a man have a secret message hidden at the back of his teeth?

'Never in all my years in dentistry…' thought Lessing, as if writing up his notes for posterity.

But then, what did Lessing know of the fellow? His breath smelt of tuna fish. His mouth was a cemetery of crooked teeth. His oral routine was rated 'average'. Beyond this – nothing, a drawing without a line. Ach, thought Lessing, did the old fool even know what was concealed behind his gums? Altering the angle of the lamp, it was possible to make out a series of tiny scratches at the very back of Jacobson's gullet, like the scuffing of a stick or the grating of finger nails: had the person who had left the message carved these inscriptions too? 'Yes, dentistry is the most mysterious of

181

the physician's arts...' thought Lessing, secreted behind mask and apron. 'In many ways the teeth are like piano keys...' – but here his metaphor started to fall down. 'So,' thought Lessing. 'What is this mouth and what is it saying?'

The fellow certainly didn't *seem* in distress, limbs relaxed, lips moist, his eyes as large and trusting as a Labrador's. Instead the old git smiled broadly at Lessing (ho, that cat-food breath!), opened wide and pulled his mouth into an enormous 'O'.

"So..." said Lessing, peering into his maw suspiciously. "Hold still, Mr Jacobson. We need to take a better look."

"Mwrr, mwrr, grrr..." said Jacobson, Lessing's fingers down his throat.

"Any pain?"

"Mmrr, wrr, wrr..."

"Yes, yes. Well, open wider Mr Jacobson! Let's see what there is to see..."

The more he thought about it, the more the fella's teeth seemed like road signs – no, not signs, *arrows* – all beckoning Lessing to step within. How lopsided Jacobson's teeth are, thought Lessing. Like swing doors on a dimly lit lobby...

At this point the dental nurse – let's call her Carol – laid a soft white hand on Lessing's shoulder.

"Mr Lessing? Ah, are you sure? I..."

Lessing adjusted his apron, heroically.

"It's alright Carol. It's ... alright."

Jacobson's mouth was open like a man-hole. His soft, brown eyes stared upwards, beseechingly. His teeth were like typewriter keys that... no, thought Lessing, they're not like typewriter keys at all...

Ho, the mysteries of dentistry! Between soft palate and tongue, the moist darkness seemed to swallow all light. Jacobson's tonsils squatted malignantly. His uvula hung like a bell. Staring in to the abyss, Lessing's expression was that of a spelunker peering into some unknown cave.

"Very nice. Very good. Good, good. Yes, yes, yes…"

There the occluded seventh and there the abraded fourth; but wither the calligraphy, wither the sign? And then he spotted it again: a tiny 'e', between the palatoglossal and palatopharyngeal arches, like some kind of aboriginal cave painting or ancient rune – definitely an 'e' or maybe a 'c', it was a little hard to tell with this amount of spit.

"Mr Lessing? Um, it's just that…"

Breathing hard, the dentist leant in a little closer. Was that some kind of tiny ladder in there? And some kind of steps leading even further in to the depths? He was about to proceed further when he glimpsed something moving around on the very first rung. But what was it: a scratch, a groove – a hand? Lessing leapt back, almost into Carol's lap. What *was* that? Carol stared at Lessing, Lessing looked at Jacobson, Jacobson gazed at the ceiling.

"Carol? Carol? I think we'll be needing the gas…"

"The gas?"

"Yes, yes, the gas, right away…"

"But Mr Lessing…"

Carol was holding onto his smock now, her lips – and bridgework – tantalisingly close.

"Damn it Carol, if you won't do it then I will!"

Frightened, Carol opened the valve on the gas tank and handed Lessing the mask. Jacobson stared at them with his brown, trusting eyes. His mouth was round as a tyre, his teeth… oh, forget it. Jacobson lay there submissively, Lessing holding tight on his tongue.

"That's it, Mr Jacobson, you relax now… that's it, breathe in…"

At the edge of Lessing's periphery vision, Carol sobbed and yanked on his smock.

"Oh Mr Lessing… not again… not again…"

Lessing's brow closed shut like a curtain.

"There now, breathe deeply, there it is…"

Jacobson made a funny little gesture, but his port-hole stayed open.

"That's it, there we go…"

"Lessing! Mr Lessing!"

The fellow's limbs fell slack and the dentist snapped a second pair of gloves on over the first.

"Ah, Carol, Carol? Would you mind popping up to the store room to get a new batch of resin? There's a box somewhere beneath the sink… the October batch, if you please…"

Carol froze.

"Yes, yes, the October batch…"

Uncertainly she started to back away, Lessing clinging to Jacobson like a murderer.

"Mr Jacobson? Mr Jacobson, are you there?"

Jacobson lay in the chair like a coat. Lessing shone the light into the darkened path, searching for rope or ladder or staircase, some manner of egress from the void below.

"A ladder, a ladder," murmured Lessing. "Where has the fool thing gone?"

And then he saw it: a ruler stretching all the way to Jacobson's epiglottis, little doll-house rungs one millimetre apart. Lessing adjusted the light and saw more marks, grazes, as if a prisoner had scratched the days on the wall. Then a pestilent wind began to blow – fishy, sour – and a tiny fist appeared on the bottom step. 'Never in all my years in dentistry…' Lessing thought, his sickle probe beginning to shake. The tiny figure slowly hauled itself up and Lessing saw that it was a miniature Jacobson, minute, but identical in every detail, except that this Jacobson was dressed in rags, his pale, emaciated wrists encased in Lilliputian shackles.

"Help," the tiny Jacobson mouthed. "Help…"

Momentarily bewildered, Lessing tried shining his torch at the little fellow's mouth, but the space was just two small. Jacobson Junior was almost at the top of the ladder now. His twin stick arms reached up imploringly, his head exactly the size of an amalgam filling.

"Jacobson?" whispered Lessing. "Jacobson, is that you?"

All at once two bony hands reached out and took hold of Lessing by the neck. Before he knew what was happening he'd been pulled inside, his shoes disappearing into Jacobson's mouth, the rest of him following close behind. For an instant Lessing struggled back to the surface, but then the ragged figure took hold of his apron, dragging the dentist down to: well, who knows – where does anything go?

When Mr Jacobson came round, two hours later, Lessing was nowhere to be seen. The receptionist and his two thirty appointment searched the surgery in vain. Carol was in the store cupboard, sobbing. Lessing's glasses lay broken by the chair.

"Mr Jacobson, Mr Jacobson, are you alright?" screamed the receptionist.

Jacobson opened his mouth, smiled benignly, and nodded. Inside his teeth were like the bars of... oh, forget it, forget it, I mean, what's the point? Nobody will believe any of it anyway.

# No Refund, No Return

Aside from the feet, the shoes were pretty good: nice strong heel, stiff leather upper, fine stitching throughout. I mean, okay, my toes were a little cramped, and the laces pinched when pulled, but still – with a bit of walking in, they'd be fine. The feet were more of a problem though. Discoloured nails, grazed ankles, greenish skin: ah, such a state! I placed the two feet side by side on the kitchen table and carefully examined them. One left, one right – size ten, I guessed, same as the shoes. Two hard corns on one sole, some kind of blister on the other. A not altogether pleasant odour. I looked in the bag, shook the box, checked the receipt. Nowhere did it say anything about the provision of two second hand feet. What was I supposed to do with them? After a while I put the shoes on my feet and the other fella's feet in the box. Then I caught the first bus back to town.

Alas it was pretty busy, with only a couple of seats near the back. Still, I pushed my way through, trying not to think about the smell coming from the box – a little like over-ripe yogurt. Some guy in a bobble hat seemed to be staring at me, maybe one of the young mums too. But what could I do? I pushed the shoe box to the far end of my seat and tried gazing nonchalantly out of the window. When an old woman tried to sit next to me, I pointed to the shoe box and shrugged. What was I supposed to do about it? Inside the blackened toes were curled up like slugs.

Luckily the shoe shop was only another couple of stops, squeezed in between Cancer UK and the bookies. Receipt in one hand and box in the other I advanced on the counter as menacingly as I could: I mean, what did they mean by fobbing me off with a used pair of shoes? But even as the shop assistant – a pale, skinny fellow with a big red nose – turned to serve me, something wasn't quite right. All the shoes on display were enormous, flippers rather than slippers, slap shoes with vast bulbous toes. What kind of joke was this? The shoes were stretched, distended, great black canoes in which one might set sail.

"Sir? Sir, may I help you?" asked the guy.

I showed him the receipt and started to open the box, but his big, red mouth grinned alarmingly.

"And what size do you say? Size ten?"

The fella shook his head. No, the store stocked nothing so dainty; I must have gotten the shop mixed up with his competitor's around the corner. Not to worry though – it happened all the time. "You're not the first and won't be the last!" His skin was very white and he seemed to have big black lines drawn round his eyes. "No harm done!" I nodded, pushing the feet back into the box and slowly backing out. The shoes really were gargantuan, like huge blind fish found at the bottom of the ocean. The bell jangled merrily on the way out.

When I left the shop a cat started to follow me, a rather mangy looking thing with reddish looking fur and one good eye. It kept rubbing up against my legs and arching its back to sniff the big white box.

"Nothing there for you!" I yelled. The smell was somewhere between compost and dead fish. "What do you want? Go find another corpse's toes to lick…"

Just as the guy said, the other shoe shop was just around the corner, poked awkwardly between Help the Aged and a tattoo parlour. I advanced upon the counter in a state of some embarrassment. What an idiot I was! How was it I couldn't even remember the right shop?

This store did look a little more familiar, but something was still wrong. All the shoes seemed to be in a state of great disrepair – some flattened, others torn, set fire to, or crushed. "These have certainly been through the wars," I said jovially.

The guy looked furious.

"What do you mean? If you're too good for them then clear off, eh? Can't you read? No refunds and no returns: that's what it says above the till. No refunds and no returns. Why come here if just to insult me?"

The guy was really cross. I tried opening the box and fishing out my receipt but he just wouldn't listen.

"Oh no, you don't. Shop policy: no refunds, no returns. All goods sold as seen. Buyer beware. That receipt won't help you here you *schwine…*"

Apologising profusely I backed into a display of fire-damaged loafers. To my horror, the stand toppled and noisily fell to the floor.

"All damaged goods must be paid for!" yelled the guy. "No coupons, no gift vouchers, no cards!"

Over my head a bell tolled mournfully.

Out on the street another three cats were waiting for me, two grey and one white. Or was it two white and one grey? Either way the gang of them were making an alarming noise, prancing around in front of me and trying to claw the box. Passers-by stared, cars braked, a small boy laughed. Shame-faced, I tried to lose the things down a series of alleyways, the cats mewling and wailing and the box smelling of mulch.

"Leave me alone!" I yelled. "What do you want? Go find an old lady's lap to warm…"

I finally lost them by an underpass in a part of town I'd never been to before. The walls were tea-coloured and the doors smelt of piss – unless it was just the box, of course. I imagined the toes snuggling against each other like little black pigs. And a horrible welt on the ankle too!

Adrift, I wandered from street to street, one eye out for cats, the other for shoe-shops. Finally I spotted a store crammed between Pet Rescue and a burnt-out florist. There was a weird stain on the underside of my box and the lid kept slipping from the top.

Was it a shoe shop? It was terribly gloomy in there and awful hard to see. A pale fella with a bald head was shuffling around in the back, the air heavy with an almost medicinal scent.

I patiently uncreased the receipt from my back pocket and absent-mindedly looked around; the shop seemed full of odd nooks and crannies and it was strangely hard to see any of the goods out on display. Was that a Wellington and that a walking stick? That a hat and this a glove? The pale guy shuffled to and fro, lugging a tall pile of white boxes.

"Just one moment sir, I'll be right there…"

"That's okay," I said. "I'm in no hurry…"

I tried reading the receipt but all I could make out was my name and the amount. Had I really been here before? Something about it was familiar but nothing really recalled the shop I'd bought my shoes in earlier. O, what was I doing here, really? The place reeked of disinfectant, the light all sickly and yellow. I wandered over to the nearest cabinet and absent-mindedly wiped the dust from the glass. Blinking myopically I tried to peer inside.

"Nearly there sir…"

"Oh, thank you, thanks…"

Inside I could see legs, fingers, ears, the merchandise arranged as if at a jeweller's. Each of the body parts had a price code next to it and I anxiously looked down at my receipt. Ho, what kind of place was this? I stepped away from the cabinet and immediately banged into a set of knees hanging from a rack.

"Sir? Sir, are you alright?"

I didn't know what to say. One of the knees was badly bruised, the other strangely round.

"Sir?"

I hugged the box to my chest and made for the door.

"M'okay!" I yelled. "I'm sorry, this is the wrong place and…"

The guy was very close now, so close I could smell his coffee-breath. I scrunched up my receipt and hid it in my pocket.

"Sit down sir. Here, let me take that…"

I hovered there as if paralysed.

"Sir? Sir, let me see…"

He reached out for the box but I immediately plucked it from his grasp, tripping back out of the door as the bell rang soundlessly. What kind of place was this? Clutching the box like a baby, I stumbled awkwardly across the road and fled in the opposite direction, making my way through what seemed to be a fairly run-down residential area. The walls seemed to slope alarmingly and the pavement was full of holes. When I found a skip filled with odd bits of building material I stopped and tipped the feet inside, the stumps lying there pale and naked, without benefit of sock or stocking or shoe. For a moment I felt kind of sorry for them: did they miss their shins, their knees?

But then I heard a voice from a near-by window yell "Hey!" and without thinking I threw the box after them and legged it as fast as I could. Listen: why invite trouble? Only a fool tips his hat to a bear…

When I got home I sat down in my favourite chair and thoughtfully examined my shoes. The toes were scuffed, the laces undone, the sole already starting to give way. Ah, what a swizz, what a con! What's happened to craftsmanship, I thought, the idea of taking pride in one's work, the sacred duty of the cobbler's art? Depressed, I placed the shoes under my bed and climbed under the covers.

A few hours later I was awoken by a terrible wailing and crying coming from outside. Stiff and achy, I rose from my bed and stumbled toward the curtains. How tired I felt! Like I'd been walking for a hundred years. When I pulled the curtains back the street was full of cats. Cats sitting on cars, cats lounging on walls, cats curled up on lawns, cats *everywhere*.

"What do you want from me?" I yelled. "I haven't got them! They're gone…"

A grey tabby looked at me suspiciously.

"They're gone, they're gone…"

I was about to yell again when I heard the sound of someone on crutches struggling up the stairwell, the thud of each crutch ringing out beneath me as clear as a bell. The progress was very slow and it sounded like whoever was out there was dragging themselves up by their arms alone. Thud, thud, slide, thud, thud, slide. Tch, what a terrible sound! I listened to the figure mounting the stairs and then retreated back to my bed. Pulling my covers up to my chin I hid myself as best I could. What did they want from me? What had I done? Thud, thud, slide, went the fella on the stairs. He was very close now. Outside my door? I couldn't really tell. Over on my bedside table the receipt opened up like a hand.

# Night School

It was well after midnight when Claire first heard the faint sound of scratching coming from her daughter's room. From the staircase, she could see her little girl kneeling in the darkness, chalking all kinds of shapes onto her blackboard: lines, waves, dots. The girl worked intently and methodically, and only after she'd filled in the very last line did she put down her chalk and climb back into bed, pulling the covers up around her throat.

Claire switched on a lamp and examined her daughter's work. The figures were drawn with great certainty and deliberation, nothing like the scribbled marks you'd expect from a five year old. The loops, dots and curves were all carefully positioned, some of the characters almost turning into letters or pictures – though Claire couldn't say exactly of what. Eventually she smoothed down the covers on her daughter's bed and switched off the lamp.

"Bobble," said her daughter, her lips a tiny 'm'.

In the morning, Tallulah seemed the same as ever. She ate her cereal, chatted happily, and allowed herself to be dressed without due protest. Although she had been fast asleep when Claire had first gone in, her blackboard had been wiped clean during the night, the chalks placed carefully inside the box. The only sign of last night's activity were the dark circles beneath Tallulah's eyes and the white dust on her hands. Claire didn't say anything – she was only playing school after all – and when she dropped her off,

Tallulah waved cheerfully and ran inside with all the others. Her teacher, Mrs Foster, tall and grey as a silver birch, took Tallulah's bag with her twig-like hand. "Say goodbye, Tallulah," she said, and Tallulah said, "G'bye."

When Claire picked her up after work, she seemed a little more subdued – tired, most probably – and Claire had to carry her all the way back to the car. In her bag, along with her school book and pencil case, was a crinkly painting of a house and garden, the sky coloured in great swirls of yellow and orange. Later, Tallulah watched TV and ate her fishcake; afterwards she announced that she wanted to go straight to bed. Fearing that she might be coming down with something, Claire took her temperature, gave her some medicine, and put her straight down. She then phoned her mother and cleaned the kitchen. When she was done she positioned Tallulah's schoolwork in pride of place on the fridge-freezer, taking time to admire her daughter's handiwork. The picture was really very good: bright colours, neat lines, the house a solid square. It was only when she looked at the windows that Claire noticed that inside the house, written in a tiny hand, were more of the strange symbols (was symbols the right word? Squiggles? Characters?), the miniscule type-face stacked up like furniture. Yet what kind of an ABC were they? Little hats, bubbles, arrows, marks. They seemed at once completely abstract and yet heavy with furtive meaning. The handwriting was spotless. Each character seemed to occupy its own space.

Creeping up the stairs, her daughter seemed to be in a deep, untroubled sleep. The blackboard was blank, the chalk untouched. Claire kissed her daughter and closed the door. Downstairs, The TV talked to itself in a whisper.

When she opened the curtains the next morning, condensation covered Tallulah's entire window, a little dribble collected by the sill. During the night more of the letters (letters?) had been finger painted onto the glass, the shapes and silhouettes fastidiously lined up in columns, the script a cross between Mandarin and some kind of ancient hieroglyphics.

"What is this, darling?" prompted Claire, gently. "Have you been writing?"

"Mummy?" said Tallulah. "Mummy, I'm very tired…"

"These marks – this writing… What…"

"Please Mummy, m'sleepy…"

The letters covered the whole window like a parchment and Claire wiped them away with the palm of her hand. How alien they seemed! When she looked back the dark rings around Tallulah's eyes formed a crepuscular number eight.

At breakfast, Claire watched her daughter carefully. The shapes in her cereal, her finger prints in the sugar, any toothpaste stains round the mouth: anything might be a clue. At work, she could hardly concentrate. Her spreadsheets were all wrong, the figures wouldn't tally, her data remained unactioned. When she picked Tallulah up again, Tallulah yawned theatrically and proclaimed she was too tired to go swimming.

"M'exhausted," she yawned.

When Claire asked what the children had been doing the teacher said, "Practising their letters." The teacher's hands were long and dry, like the straw switch of a broom.

That night Claire again heard movement, but when she raced up the stairs, Tallulah hadn't stirred. The board was still empty, her chalks untouched. Claire suddenly remembered Tallulah's felt tips. Scurrying under the bed she urgently pulled them out, but the tops were still on, and there was no sign of any paper. Claire turned the central heating down and slowly tip-toed out of the door. Shadows ran from the lamp.

The next day, Tallulah was almost impossible to wake. She moaned and whimpered, rolling herself up in her blanket. But, of course, there was still work, so she had no choice but to scoop her listless child up and place her in her uniform. Tallulah refused to eat anything, so Claire placed a breakfast bar in her satchel. Pushing it to the bottom, she came upon her work-book, the pages all crumpled, the cover pulled back. The pages were all filled with the same weird, alien-looking characters: not really squares or circles but odd stamps and streaks, the patterns unfamiliar but the manuscript somehow terrifyingly precise.

"What is this?" Claire asked her daughter. "What does it mean?"

"I don't feel so good," said Tallulah. "Mummy, can I stay at home?"

Claire looked at the calligraphy and looked at her daughter.

"Get in the car," she said. "We'll see what your teacher has to say about this…"

Of course when Claire confronted the tall, birch-like woman, demanding to know just what the school thought it was teaching, Mrs Foster merely looked confused, her long arms swaying in the wind.

"Teaching?"

"Here – in her book."

Claire handed over the evidence with a flourish. Here, she thought: let's see what the withered old stick had to say about that!

"Mrs Robertson," said the teacher, dryly. "This is clearly not school-work, and clearly not the work of a five year old either. There must have been some kind of mix up. I assure you that we rigidly defer to the statutes of the national curriculum…"

Claire felt an angry glow rising to her cheeks. "But these signs…"

"If you wish to see a list of the learning outcomes then I suggest that you refer to the relevant document on the school's website. In the meantime I have several crying children and the school day is about to begin…"

The old bint wasn't kidding: half the class seemed to be sobbing, the other half asleep. Mrs Foster's expression was so wooden you expected a bird to come out of her mouth at any moment. Then the school bell rang and everybody jumped.

Driving to work, all Claire could think about was the school-book. If not at school, where else could she have filled it in: Grandma's?

She sent an angry text to her mother and then realised that it made absolutely no sense. She then sent a second text to explain, but realised that without the notebook, this second message didn't really mean anything either. In her exasperation she sent a third, even more incoherent text, and then switched off her phone. What else could she do? She was late for her enabling seminar. Her action plan was unfulfilled. She missed her target.

Wednesday afternoon after school was always when Tallulah's little friend, Amelia, came round to play. She too seemed spent and sluggish. Instead of their usual loud games, they huddled together in Tallulah's room and whispered. When Claire asked what they were playing, Tallulah said, "Schools." Amelia was chewing a torn piece of paper like a cow.

That night, instead of going to bed, Claire stationed herself outside Tallulah's room and settled down for the night. How vulnerable she seemed! Tallulah lay curled up like a tiny question mark, her little lump rising and falling as she dreamed.

After just a few minutes, Tallulah's shadow hopped out of bed and crept toward the window. At first it peeled itself away from the night-lamp, and then it formed itself out of the darkness in the hall, a perfect silhouette of Tallulah's pyjamas, save for the strange pointed hat on her head. As Claire watched, the shadow passed through the window and descended the outside wall, growing and then shrinking as it crossed the lawn.

At the junction with Wilson Street, a yellow school bus was waiting for her, its windows filled with vague shapes. Tallulah's shade jumped on board and the bus pulled off. Everybody on board seemed to be wearing the same pointed hat, the headgear somewhere between a dunce's cap and a witch's peak. The driver was a shadow too.

Claire's limbs felt as heavy as clubs. She could run and get her car: but how could she be sure that she could catch up? Should she ring the school, the bus company, the council? But Tallulah was still inside, sleeping in her bed: how could she even think of leaving her now?

Uncertain, she drew up a chair and decided to wait for Tallulah's shadow to return. It was nearly light and the first few birds were singing before she heard the sound of air-brakes and glimpsed her daughter's likeness skipping up the path. The shadow passed through the wall, climbed the stairs and went back to bed. Ten minutes later Claire's alarm clicked on and it was the start of another working day.

Pale and irritable, Claire sat at her desk like the sketch of a person waiting to be filled in. The files didn't seem to make any sense, her coffee tasted strange, she couldn't log onto Shared Services.

At eleven she went along to an envisioning meeting, only to discover the knowledge-transfer room empty, a naked flip-chart in the centre of the room. And on the other side of the blank page? She didn't want to know. Walking back to her car she saw that somebody had spray-painted almost the entire wall of the stairwell with strange logos and designs. Were they the same as the ones in her daughter's notebook? Claire switched on the radio and drove fast.

"Are you okay sunshine?"
"Just a little tired."
"Are they working you too hard at school?"
"School? No…"
"Is Mrs Foster ever mean to you?"
"She has very bumpy hands."
"Mm?"
"Her hands are very bumpy…"
"Well…"
"Jack Whistle says leaves grow in her hair…"
"I see…"

That night Tallulah's shadow once again clambered out of bed and trotted off to night school. Claire tried taking a picture with her phone, but she couldn't really see anything. The shadow's hat pointed at the sky like a finger. The bus was a little late but it turned up eventually, its engine turning over quietly in the gloom.

At work Claire could hardly keep her chin from her desk. When she received an e-mail from batch management listing row after row of figures she typed 'What does this mean?' and hit reply. A few minutes later she got a call from IT informing her that they were going to have to re-migrate information from her work station. "A-huh," she said, and minutes later the screen went blank. Seconds later, the phone rang again: "What do you want?" she yelled. This time it was the school – Tallulah wasn't feeling so well and needed to come home. Claire said "A-huh," and walked awkwardly to her car. In the ugly light of the multi-storey she felt terribly queasy, as if either Claire or her shadow were about to collapse. Fortunately

Tallulah was okay, just a little run-down. "Can I get in my pyjamas?" she asked. Mrs Foster handed Claire a form to sign, and informed her that this would be factored into Tallulah's attendance figures. Mrs Foster's fingers were as long and pointed as pencils. When she typed the release code to let Claire out, both the door and Mrs Foster seemed to creak.

Tallulah was asleep before they even left the school car park; all that was left to do now was drive around until it was time. It was autumn and the lights came on early: first the shops, then the cars, then the streetlights. When they pulled in to the petrol station for crisps and an energy drink, Tallulah didn't wake up. When it was finally night time, Claire drove to the end of their road and waited. The radio played soothing classics and Claire ate her crisps. The car was hot and the windows misted over.

"Blue," said Tallulah.

This time, when Tallulah's shadow left by the passenger door and took off toward the bus stop, Claire was ready. She edged the car forward and watched her daughter's engraving cheerfully climb on board. The bus turned left and she turned after it. There was no other traffic around and all the lights were green.

After half an hour or so the bus pulled into an out of town industrial park, coming to a rest outside a series of ugly concrete units housing (according to the signs) a carpet warehouse, storage depot, and soft play area. The bus stopped in the car park and the shadows jumped out, pushing and shoving to get to the front. Claire parked on the opposite side of the lot, watching the crocodile of cut out figures cross the empty yard, entering the central block two by two. Needless to say, all were wearing (wearing?) those funny pointed hats, and, as far as one could tell from their outlines, their night-wear. Claire checked that Tallulah was still asleep before inching out of the door and following the parade of shadows. Fortunately her footsteps didn't make a sound.

Both the outside door and the dull, functional corridor were covered in sheets of A4 paper, all bearing the same signs and logos inscribed in her daughter's notebook, badly photocopied and printed a little off centre. Of the line of shadows, Claire could see nothing; instead she followed the long stripe of paper, passing heavy fire doors, locked offices and stacks of abandoned chairs, the light so dim her hand looked like a glove.

At the end of the corridor she spotted the smudgy imprint of a dressing gown disappearing through an open set of double doors; inside was a large hall filled with desks set out as if for an examination. Shadowy pupils sat at each place although they were by no means all children: many of the shapes were of adult sleepers, their outlines squeezed uncomfortably onto the tiny plastic chairs. Claire was handed a tall, conical hat and led to her own desk. Waiting for her there was a large pad of paper, an eraser, calculator and a pencil. When she looked at the calculator she realised that she couldn't recognise a single button. The nib of her pencil was broken and blunt.

She was just about to say something when some guy – not a shadow, but some joker in an ugly brown suit – strode up to the front of the hall and started to talk in a low, monotone voice. From where Claire was sitting she couldn't hear a thing; nor could she make head nor tail of the strange letters (letters?) he marked on the whiteboard with his thick black pen.

"Hey," she said to the shadow next to her. "Hey, you…"

The shadow and its pointy hat turned round. "Me?"

"What is all this stuff? I don't understand a thing…"

The shadow glanced round anxiously. "What?"

"I don't get it…"

"Did you do your homework?"

"What?"

"The take-away. Did you…"

Somebody hissed, "Shhh," and several heads turned in their direction.

"Ah, I don't think…" Claire whispered.

"But you know what day it is today, right?"

An overcast invigilator swooped toward them from the next aisle along, her shape half-seen and blurry. "Shhh," someone whispered. Even the drab voice of the speaker seemed to pause.

"I don't know anything," said Claire. "What is this stuff? What…"

The official drew nearer and Claire's pencil fell from her desk, rolling loudly across the parquet floor.

"But today," said the shadow. "I mean, today, you know…"

Before the examiner could reach her, Claire knocked over her chair and fled, a wave of disgruntled murmuring following her across the hall.

"Will you please be quiet!" yelled a particularly agitated voice.

As Claire stumbled along the aisle she suddenly spotted her daughter's outline, crouched over one of the desks.

"Tallulah? Tallulah, sweetheart, is that you?"

"Mummy, I'm *writing…*"

"Tallulah, come here…"

"The teacher…"

"Shh…"

Dragging her daughter by the hand, Claire awkwardly exited the hall, aware of a strange movement in the desks behind her.

"It's alright darling. Mummy has to go now…"

"But Mummy…"

"Mummy has to go…"

Without looking back, Claire pulled her daughter past a long line of disconnected terminals. The light felt like it had been filtered through a cloth.

"Mummy? Mummy, I've forgotten my bag…"

"It doesn't matter…"

"But the teacher…"

"The teacher doesn't matter…"

Claire moved through the outer doors and swept across the dingy car lot. Her car was just where she'd left it, parked up between the traffic cones and the bins. Inside she could see herself and Tallulah curled up in their seats and fast asleep. Claire stopped in front of the door and paused. No, it wasn't a reflection: she really was slumped to one side on the driver's seat, her mouth slightly parted, an empty crisp packet on her lap. In the back Tallulah stirred.

"Tallulah?" said Claire, but her shadow had gone. "Tallulah, I…"

Atop her head, her hat narrowed to a cone. The crook of her arm seemed to lengthen and bend. She no longer looked like her shadow now, more like something in Cyrillic, or some kind of script.

"Tallulah? Darling?"

On the back seat Tallulah silently mouthed the alphabet, her tiny mouth opening and closing as she did so.

# The Honeymoon Suite

They arrived at the palazzo just after midnight, the boat nudging its way cautiously between the jetty's smooth wooden posts. From a distance the hotel seemed to slump into the water like a great upturned cake, but from the water's edge it appeared more delicate, its filmy, lace-like façade framing a series of elegant arches, snub balconies and tiny trefoil windows. Torches ringed the landing bay, illuminating a long white corridor leading to a thick, red curtain. Adam fumbled pulling their suitcase through and Zdenka, giggling, had to bend down to help him. In the lobby Adam removed his waterproof and gave his umbrella a shake. The pair of them were soaked and there were puddles of water everywhere. By the empty desk a sallow-faced man in a red cap eyed them up suspiciously. The guy had some kind of squint and gazed at the pair balefully with his one good eye.

Adam sauntered to the counter and rang the bell.

"Um, hello? Hello *por favor…*"

"That's Spanish…"

"Who's Spanish?"

"You, you *blbec…*"

Adam re-rang the bell and glanced up and down the deserted lobby. A step ladder and an old, spattered dust-cover suggested that it was in the process of being re-decorated, though there was no sign of any paint – or painters for that matter.

"Ah, hello. Hello, is there anyone there?"

"Shh," said Zdenka, "it's late…"

"Late? It's a hotel." Coughing, he turned to the guy in the red cap. "Excuse me, um, *signore*. Ah, do you speak English? You see, well, my, ah, wife and I…"

"*Passaporto.*"

"Sorry?"

"*Passaporto.*"

"He wants to see our passports," said Zdenka, rooting in her bag.

"You think? Look I'm just…"

The guy in the cap squinched up his working eye and examined Zdenka's photo. He then flicked to Adam's picture and made an odd noise – bleh, or something similar.

"Sorry?"

"Married?" asked the man. His voice was deep, mournful, and sounded oddly dubbed.

"Honeymoon," said Zdenka, beaming.

"Honeymoon?" The man looked sceptical. "Feh." He took out a large black pen and started to scribble on several of the pages.

"Um…" said Adam, but just then the desk clerk arrived, a short, barrel-chested man in a wig.

"*Signore, signora…*"

The concierge spied the man with the red cap and immediately launched into a furious argument conducted in equally furious Italian. The guy in the cap made an obscene gesture, the desk clerk yelled, and eventually the fella and his cap slunk away.

"I am most terribly sorry," said the concierge, handing the couple back their passports. "Please, please, sign here and let me arrange for somebody to take you to your room…"

"Who is that guy? Does he work here?"

"God protect us! No, no, signora, there is no place for him here…"

"But…"

"Sign here, here, and here, if you would be so kind…"

A sleepy, red-cheeked porter took their bags and led them to the lift. The interior was decked out in gaudy zebra prints, and smelt obscurely of egg. Adam flicked through his passport and showed it to Zdenka. The guy had drawn a something long and rude right over Adam's face. Zdenka started to giggle and by the time they arrived at the right floor she felt as if she might collapse.

# Z

Zdenka was still laughing in the shower. How funny marriage seemed, how nonsensical! It was as if she and Adam were two naughty children, engaged in some kind of impromptu yet elaborate prank. Even her new, awfully expensive, wedding ring looked like something found in a joke shop, a ridiculous toy. She held it against her bare middle and imagined that it winked. Then she started giggling again.

When she emerged, wrapped in a hotel gown several sizes too big, Adam was still dressed and watching TV. A priest in heavy red vestments was interviewing a young woman in an extremely low cut dress – or the woman might have been interviewing him, who knows?

"What's this?"

"Something Italian."

"Mm."

The audience were laughing crazily and Zdenka felt on the edge of hysteria herself. Only her new husband remained poker faced.

Still sniggering, she combed out her hair and watched as Adam stared motionlessly at the screen.

"It's free," she said.

"What?"

"The bathroom, it's free."

Reluctantly Adam dragged himself away from the TV. The bishop suddenly uncrossed his legs, revealing a flash of hairy flesh above the ankle.

"Oh, okay, I just need to…"

"Be my guest."

Whilst Adam showered and shaved, Zdenka stared at her various night things, especially chosen for their first night. Or should she simply get into bed as she was? No, she slipped on something sheer and romantic, her heart beating a little faster, her whole body feeling a little giddy. She then switched off the TV and dimmed all but one of the lights. A boat moved slowly past the hotel in the darkness, and for a moment it felt as if the hotel were moving too.

Staring out of the window, Zdenka could make out a figure in grey on the back of the boat, signalling wildly. She couldn't see his face very well, but the man looked agitated and dirty, half-crushed by the bags. Great sacks of rotting rubbish were piled up on the back of the barge, and the whole thing stank of shit.

Suddenly the canal worker seemed to catch sight of her, and with a gasp Zdenka quickly let the curtain fall back. Shouts were heard: something coarse, no doubt. Strangely, Zdenka only thought of her husband, as if afraid such language would bring a blush to his innocent cheek. Adam was still locked in the bathroom though: honestly, what was he *doing* in there? That a husband should take longer preening himself upset her Central European values. Besides, she was feeling kind of sleepy herself and didn't want to wait any longer.

Lying down on the simply enormous white bed she heard a child softly crying in the next room along. At first she smiled – what an omen for a wedding night! – but after a while she began to feel a little cross. What on earth were the parents doing? Were they deaf, or had they left the poor little thing all on its own?

Climbing out of bed again she padded across the floor and put her ear to the smooth wooden wall. It was obviously a very young baby, and sounded as if it had been crying for some time. Incensed at the indifference of the parents, Zdenka pushed against the wall and was astonished to find that it gave way: a panel opened and in a moment she was standing in the next *camera* along, the room a slightly darker variation of their own. Thankfully the bed was empty, but at its base was a small wooden cot, in which a tiny figure lay mewling. Without thinking, Zdenka stole across the room and embraced the child. As she did so the baby – a boy – stopped crying and instead stared deeply into her eyes. His tiny bud-like lips moved, his fat pink fingers flexed, and Zdenka pulled down her night-dress and held him to her chest. Immediately a feeling of intense pleasure washed over her and she felt as if she might swoon with joy. She felt his diminutive mouth encircle her, watched his blue eyes widen in surprise, and then took several steps backwards, stalking angrily around the room. How long had he been sobbing? How could they abandon such a wee, defenceless thing? A suit was strewn across the bed, and in an open wardrobe cocktail dresses floated like phantoms. No, it was simply unacceptable! Holding the babe carefully to her chest, Zdenka unlocked the door and made her way out into the corridor beyond.

# A

Adam could simply not get the damn thing to flush. Whenever he pulled the handle, a tiny spritz of water trickled into the bowl, nothing more. What would Zdenka think? Of course, since she'd clicked off the TV, she'd probably heard the whole sorry saga anyway. Adam switched the shower back on and sat down on the seat in despair. He tried the handle again: a miniscule splutter, a squirt. Then, just as he made to hide the brute with toilet paper he spotted them: a pair of eyes staring back at him from behind a grill in the ceiling, the pupils blazing before ducking back in to the darkness. Adam leapt up as if from an electric chair. What on earth was that?

"Hey!" he shouted. "Hey, you!"

Angrily he climbed onto the top of the seat and stared hard at the striped mesh of the grill. He could hear some kind of movement, but not that of an animal – a tiny person maybe. When he touched the dusty screen it easily gave way, revealing some kind of service shaft, the sides strangely damp.

"I know you're there!" he yelled. "Stop! Thief!"

Nothing.

Adam replaced the screen and then sat down by the basin again. Should he tell Zdenka? It might be some kind of pervert or maniac. But then, did he want to go and spoil the mood on their wedding night?

Opening the bathroom door, Zdenka was nowhere to be seen. He checked the balcony, the walk-in wardrobe, under the bed. His first thought was that this was some kind of romantic game, but after a few minutes of patient searching he began to have his doubts. Had someone come to the door? Had the desk phoned whilst the shower was running? He thought about the eyes and the fella in the red cap and sprinted out in to the corridor calling out his wife's name.

Their room was at the very end of a hallway, a series of low stairs leading down to the next landing. The carpet felt surprisingly coarse under his bare feet, and as he sprinted along the hall, Adam felt as if tiny brushes were scrubbing at his toes.

The corridor – a rich, burnished orange – snaked erratically left and right, each turn revealing another staircase, landing or narrow, slit-like window, the view opening out onto the mysteries of Venice beyond. The palace opposite looked like a jewellery box, the canal an elegant mirror. Lights moved about capriciously, seemingly untethered to street lamps, buildings or places, and Adam imagined himself as some kind of master thief, a cat burglar coolly casing the joint...

Directly across from a rather explicit nude he spotted the call button for the lift, but for some reason he felt embarrassed about going down to the lobby to ask about his wife. It seemed vaguely unmanly, somehow, to have lost one's bride on one's wedding night, and Adam feared the clerk's knowing smile, the manager's sideways glance. No, Zdenka was no doubt already back in their room and that was where he should be too – not gallivanting about after midnight, dressed only in his pyjama bottoms. His eyes lingered on the nude and he suddenly became aware of a desperate fear of being found out, of being discovered in some kind of compromising position... Shaking his head he retraced his steps back down the corridor, all the time looking out for the small left-hand side staircase which would take him back up to the right floor.

The passage was deserted save for a long line of shoes carefully placed outside each of the porridge-coloured doors: some men's, some women's, stout walking shoes, mules, expensive looking high-heeled affairs. It was as if the occupants of the various chambers had, on the spur of the moment, vanished, leaving only their empty footwear to mark their passing.

Stopping outside one of the doors, Adam caught sight of a pair of duck-egg court shoes which looked exactly like Zdenka's: same style, same size, same scuff. His heart racing, he picked the shoe up and examined it, investigating the instep as if it were some kind of expensive jewel. Yes, the same pale blue flower at the top, the same strap, sole: but did it smell of Zdenka? Glancing round the hallway Adam lifted the shoe up to his nose and sniffed. He then placed his hand inside and felt his way toward the toe. Inside the soft, fur-like lining there was something wet and sticky. He pulled his hand back and upturned the shoe: milk.

Startled, he moved to the next shoe – a doughty pair of men's brogues, and placed his hand inside again. This time he felt something cold and greasy: scrambled eggs. Inside a pair of smart Italian walking boots he found a great congealed mass of beans and ketchup, and inside a delicate woven slipper, a small crisp slice of bacon. A pile of dirty plates had been abandoned at the very end of the corridor, and Adam supposed that someone must have distributed the contents as some kind of gag. Still, the sensation of placing his hand inside the various openings stayed with him, and he backed away uncertainly, wiping the whole sticky mess on his pyjamas.

A hallway of shoes, abandoned like the footprints of a departed army... Adam stared at his wife's shoes one more time and then heard the sound of footsteps approaching from a stairwell nearby. He looked down at the breakfast dishes, the smeared cutlery and sticky plates, and immediately felt a stab of guilt: what if the passer-by should think that it was he who had scooped the food into the various receptacles?

Hiding his hands down his pyjamas, he fled down the corridor and hid in some kind of stock cupboard, the closet smelling of fresh linen, cleaning products, and pork. Unfortunately it was desperately dark in there and impossible to see a thing: one foot nudged a brush pan and the head of a mop tickled his nose. It was only when he heard a drawer closing that he realised that there was someone else in here with him, the figure extremely close, virtually right on top. Before he knew what was going on, Adam felt a hand pat down his pyjamas and then give them a healthy tug. Something touched him softly between his legs, and Adam leapt out of the stock cupboard yelling, the mop stumbling after him as if some kind of accomplice.

"Adam?" cried a voice. "Adam, is that you?"

# Z

Zdenka moved cautiously along the corridors, the tiny, pink fella pressed tight against her breast. There was no sign of life anywhere. The carpet was soft and yielding, almost like a mattress, and beyond the walls she could hear the dark waters of the canal lapping gently against the stone.

After a while the deep red corridor turned a rich purple, the doors the colour of oatmeal. It was very warm here, the heating equipment purring like an animal. Condensation dripped from the windows and the hall smelt vaguely of breakfast.

To one side a staircase spiralled up and down, but for some reason Zdenka couldn't face the idea of going down to the lobby, handing over the child, registering an official complaint. No, the more she thought about it, the more the child seemed to belong to her now – and to Adam, of course. Instead she walked right past the staircase and padded softly along the plum-coloured passage, her feet sinking into the carpeting as if she were skipping through a meadow of freshly mown grass...

The baby cooed, water slopped against the foundations, and Zdenka heard a gentle moan come from an open *camera* someplace off to one side.

"Hello?" she said. "Ah, is everything okay?"

The moan – a pale, scrap of a thing – drifted across the corridor and into Zdenka's ear, more of a whisper than a cry really – a breath.

"Hello?"

Zdenka and the babe entered a large, extremely well-appointed room, its gloom magnified rather than banished by a dim, antique lamp. In the middle of the enormous four-poster bed lay a tiny, almost mummified figure, its skin, teeth and hair the same unhealthy shade of yellow. The figure – a woman, though her sex seemed to have atrophied with the rest of her – lay on the bed like a discarded husk, the top half of her body sticking out of the covers like a corpse sitting up in its grave.

"*Signora?*"

A low wheeze departed the granny's body and Zdenka thought for some reason of her late aunt, Ljuba, a thin, chalk-drawing of a woman who had given her buttons once, as a child.

"*Signora?*" said Zdenka, uncertainly. "Ah, *bene, stai bene?*"

The old lady lifted a desiccated claw and beckoned Zdenka to her side. On a tray to one side were a wine-glass, knife and fork, and an egg.

"This? You want this?"

The old dear pointed to the glass.

"A drink?"

The woman nodded. Her lips were as dry as an envelope and when Zdenka moved the glass up to her mouth, the *babička* gulped it down greedily.

"*Grazie*," she said, her voice no more than a sigh. "*Grazie milli…*" With that her eyes seemed to focus, and she immediately caught sight of the child.

"*Che bello, che piccino…*"

Reaching out her hands, she stroked the baby's head with one, long finger. "*Těšit se dobrému zdraví, mláďe…*"

"You speak Czech?" said Zdenka, astonished.

The woman made a broad, dismissive gesture and the egg rolled off the tray.

"Oh," said Zdenka, "here, let me…"

Planting the baby on the bedspread, Zdenka footered about under the bed for the missing shell. O, if only there were more light! But no, there was the egg, resting in a nest of dust and cobwebs. When she looked back up, the baby was sucking on the old lady's finger and waving his arms excitedly.

"He likes you," said Zdenka, before pausing and translating her words into Czech. The old lady smiled and murmured something, but Zdenka couldn't quite catch it. Eyes sparkling, the granny pointed first at the egg and then at her mouth.

"This? Well…"

Zdenka uncertainly brought the egg towards her and before she knew what was happening, the old dear had taken the thing in her mouth and swallowed it, shell, cobwebs and all. Zdenka looked on in horror but the old woman simply smiled and whispered "*hladový*" – hungry.

"Hungry? No, no, you mustn't…"

The woman shook her head. "*Hladový.*"

Zdenka stared about the room. "But what is there to…"

The granny pointed her long, shrivelled finger toward a desk nearby and then circled her mouth. "*Hladový*."

Hesitantly, Zdenka walked over to the desk and began to rifle through the drawers; to her astonishment she found a long piece of smoked Polish sausage, some kind of black pudding, and a mushroom. She obediently brought them back to the invalid, and with a slight air of reluctance, poked the whole lot through the old woman's pale grey lips.

"*Hladový*," said the granny.

"Still hungry?"

"*Hladový*."

Behind the granny's pillow Zdenka retrieved a thin slice of Yorkshire ham, and from beside the bedside lamp, an old stump of hard, yellow cheese. These too disappeared terrifyingly swiftly into the same black hole.

"*Hladový*," said the granny.

The baby squealed happily, the old woman smiled, and Zdenka scoured the room for other tidbits, locating a kipper in a slipper, toast behind a post, and a bedpan of grey, brackish water, cradling a cold poached egg.

"*Hladový*," said the granny, her little black tongue licking her lips.

No sooner had Zdenka presented each treasure than it was immediately consumed, sucked in to the void. Zdenka had to venture further and further afield now, hunting around in the bathroom, the toilet and the dark, narrow vestibule too. Ach, when *would* the old dear be satisfied? Zdenka could hear the baby giggling, the old lady breathing, and the sound of the water thrashing against the outer walls. Would Adam be looking for her, would he be worried, cross, upset? It was their wedding night after all...

Just then Zdenka heard the crash of a tray falling from the bed and she hurried back to the room, dusty tomato in hand. At first she couldn't work out what was going on. The lamp had fallen over, and the room seemed broken up into shadows. Was that the bedspread and that a figure? Then, as her eyes finally started to adjust, she saw the granny pulling the tiny baby toward her mouth, the old lady's long, pencil-like fingers holding tight to his head.

"Jiri! Little one!"

With a cry Zdenka threw herself on to the bed, trying to pull the baby back to her breast. "What are you doing?" Zdenka yelled at the woman in a mixture of English, Italian and Czech. "What kind of a mother are you?"

"*Hladový*," whispered the granny, and Zdenka felt long nails ripping through her night-dress, piercing her side.

"Bad mother! *Zlý člověk...*"

Panting, Zdenka scooped up the babe and fled, racing along the indigo corridor, hammering on every door she came to. Was the witch close behind – but how could she leave her bed? Nevertheless, Zdenka continued to bang on every door, and when one opened, she threw herself inside, her body shaking as if she had just been chased by a bear.

"It's okay, it's okay," she told the crying child, and when she pressed him to her chest, her nipple stood out like a light-switch.

Rather than a bedroom, they seemed to be in some kind of art gallery or wing of the hotel devoted to temporary exhibitions and the like. The room itself was very badly lit, but by each painting was the tiny stub of a candle, the puddles of wax easily giving off as much smoke as light.

"Shhh," said Zdenka to the baby. "The naughty lady has gone. We're safe here, shh..."

The room was very different to the nearby bed chambers, more like a hall or a strangely convoluted corridor, constantly twisting and turning around alcoves, inset spaces and dead ends, the latter blocked by thick red drapes.

"Don't cry," said Zdenka. "Mummy's here, there's nothing to fear, shhh…"

Despite her fears, Zdenka drifted closer to the paintings, all of which were nudes – male and female, young and old, hung up in the room seemingly without sentiment, decoration or decorum. Yes, everything was displayed as openly as one's sheets on laundry day, but the overall feeling was of an odd kind of indifference, as if these were things of flesh and bone, nothing more. Zdenka stared at the crowd of naked torsos without the faintest flicker of arousal or embarrassment; if anything her only thought was how much nicer her own body looked than all this sagging meat, how she had, in her twenties, so far escaped the wrinkles, bags and drooping appendages of age… yes, she was young and so was her husband, their bodies newly minted things, unbruised or tarnished…

Thinking of her husband, Zdenka moved swiftly on her way, picking her way between the gold frames and the endless sea of skin tones, navigating the patches of hair and the rounded stomachs…

Rounding the next corner she found herself in a smaller gallery, the canvases portraying a series of tiny, almost miniscule still lives. On one side of the room, in startling detail, she could see lovingly reproduced hats, overcoats, ballpoints and sabres, whilst on the other there were exquisite paintings of bottles, boxes, trunks and stoves. The smoke from the candles softened the edges and to Zdenka it seemed as if these inanimate objects were vastly more alive and intimate than the unclothed strangers hanging around next door. One beautifully ornate bottle appeared infinitely desirable and seductive, whilst a wide earthen jar seemed to wink playfully, its cork stopper pulled roguishly over one eye. As for the watering cans, the spears, sabres and rifles, Zdenka felt her cheeks redden as she approached them: how long they were, how perky! Passing by an enormous walking stick, she felt as if she should avert her eyes – or at least cover the face of her child. And with that she virtually collided with the guy from the lobby in the red cap, the fella engaged with removing a picture of an open cupboard from the wall, a torch and pair of half-filled sacks lying by his feet.

Zdenka started, the guy belched, and with that he turned to stare at her and the baby, sizing up the pair of them with his one good eye. He spat, shoved the painting in the smaller of the two sacks, and started towards them.

"What are you doing?" yelled Zdenka, "what do you want?"

She scowled, shook her fist, and then started to run, dodging to one side and sprinting through the seemingly endless gallery like a lunatic. Her bare feet barely seemed to touch the springy carpet, her sheer night-gown floating past the canvasses like a scarf. Was the fellow chasing her? Yes, yes, he was. When she glanced back over her shoulder she saw him following with his one red eye – as red as the cap he wore on his oversized head.

"Bleh," he spat, shaking his head from side to side, and Zdenka felt his breath in her ear – as close as a finger and a nail.

The pictures seemed to be getting larger again, but there was no time to inspect them now: breathing heavily the man in the cap was hard on her heels, and she could hear the *protiva* grunting and snorting, make out the whistle of air through his teeth.

'Adam,' she thought, 'Adam, where are you?'

Both pursuer and pursued reached the dimly illuminated exit at precisely the same time, finding themselves at the base of a navy-blue set of stairs, the carpet as soft as rabbit fur. Breathless, Zdenka sprinted up the staircase, fear – for the child, herself, her night gown – propelling her to the next floor. Fortunately Red Cap seemed weighted down by his sacks, and it wasn't long before she started to out-distance him, his wheezing groans falling further and further behind. Who was he anyway – some kind of art thief, a burglar? Zdenka's cheeks were flushed and strands of hair stuck to her face, but she nevertheless made it to the very top of the stairwell, throwing open the fire-door and falling out onto the roof.

The rain seemed to revive her, and as she carefully barred the large, heavy door behind her, she suddenly started to titter and laugh. Behind the door, she could hear the man in the red cap bang and bang on the barrier, and then stop. Zdenka placed her ear to the door and listened: the man's breathing was ragged and noisy, eventually turning into large and inconsolable sobs.

Still laughing, Zdenka backed away from the door and looked out at the incomparable, matchless city, a ravishing corpse laid out in its most extravagant jewels and finery. Only then did Zdenka realise that the babe was gone.

# A

Adam reached the main staircase before realising he was no longer wearing his pyjamas and had no idea where he was going. Worse still, he seemed to be in a state of some consternation or excitement. How terribly misplaced, he thought – what kind of a wedding night was this? Ducking behind a curtain he hid himself within the drapes as best he could, re-arranging the folds to make himself less conspicuous. What a place to find oneself! He heard footsteps and pressed his bare bottom back against the glass: beyond lay the most beautiful city in the world, all the bells of the city tolling mournfully. Waves splashed against the hotel, rain fell from the sky and Adam felt a powerful urge to urinate; but he fought the feeling and instead hopped awkwardly in the direction of the nearest open door, holding himself between his legs.

A row of stained white lockers faced him, but all seemed locked, and the cracked tiles of the floor felt very cold. Blinking at the strip lights, Adam paddled quickly across the puddles and the leaks, ignoring the shuttered desk and the vending machine, and heading down a series of yellow, uneven steps.

At the bottom was a small, almost circular swimming pool, the dull yellow lighting making the pool resemble a great bowl of soup. The place stank of chemicals and the light hurt his eyes, yet Adam felt an enormous sense of relief; this was a place where he was encouraged to take his clothes off, a room in which a certain state of undress was to be expected. Placing one toe in the surprisingly warm, vaguely sulphurous *aqua*, Adam realised that he had stumbled upon the one place in the hotel in which he might hide. Sure, the piss-colour was a little off-putting, as was the amount of hair drifting upon the surface (what did they do here, shave the cook's sausages?) but at least for the moment his nudity was acceptable, his embarrassment submerged beneath the surface.

Taking a breath he flopped awkwardly into the pool, the splash rather louder than he might have hoped. A long, dark hair immediately stuck to his lips and his nostrils burned, but he nevertheless swam a number of swift lengths, unsure as to what else to do. After a while the water seemed to soothe him and he felt his muscles start to relax; it was as if his body knew what to do whilst everything above the neck felt heavy and confused.

After several laps Adam paused and clung to the side. Fuzz and frizzies were glued to his fingers, and he had a bristly thatch of whiskers stuck to one cheek. Carefully, he extracted a long strand wrapped around his ring finger: a strange kind of omen, though he couldn't quite think what of. And then he saw it – his wedding ring was gone.

A jolt of anxiety shot through him. How could he lose his ring – on tonight of all nights? What would Zdenka say? Adam ran his fingers through the water and gazed into the citron depths warily. A carpet of hair floated past, spiralling gently. Ho, what kind of start to their married life was this? Besides, the ring was the very last thing he still had to wear…

Diving down (the pool was no more than a few feet deep) Adam groped blindly through the fronds of hair, expecting at any moment to see his ring flash or wink. But all he could see down there were sticks, branches and bits of grass, almost as if instead of a swimming pool it was the base of some kind of underground pool or lake.

Coughing, and spitting, Adam bobbed back to the surface and felt his eyes sting as if rubbed with pepper. He rubbed the lids, shook his head, and dived back under the water, groping blindly along the bottom. When he resurfaced for the third time, a middle-aged woman was sitting atop a rickety step ladder near the centre of the room, the woman dressed in a grey, ill-fitting tabard and head scarf. From her vantage point atop the stool she watched him struggle to hide himself in the water, not even the tiniest flicker of emotion crossing her thick, fleshy mouth.

"Um, *ciao*," said Adam, hopefully. "Ah, swim, swimmo, ah, *piscine…*"

The woman stared at him blankly, and took out a packet of boiled sweets from her pocket. She resembled the old Hollywood actor Ernest Borgnine, albeit rouged and fully made-up.

"Si, si, um, *essere immerse, immero toto…*" Adam smiled his most winning smile but the woman wouldn't fall for it. Rather she looked at him as if he were a difficult thing she was going to have to laboriously scrape from a plate.

"I, er, I seem to have lost…"

Adam's Italian escaped him and instead he mimed how his ring had fallen from his finger – only when he had finished did he realise just how unfortunate the gesture looked.

"Um, *il ring, matrimonio…*"

The woman's face was as glacial as the arctic, as if she were some kind of cut-out placed there for a gag.

Adam nodded. "Yes, yes, ring, marriage, ah, *matrimonio…*"

The woman sucked her sweet.

"Yes, lost, ah, on the bottom…" He gestured toward the pool. "Bottom…"

Removing a cloth from her tabard, the woman began slowly rubbing the top of the ladder. "*Matrimonio? Le nozze?*" she said, her tone absolutely neutral.

"Yes, yes, um, honeymoon, *il ring…*"

Covering himself as best he could, Adam paused: had he just proposed?

"Ring?"

Adam nodded. "Um, *parla inglese? Potete…*help? *Assisto?*"

The woman stared at him unblinkingly and then said, "*Aspetarre,*" in a low, almost toneless voice, climbing down the step ladder in a painfully slow manner before padding up the stairs in her soft, plastic-looking crocs. A few minutes later she returned with a second tabard-clad woman, this one much shorter and thinner, with a tanned and smiley face.

"Ah, um, you speak English?" asked Adam, but the woman merely shook her head and stared at where he kept his hands. The two women looked at Adam, looked at each other, and then began to converse in Italian in an unhurried and perfectly casual manner.

Adam cupped himself as best he could, feeling like a naughty boy caught doing something naughty in some nearby, naughty thing. He wondered whether he should head back into the waters again – perhaps the ring might still be found – but then the second woman waved and gestured for him to follow them toward the lockers.

"*Venire, venire,*" she said, and from one of the lockers she produced a small pink towel – more of a facecloth, really – made of some kind of material Adam had never seen before in his life.

"Thank you, *graci,*" he said, but as soon as he began to dry himself he realised just how abrasive the towel really was: more like sandpaper than cotton.

He paused in his ablutions, but the two women were staring at him intently, the second woman smiling eagerly, making the gesture for him to dry his bottom. The first woman – Ernest Borgnine – noisily sucked another sweet.

Swabbing himself as gingerly as possible, Adam awkwardly wrapped the towel around himself, though there was no way it was going to go around his middle. He looked at the women, the women looked at him, and both the smiling woman and Ms. Borgnine seeming to be awaiting some kind of response. Adam held on to his face cloth and tried a smile.

"Ah, thank you, very good, *graci,* um…"

The first woman measured him with a practiced eye, and then, removing a fob of keys, opened one of the rusted whitish lockers. Various items of clothing were kept inside – all of them musty and rather unpleasant smelling – from which she removed trousers, a work shirt, and some kind of reflective jacket.

"*Qui … usura,*" she said, her expression as cold and empty as the room.

"Me? No, no, I…"

"*Si – per te…*"

Better work clothes than no clothes at all, thought Adam, and he abandoned the towel and stepped squeamishly into the trousers, trying not to think of his bare skin touching the stained, rubbery fabric.

"Good, good," said the smiley woman, appraising his attire as if he were standing there in his wedding suit. "*Prestante...*"

With that the two women led him out of the locker room and along a dull grey service corridor, Adam's feet uncomfortably cold on the coarse, wiry carpet.

"My ring..." he said to them, but it was no use now. The two women appeared to be very certain as to where they were taking him, and after several more turnings he could no longer remember the way back.

# Z

From the roof, Venice resembled a great jewelled cloak thrown over an enormous puddle, the rooftops, chimney pots and turrets clinging precariously to its folds. Somewhere amongst the soot of night, muffled alarm bells tolled monotonously: *aqua alta,* the autumn flood. Though it was too dark to see, Zdenka could easily imagine black waves sweeping along the ancient arcades, hands of brackish water poking through cracks and fissures, *piazzas* transformed into tranquil lakes, ancient arcades into deep dark wells.

Zdenka looked down at her naked breast and thought about the baby. Had she misplaced him somehow, lost him during the chase? For a moment she considered heading back through the barred door, but could still hear the man in the red cap behind it, the fellow disconsolately weeping. Instead she cautiously edged her way across the roof, the rain a kind of fine mist now, soaking her night-dress and her skin. The stone was flaked and worn here, the stone covered in tiny cracks. A small black cat watched her from a tiny recess up above, but when she reached out her hand it immediately scampered away, gingerly stepping from tile to tile. It too was drenched to the bone, but nevertheless it steadfastly refused to approach her; instead it watched her from afar, its tail flicking slowly.

"Adam," said Zdenka. "Adam, *kde jsi?*"

Still several feet apart, Zdenka and the cat carefully made their way across the slippery tiles and gulleys, the pair of them perilously perched above a grand stone balcony, able to peer down its décolletage but without any hope of climbing down below. The cat mewed and Zdenka shivered: the night was cool and she was wearing the flimsiest of garments. Ah, how distant the rest of Venice seemed! Capsized churches bobbed next to the shipwreck of a bell tower, the lights of an occasional boat sweeping the waves as if looking for survivors. The cat licked its fur and the lagoon licked the *palazzo*; even the bells sounded full of water.

Near the summit of a carved window-arch, its gothic frame adorned with rich foliage and grotesque faces, Zdenka could see a small service hatch, the grill partly open. Pulling hard, the rusted metal gave way to reveal a darkened shaft leading back down into the hotel – more of a pipe really, but large enough to swallow a human being. The cat hissed angrily, but Zdenka ignored it, squeezing her way carefully through the gap. She heard a tearing sound as her gown snagged on the broken catch, but there was nothing she could do about it now: an ogre with an obscene nose leered at her from the window-arch and Zdenka stuck out her tongue in response.

A rough, cracked ladder led down the shaft and Zdenka inched her way slowly from rung to rung, an unpleasant breeze blowing up beneath what remained of her night-dress. She could hear water trickling from a great height somewhere, and for a terrible moment she thought that she might piss too. O, what kind of place was this? The chute narrowed and her bladder shrunk. Then, just when she thought things could get no worse, the hatch abruptly tilted and the last remaining square of light immediately vanished, the space below as dark as beneath an undertaker's hat. Dust tickled Zdenka's nose and invisible bugs crawled across her naked skin: 'I must not panic,' she thought, 'I must not drop.' Eventually she spotted a bright grid of light and crawled gratefully towards it, the grill forming a fuzzy mosaic of dazzling light. Elbowing her way forward, Zdenka pushed her face up against it, trying to make sense of the shapes and blurs moving before her eyes. To her astonishment she realised that she had somehow crawled her way to just above their bathroom. There were her bottles and lotions, still sitting on the shelf, and there was her toothbrush, nestled up next to Adam's, by her face cream and tweezers. And there was Adam too, staring in to the toilet bowl and pushing the handle up and down. But what was he doing? He tried the handle again and again, and Zdenka watched his face redden, his cheeks puffing in and out. How strange it was to see him like this – and how ridiculous he seemed! The man around whom she had fashioned such romantic ideas, staring sour-faced into a toilet bowl. Trying to stifle her giggles, Zdenka moved to get a better look, and in that instance their eyes met, Adam staring into the gloom, Zdenka blinking out at the light. But what should they say? Zdenka felt ashamed, as if she were staring at something she should not, whilst Adam looked angry and upset, his lip curled back like a dog. She shrunk back from the grill and Adam leapt up as if from a hot stove.

"Hey!" he shouted. "Hey, you!"

His face a fierce shade of crimson, he climbed on to the seat and stared hard at the striped mesh of the grill.

"I know you're there!" he yelled. "Stop! Thief!"

Zdenka frantically pushed her way back into the shaft, a feeling of shame stretching from her damp, frizzy hair to her ripped, barely present night-gown. How could she explain what she was doing here, where she had gone? What could she ever say to her husband about what had happened on their wedding night – the baby, the man with the red cap, her hazardous journey across the roof? So instead she crawled backwards, following a different shaft, this one a little darker and narrower, Zdenka losing the last remains of her gown as she dragged herself along.

A second grill looked down upon another bathroom, albeit rather plainer and smaller than the suite she'd booked into with Adam all those hours (hours?) before. The room was empty and unlit, the only illumination coming from under the porridge-coloured door. Straining her ears, Zdenka was pretty sure the *camera* was unoccupied and urgently pulled at the grill. Ach, why wouldn't it come? But then the dusty mesh gave way and Zdenka fell as if dropped from a trapdoor, flopping painfully on the plastic tiles, shivery, damp and bare. Stumbling across the room she checked that no one was asleep and then opened the curvaceous wardrobe – empty, sad to say. Nor were there any coats or robes hanging behind the door, no, not so much as a hotel slipper.

Swearing softly in Czech, Zdenka inched open the door and surveyed the corridor: deserted also. A decorator's ladder was left abandoned by a fire-door, a rubbery mat thrown across the floor. The whole passage smelt of paint. Half of it was red and half blue: the brushstrokes stopped as if the mysterious painters had melted away invisibly into the night.

Zdenka stepped over the blobs and spills and warily stalked along the corridor; the carpet coarse and prickly and the mat cold and spongy, her feet sticking to the tacky surface. O, what if the man in the red cap should come upon her now? Or her new husband for that matter – what possible justification for her naked state could there be? Venice reclined on the invisible lagoon as if on a dark, endless bed, yet instead of curling up next to her husband there she was, stalking the corridors like some pale, dark eyed ghost... By the entrance to the lift Zdenka spotted a life-sized nude and shivered: was it a canvas or a mirror? She stared at the painting's eyes and blinked.

Beyond it the corridor snaked erratically left and right, each turn revealing another staircase, landing, or narrow, elegant arch. Expecting to be uncovered at any moment, Zdenka cautiously paced along the passages, the hotel evacuated save for row after row of forgotten shoes. Occasionally she thought she could hear feet pacing the hallways some distance away, but they never seemed to draw nearer, the *palazzo* so silent she could almost hear the dark water rising behind the wall. The corridor arched like a gracefully extended arm, whilst behind the heavy drapes of a nearby curtain something poked up against the curtains – a handle, or some kind of discarded tool, she guessed. Every door was the colour of oatmeal, every door was the same. Numbers? *Nijak, nessuno,* no.

Just when she felt certain that some nocturnal guest or officious member of staff was bound to finally appear, she came upon the door to a stock cupboard, the space smelling of fresh linen, cleaning products, and, for some reason, cured ham. Pulling on a cord, Zdenka saw that the closet opened out onto a surprisingly expansive room, rows of maids' uniforms neatly folded on shelves next to those of kitchen staff, bellboys and security guards. Zdenka dressed swiftly, pulling on the brown apron and white dress of a chamber maid. No sooner had she finished when she heard footsteps again, this time unquestionably coming closer – running, even. Immediately she switched off the light and hid at the back at the closet. At that moment a shadowy figure burst in, shutting the door behind him. Squeezed back into a kind of recess Zdenka hardly dared to breathe: what if he were to speak to her? Strangely though, nothing happened; no one spoke, moved or sniffed – instead the darkness deepened like a well. Had she imagined everything? When she reached out a hand she bumped into an open linen drawer. Closing it, she groped blindly in front of her, finding some kind of fabric which she swiftly gave a firm tug. The next thing she felt was something else entirely. The figure moaned, the door flew open, and a mop crashed across the doorway like a sword. Lying at Zdenka's feet were a pair of pyjama bottoms exactly like those of Adam.

"Adam?" she yelled. "Adam, is that you?"

But by then the bare bottom was gone.

# A

"*In questo modo, ci seguono,*" said the smiley woman, gesturing to Adam as if he were some kind of stray dog. "*Si, si, non lontano…*"

Adam followed the woman's tabard along the dull and functional corridor and out toward a fire-exit. The alley outside was wet and narrow and smelt of fish. In the pocket of his high-visibility jacket he found a small, flattened pastry.

"Um, reception? *La reception?*"

The women looked at each other inscrutably.

"Um, I've lost my wife…"

"Ring?"

"Wife…"

*La Borgnine* sucked on a sweet and the smiley one patted down his jacket.

"*Si, questo è il modo giusto…*"

Adam could smell silt, garbage and petrol: the canal was close by.

"*Grazi*, um, you've been very kind…"

The smiley woman nodded and continued patting him down as if searching for explosives.

"Ah…"

But where were her hands going?

Red-faced, Adam waved goodbye and stumbled along the alleyway, the ground feeling terribly cold and wet on his poor bare feet. Unlike the rest of the *palazzo*, the cement wall looked newly built and great mounds of sand kept blocking the way. For some reason Adam thought suddenly of the corridors leading backstage behind some kind of theatre – the space where props were kept, or the scenery stored for the next change of act. Everything here felt forsaken and neglected, from the piles of bricks to the abandoned cement mixer, rejected objects not intended for public view. Was the hotel just some kind of derelict set after all?

The cement passage led into a small, self-contained courtyard, whose principal feature was a large ugly fountain, decorated by a series of stone fish all with obscene, droopy mouths. Though the bowl was full of rain water, the fountain itself produced barely a dribble, little more than an embarrassing drip, and Adam stared at the liquid unhappily, a vaguely unhappy memory turning round and round in his head. Although the setting hardly looked imposing, little coloured lanterns had been hung here and there, and there were even some half-deflated balloons strung amongst the alcoves, flaccid and exhausted.

Adam drifted over to the fountain and stuck his fingers into the pool. The porches were very dark and the sky lacked a single star. A litter bin was filled to the brim with dead, wet leaves, though oddly Adam couldn't seem to see any trees. Over in the arcade, a solitary wheelbarrow looked on.

Was this a public space for guests or some private, backstage area, intended for chefs to smoke a crafty cigarette or tired housemaids to take the air? Adam wasn't so sure. He rolled the pastry back and forth in his pocket and watched the thin spits of rain fill the empty wheelbarrow. Beyond the wall the canal splashed like an overfull pail.

Ah, how tired he felt! He knew that he would have to gather up the energy to head back inside, find reception, speak to the duty-manager, explain his situation: but all this seemed beyond him right now. He couldn't imagine where Zdenka might be, or how he might find their hotel room again either. Across the way, instead of a door, he could see a pair of thick, russet drapes, and again he felt he was somehow behind the stage, the pearl-grey facings of the hotel no more than a *trompe l'oeil* illusion.

As if to confirm these impressions he turned to watch a slender figure standing in the wings, staring toward the curtains as if waiting to go on stage. The figure – a chambermaid by what he could see of her dress – was staring into space in what he felt to be a slightly affected, *faux*-dramatic manner. He couldn't see her face, just her torso, but everything about her pose suggested a tragic heroine awaiting the last act.

Unmoving, he watched her for a little time, the pair of them seemingly unaffected by the falling rain or endless darkness. A black cat padded past. Water gurgled in a blocked drain pipe. Somewhere muffled bells tolled half-heartedly and it felt as if all of Venice were sinking slowly beneath the waves.

Adam shook his head, swallowed, and started towards her – just as a series of bangs and yells suggested the arrival of something large on the other side of the wall, the light of a lantern swinging crazily across the yard.

To the sound of loud Italian curses, the curtain was pulled open and a team of garbage men rolled into the yard, searching out the piles of black, plastic bags kept in a closed alcove to one side. The men, dressed in black caps and heavy reflective jackets, laboriously picked up the rubbish and dragged the stinking sacks of plastic back through the curtains and toward their barge, the bags wobbling disgustingly. All the time they yelled loudly, but Adam couldn't make out a word.

As the bin men spread out the maid melted away and Adam crouched down behind the fountain. When he looked up he could see a pair of stout black boots and a pair of rubbery protective trousers standing over him: one of the bin men was watching him intently, his dark brow furrowed. Smiling inanely, Adam raised his arms as if in a movie, and walked over to the rest of the team. One of them – a bearded guy with a wide, bulbous nose – pointed to the pile of bags and Adam reluctantly picked one up, the wet plastic and ripe smell deeply unappealing.

"But I'm not…"

The bin-man glared at him and made some kind of gesture – one with coarse overtones, no doubt. Adam pointed to his bare feet, the bin-man pointed to the curtains, and grudgingly Adam pulled the sacks awkwardly out of the yard, all the time egg shells and potato peelings leaving a haphazard trail behind him.

A rough, slippery plank led to the back of a large barge, the rear already piled up with a mountain of stinking plastic. Adam tottered across and added his fat sacks to the pile, slipping and sliding on the surface. Then, just as he started to make his way back to the gangplank, one of the workers whistled, a rope was cast off, and the barge started to pull away from the rear of the hotel, joining a cortege of barges sailing sombrely through the gloom.

"Um," said Adam. "Ah, that is…"

Yes, there was no doubt about it: the pearl-grey façade was already vanishing, the waves high and choppy. The red lights of the barge gave the vessel a strangely unearthly feel, and as the barge passed the side of the *palazzo* Adam felt as if he were slipping away from the known world entirely.

In an upstairs trefoil window, beneath an elegant arch of Istrian stone, he spotted Zdenka, dressed in her night gown and gazing down at the canal, an unreadable expression upon her face.

"Zdenka!" he cried. "Zdenka, down here…"

He waved and gestured, but at the vital moment lost his footing and flopped back clumsily amongst the garbage and the scrapings. The curtain fell back, Zdenka vanished, and the barge moved on. Adam tried to right himself but more and more bags kept slipping on top of him till eventually he couldn't see anything at all.

# Z

When Zdenka found him, the little boy was busy scraping the contents of a deserted breakfast tray into a deserted line of shoes and boots, pushing down the scrambled egg and tomatoes with his fat, jammy little fingers.

"Jiri!"

The boy looked at her without any acknowledgement of wrongdoing; instead he toddled cheerfully over, abandoning his croissant to caress the fabric by her knee. He couldn't have been more than two or three; a slightly pale boy with sandy hair and fine features.

He reminded her of the baby she'd found earlier, and once again she felt a shiver of anger toward the negligent and thoughtless parents, abandoning their child in the maze.

"Where have you come from, eh? What are you doing little monkey?"

He pulled at her hem and tried to bury himself under her skirt, his fingers sticky with egg and jam.

"Where are your mummy and daddy? Is this the door, sweetheart...?"

The boy wiped his face on Zdenka's dress and nodded. His eyes moved toward the door behind him, but his face stared up at her as if she were a large balloon.

"This one? Here?"

Zdenka edged open the door and, despite the gloom, could see two figures engaged in vigorous adult activity. She closed the door again, swiftly.

"Come with me," she said, taking the little boy's hand. "Are you hungry? Foo, leave that mess, come here..."

"*Hladový*," said the boy, squeezing Zdenka's ring finger and nodding. His pyjamas had rocket ships on and were pale blue.

Together, the two of them walked along a recently re-decorated passageway – now green but with little specks of orange still shining through – and down toward the main stairs. Paintings of the Grand Canal adorned the walls, the city a giant chocolate box housing tiny gold churches and delicately wrapped silver *palazzos*, the canal a glittering blue ribbon surrounding them. The boy beamed at Zdenka and Zdenka smiled back. His hair was as dry and golden as straw.

In the lobby at the bottom of the sea Zdenka spotted the concierge chatting casually with the sleepy red-cheeked porter, the two of them laughing as if at some kind of dirty joke.

"No," said Zdenka to the child. "Not this way – back up the stairs, darling. We'll find someplace else to eat."

Pushing open a plain door Zdenka led the boy into what looked like some kind of conference room, containing a long table, a series of high, leather chairs, and a bowl of slightly spoiled fruit. Zdenka inspected the produce and handed the boy a brown, rather bruised apple. The boy took a bite and pulled a face. "*K ničemu*," he said – no good.

Zdenka scowled and squeezed a limp and blackened banana. "Wait here," she said. "I'll find you something else."

The boy nodded but held on tight to her apron.

"*Ne, ne*," said Zdenka. "You stay here – I'll be right back."

A frown passed across his forehead but he nevertheless let her go. Soft golden down covered his cheeks like sugar.

"Stay," said Zdenka. "Shh, don't cry – stay."

Gently closing the door Zdenka raced along the corridor searching for some kind of kitchen or store cupboard. The split landing led to a series of shallow stairwells leading left and right, whilst the corridor itself kept vanishing into hidden alcoves and tiny nooks. Cast-off shoes waited outside the doors like absent sentries and the radiators hissed and popped.

Turning a blind corner Zdenka stumbled straight into the arms of a tall, robed figure dressed in some kind of carnival garb: long black habit, elaborate golden trim, and a hideous beaked mask, the barb extremely long and pointed. Zdenka thought she might cry out, but the figure apologised, bowed, and moved to let her pass. He was carrying a large doctor's bag and walked with a steady and professional gait. Zdenka watched him ascend the stairs but he didn't look back; she found it hard to believe that he had ever been there at all.

Scrutinizing the various passageways Zdenka realised that she had completely lost her bearings. Which way their hotel room and which way the child? She glanced up and down the halls of oatmeal doors and neatly lined footwear and decided to retrace her steps: perhaps the man in fancy dress could help after all. Forgetting that she was still dressed as a maid, she trotted swiftly after him, calling out *"Signora,"* in an uncertain voice. At the top of the stairs a door flew open and a maid appeared, passing over a tray with wine glasses and olives and whispering *"Camera due Quattro a sei."* Startled, Zdenka took the tray and curtsied: what else could she do? There didn't seem to be any numbers on the doors but that didn't matter: a steady of stream of guests and catering staff were heading toward the same open door, the hum of subdued conversation emanating from within.

Unlike the rest of the apparently uninhabited and empty hotel, the suite was crammed with people, the men in black suits, the ladies in elegant yet sombre dress. All around waiting staff served drinks and collected glasses, the subdued small talk carried out in a mixture of Czech, Italian and English. Zdenka transported her tray over to a long trellis table and handed the glasses and olives to the tall, good looking caterer; she then picked up a bottle of white and automatically set about re-filling glasses.

Many of the guests in the room looked vaguely familiar to her, though she was hard pressed to think from where. Recipients accepted their drinks and murmured thanks in various languages but no one met her eyes and Zdenka felt an odd sense of melancholy creeping over her, a sadness tinged with a vague sense of unease. She stepped backwards onto the feet of somebody behind her, and turned to see a light-haired young man whose fine features and apologetic smile felt oddly intimate.

*"Pardone,"* he said, "here let me…"

The tray was leaning at an alarming angle but the young guy

swiftly supported it, holding on to Zdenka's arm as he did so.

"I'm sorry," she said, embarrassed. "I'm not really a waitress…"

"No?"

"No, um…"

Ho, why did he look so recognizable, his features so familiar?

"Are you okay? Come and sit over here, next to Father…"

Zdenka took his arm and allowed him to escort her over to a small reception area, where a middle-aged man sat talking with a much older, rather matronly woman. Despite her age, the woman had strikingly red hair, speaking in a hoarse voice with a pronounced Central European accent.

"Here, no here, sit down," said the kindly young guest, manoeuvring Zdenka onto the chaise next to the middle-aged man. "Dad? Dad, let this young lady sit down…"

The pair were instantly identifiable as father and son, both with the same fair hair, high forehead, and virtually invisible eyebrows. But whilst the father's eyes were pale and watery, the son's were as black as a crow.

"Are you alright, miss? You don't look so well. Would you like a drink? Or would you rather sit by a window?"

To be honest, Zdenka didn't feel so good. The room was very stuffy and there were far too many people crammed between the reception area and the bedroom. She tried to focus on a painting of the *Basilica San Marco*, but the colours were too bright, the lines bending and distorting as if underwater.

"Miss? Miss, can you hear?"

Try as she might, she just couldn't work out why the faces of the father and son were etched so intimately in her mind. Even the old woman seemed known to her, the old dear's hands trembling a little as she held tightly onto her glass. "Danka?" she asked, leaning in closer, and Zdenka felt the liquorish breath of *Hašlerky* on her cheeks.

236

"The doctor is just in the next room," said the son, holding on to Zdenka's hand with some concern. "Maybe he should just…"

"The doctor? Well, yes, of course," said the father, helping her to her feet. "This way, my dear, just through here…"

Despite her protestations, father and son firmly guided her through the maze of people, her feet dragging a little and several guests starting to whisper and stare. One trailing arm knocked over a lamp, and though the father caught it, a hush fell upon the room.

"Miss? Don't worry miss, there's a doctor right here…"

A stab of dismay swept over her, and Zdenka struggled in their arms. "*Ne, ne,* I'm fine…"

"S'okay," said the son, "he'll make sure you're okay…"

They seemed to be propelling her inexorably toward the bedroom and Zdenka twisted and wriggled, her feeling of dread steadily becoming more acute. The crowd parted and the room swayed like the cabin of a ship.

"No," she said. "No, I don't want…"

A yellowish figure was lying prone on the bed, but Zdenka didn't want to look at it. A feeling of revulsion and foreboding grew the closer she got to the bedside. A gaunt claw poked out of the bed clothes and thin strands of tobacco coloured hair trailed across the pillow.

"No," said Zdenka. "No, no, no…"

Seated by the bedside was the plague doctor in his long black gown. His beak turned toward her, his long fingers clicking like pincers.

"Miss?" he said. "Miss, can I help?"

"She doesn't feel so good," said the young guy.

"She's awful pale," added the father.

The doctor nodded and rooted around in his black doctor's bag. As Zdenka jerked and squirmed, he produced what seemed to be a long syringe and a hard boiled egg.

"No," she said. "No, I'm not…"

The doctor removed his mask to reveal the sallow face of the one-eyed man, his face crunched up as if peeping through a keyhole. Zdenka screamed and tried to extricate herself from her rescuers, pushing her way back through the crowd as the room rocked from side to side.

"Miss?" cried the young guy. "Miss, are you alright?"

Behind her she could hear the woman with red hair, crying.

# A

Struggling to breathe, Adam's head poked out from the plastic like a snail. Above him, the silhouettes of ancient apartments rolled slowly past, whilst below curls of orange peel and slices of tomato bobbed in the oily water, the light from the barge cutting the waves like a blade. The canal was very narrow here, no wider than a gate, and the barges drifted perilously close to the sides, workmen jumping off from time to time to add more sacks to the heap. Adam flinched and wilted greenery and sodden paper spilled from a gap. The stink was unbearable, a mixture of rot, sweetness and waste.

As the barge passed under a low bridge he glimpsed a bare bulb kept in a cage above a statue of the Madonna, her carved face looking directly at him.

"Danka," whispered Adam, "Danka, I'm here…"

Ah, it was no use: the bridge rolled back, shadows covered the Madonna's face, and soon the holy mother was gone. By now the line of barges had already reached the Grand Canal, ghostly *palazzos* and crouching churches crowding in around the canal for a better view. The arched bridges were much higher here, but seemed somehow unfinished, closer to scaffolding than completed erections. There were no pedestrians, no tourists, no statues: the whole city seemed to have been emptied of any human form. Instead the black sky reached down to the inky waters, the cortege of barges passing without sound or impression or witness.

After a while Adam realised that his barge was heading out into the lagoon, the wind a little stronger, the waters a little rougher. The view seemed closer to Turner than Canaletto, everything felt slick with moisture, sliding surfaces refusing to meet. Clouds slipped down from the sky and the lagoon rose up to meet them. At least the stink of the bags didn't seem quite so bad here though; gusts from the *Golfo di Venezia* blew the stench back to land, and Adam could smell the sharp tang of the sea.

"*Excusez moi monsieur policier,*" he murmured, "*pourriez-vous directez diriger vers la piscine?*"

Deep Italian voices conversed at the prow but nobody seemed to care that the Englishman was still on board. Whenever Adam tried to move more bags rolled to fill the gap and he felt as if he were trapped on some great rolling bed from which it was impossible to rise. O, what was he doing here? One bag contained something sharp and pointed: a broken umbrella. In another was a torn coat, a lost hat, and some kind of cloak. Another contained soiled nappies and coils of hair. All human life was here – death too. Bones, meat, the chopped claws of a cock. Adam could no longer prop up his elbows or move one leg. A great black sack blocked out the sky. Then he felt the barge lurch against some blockage – perhaps those rubber floats employed to prevent boats from smashing up against jetties – and the bags rolled back the other way. Where was he? The engine of the barge fell quiet and Adam could hear his co-workers softly cursing and yelling, their voices seeming to drift further and further away.

"Hello?" he croaked. "Hello, is there anybody there? *Signor?* Hello?"

Slowly, painfully, he managed to claw his way to the surface, bin-juice trickling down his chin. Illuminated by the lights of the barge and the mooring strip, all he could see was a great terracotta wall before him, its red bricks seeming to stretch the whole way around the world. Behind the jetty the flaking cupola of a large white church lay like the moon, a dark tower peeking officiously over the top.

"Ah, excuse me," said Adam. "Um, does anybody have a phone…?"

Now that the barge was no longer moving, Adam managed to lever the bags from him, stumbling to his feet in a mess of peelings, newspaper and filth. The night was very quiet. Dark Cyprus trees tried to hide the gate and Adam felt as if he had travelled to another world completely. A sign read *Isola di San Michele* – the Venetian Isle of the Dead. A floating carpet of sea-weed drifted slowly toward him and a crushed beer can bobbed mournfully upon the deep.

# Z

Pushing her way past the waiters and the guests, Zdenka sensed the plague doctor just behind her, his sharpened pecker pointing toward her like a sword.

"Miss, *Fermasi, aspettare…*"

Zdenka stumbled over the convoy of shoes, almost falling down the stairs. The doctor (doctor?) was right behind her now, his nozzle terrifyingly close.

*"Počkej, zastav…"*

Leaping the split level, Zdenka managed to evade his nib, her bare feet covering the ground more quickly. Breathlessly, she climbed the stairs to the next floor, squeezing between the step ladder and the tins of paint. Fortunately the be-robed doctor was not so swift and when she turned she saw his snout caught between the rungs, his doctor's bag too fat to pull through. Zdenka turned the corner, hid in a shallow alcove, and watched the fella's dark habit rush through. Then she swiftly retraced her steps, descended two more flights of stairs, and shoved hard against an external door.

Outside was a small walled courtyard, its sputtering fountain ringed by odd coloured lanterns and shrunken balloons. Slamming the door behind her, Zdenka crouched down behind the fountain and waited. The fountain dripped and the gutters splashed. Only when she was certain that the physician had lost her did she straighten up and turn her face to the rain. When she noticed a stone fish in exactly the same pose she immediately started to laugh.

Yes she thought, it was all ridiculous, some kind of nonsensical pantomime. Zdenka felt the giggles come with great force, her whole body starting to jump and tremble. Worried that she might draw attention to herself she moved toward the darkened arcade, stepping between the puddles of rain water and wet sand. Laughter still bubbled up inside her and her shoulders shook with merriment. Was that the sound of the canal beyond the wall? She listened to the waves licking at the stone, the nocturnal tide rippling and splashing against the jetty. What was Venice? A drowned queen, a spilled glass, the exquisite corridors of a sinking ship… feeling in her apron she found a boiled sweet and sucked on it thoughtfully: mazes within mazes, *il dedalo*, the labyrinth…

From out of the shadows a familiar shape strolled nonchalantly toward her, the same black cat as before, but interested now, curious as to what she had found in the folds of her tabard. Zdenka knelt down and the cat climbed up into her lap, its fur soft and wet. Stroking it, she felt an enormous wave of contentment, an irresistible surge of pleasure and relief radiating from the small furry bundle and spreading out through Zdenka's entire body. The cat purred and Zdenka sighed. As she petted and caressed its black, downy hair, its mouth opened a little, its tiny pink tongue licking the air. Zdenka placed her finger inside its mouth and rocked it like a baby; how could such a small, wet thing generate so much heat?

Humming gently she failed to notice the guy in the reflective jacket, standing by the fountain and dipping his hands in the muck. The cat however glared at the intruder and hissed angrily, wriggling in Zdenka's lap before scampering away and hiding someplace in the gloom. Zdenka tried concealing herself behind one of the damp stone columns but it was no use: the fella was looking straight at her.

"Adam?"

Water gurgled in a blocked drain pipe and somewhere muffled bells tolled half-heartedly.

"Adam, is that you?"

"Zdenka?"

Zdenka approached the figure and placed one hand upon his reflective jacket. "Adam, what is this? A workman's jacket?"

"Ah, well…" Adam picked at the reflective panel and shrugged. "You see, um…"

She carefully removed it and placed one hand upon his dirty off-white shirt. "And whose is this shirt? Pff – you're so cold you're trembling…"

Adam nodded and reached out to Zdenka's apron. "And what about you? A little moonlighting, eh?"

"That's right," said Zdenka trying to slide her apron out of his grasp. "Don't all men want to see a woman dressed as a maid?"

"Dressed?" Adam undid the string as Zdenka pulled the shirt from over his head. Somewhere out on the lagoon a horn blew lugubriously.

"Ho!" she smiled. "And these rubbery trousers are supposed to turn me on, I suppose..." When she held him, the plastic was springy and squishy, terribly cold to the touch.

"No, no, that's just a safety feature..."

"Right..."

"To prevent unwanted contact..."

"I see..."

Adam shivered. "Besides, your dress doesn't even fit," he said. "Look, it comes off so easily..."

"Mmm..."

"Just one pull..."

"Well, at least I remembered to wear underwear and shoes," said Zdenka, gazing at Adam's bare limbs. "What on earth happened to you anyway?"

"Me? What about... hey!"

Zdenka scooped a great handful of water from the fountain and tossed it at Adam's bare bod. Laughing, he dodged around the other side and splashed a fistful of rain water back.

"Ahah!" said Zdenka, but as she plunged her hands into the water to splash him again, she noticed something small and gold at the bottom, its surface reflecting the lantern's rosy light.

"Wait, hold on," she said, dipping her fingers in the murk. "Adam – is this yours?"

Adam walked up to her and examined the ring. "But..."

"Adam, what on earth..."

Adam turned the ring this way and that.

"Ah..."

At that moment a series of bangs and yells suggested the arrival of something large on the other side of the wall, the light of a lantern swinging crazily across the yard.

"Quick!" she yelled. "Over here…"

Still laughing, the two of them plunged back through the door and along the empty corridor. The carpet was soft and yielding, the passage a pale pink.

"Um, is this…"

"Shh…"

"But I don't recognise the…"

"Adam, be quiet…"

Zdenka pulled him into a narrow alcove where Adam removed the rest of Zdenka's clothes. There they stared at each other meaningfully.

"This night," said Adam, "I mean…"

"Don't speak," said Zdenka. "Just touch, don't…"

"But this night, ah, what do you think…"

"No words," said Zdenka, "*nikdo…*"

At the end of the corridor they saw the open door of their hotel room and raced toward it, Adam's dark shoes and Zdenka's highest heels still waiting faithfully outside. Giggling like children, they entered the room and firmly shut the door.

Their first night in Venice, the beginning of their honeymoon. The stilts on which the hotel was built seemed to creak whilst the light in the corridor shifted and changed, the passageway somewhere between grey and blue and white. A wave broke over the jetty, only to fall away again, back into the depths. Yes, they had finally arrived. In the next room along a baby cried out and the parents began to wake.

# A

Behind the funeral gates the cemetery stretched out onto a wide expanse of serene gardens and long colonnades, the dark Cyprus trees bending like mourners by the graves. The wind had blown over and a gentle mist settled between the cloisters of the old monastery and the funeral gates, a Venetian cloud fallen to earth. Everything felt cool, damp, forgotten, the island vacated by all except the dead. Not a single sound could be heard: instead the mist turned from air to water and back again, a never ending conversion or exchange.

Adam slowly walked up the walkway from the jetty, passing the white stone of the Church of San Michele and the adumbral arcades surrounding it. Hundreds upon hundreds of tombs covered the island, from monumental crypts to modest headstones, Adam passing high walls of stacked bones, like enormous filing cabinets of the dead. Flowers were strewn everywhere, though many looked as if they'd seen better days; likewise whilst most of the cemeteries were neat and well tended, other sections looked unkempt and half abandoned, turning back into scrub land or swamp. A long line of angels pointed to an avenue of trees and the high terracotta wall beyond.

Of the bin men, there was absolutely no sign. Whilst the barge remained moored by the rough wooden jetty, its occupants seemed to have departed, dissolving someplace amongst the moisture and the spray. How tranquil it seemed here! No monks, no visitors, no guards: though of course it was either very, very late or very, very early – the light was such it was almost impossible to tell.

Adam made his way along an ancient, crumbling cloister and up onto a rather precarious stone balcony pointed back toward

Venice, the city a silvery ghost haunting the bleak and caliginous sea. Adam gazed out across the waters and slowly wiped his eyes. Despite all that had happened to him, he felt calm and stoical, resigned to the vagaries of fate. A sea of tears before him, a sea of the dead behind: and between them? Venice, that spectre of the past, history's shadow.

Zdenka felt very far from him now, separated not by miles but years. Even their wedding night seemed distant, as if it were a story told by an acquaintance many moons ago, a rude joke whose punch-line had to be told in a whisper. Perhaps it really had happened many moons ago – or perhaps it was something he'd read in a newspaper, the disappearance of a foreigner's wife on their wedding night. But how it all pertained to him, Adam could no longer be so certain. Ho, why worry about it now, fill in forms, alert the authorities: would any of this bring her back? No, it was right to stay here, thought Adam, marooned amongst the dark trees and the mist, a solitary mourner lacking even the consolation of a grave. He could ask the garbage men for a job, learn to fish, perhaps even join the monks, his days austere and thoughtful, the rhythm of his days re-set to eternity.

Adam stretched and smiled. Who was to say what was the end and what was the beginning? Perhaps life didn't travel from A to Z but constantly traded and changed; from here it was Venice which seemed like a dream and the island of tombs which chimed the one true hour.

Adam sniffed. Above him the light shifted and changed, someplace between grey and blue and white. A dark wave broke over the jetty, only to fall away again. The trees swept the dirt from the graves. Yes, thought Adam, I've finally arrived. Then a gull cried out and the day slowly began to awake.

# Love in an Age of Austerity

For their first date, Stefan and Emily went to a little French place, *coup de fonde* (literally, 'cup of fondness' or 'cup of fondling' depending on where you put the accent), over on the far side of town. Alas, one look told them the joint was way out of their league: discreet entranceway, thick velvet curtain, not even the faintest sniff of a menu.

"It's okay," whispered Emily softly, "we don't have to go in here. I'm not so hungry, you know?"

"No, no, s'all right," said Stefan, nervously fingering his wallet. "I'm sure this place is fine…"

Stefan stepped past the golden rope, handed over Emily's coat at the cloakroom, and followed the immaculately dressed maitre d' to a table in the very centre of the room. All around them diners nibbled on the finest delicacies, sipped fine wine. Emily looked terrified.

"Stefan? Stefan, I…"

"Shh, it's all fine."

Before they even had time to pause for breath, chairs were pulled back, napkins positioned, and the wine-waiter appeared as if pulled out of a hat.

"Sir?"

Stefan's jaw involuntarily tightened. He couldn't make head nor tail of the *carte des vins* (literally, the wine cart) at all.

"Mm," he said knowledgably. "Hm, let me see…"

He glanced across at Emily but she'd opened up her handbag and seemed to be trying to fit her whole head inside.

"Yes, wine…"

Snapping the menu shut like a clam, he said confidently, "The *Chateau Margaux*," and beamed at the waiter helplessly.

"The ninety four?"

"Mm."

"The ninety four?"

"That's right, the ninety four."

Stefan beamed at Emily but she couldn't help but notice a strange rash creeping up from his neck.

"Well, this is nice," he said.

When the wine came it was very, very dark – almost black. When Stefan took a sip it was as if he'd been drinking ink.

"I hope this isn't too…"

"Pff, no, no, it's fine," he said, frantically sizing up the bottle. "You look terrific, you know. Your dress is a knock out. And your hair…"

He struggled to find the word.

"Extortionate."

"Sorry?"

"Exquisite. It's exquisite…"

Just at that moment a second waiter was whipped so and they had no choice but to order the *amuse bouche* (literally: funny bush), *hors d'oeuvre* (whore's egg), *plat principle* (the headmaster's plate), *du pain* (the pain). By now Stefan's tongue was as dry as a roller-towel.

"Oh, and another bottle of that wine please…"

Some of the other customers – wealthy looking businessmen, model types, investment bankers – seemed to glance their way. Emily blushed.

"Do you think that seems an awful lot? We could just go to

*Nandos…*"

"What? No – you're a special lady and you deserve the best…"

"Um."

And the food *was* great – little truffley things, some kind of pate, strange wee pastry things filled with some kind of goo.

"This is nice, eh?" said Stefan. "Hm? What do you say? Eh? Eh?" He had a wild look in his eyes and distractedly mopped his brow with a slice of bread.

"Stefan, I…"

"Shh. Eat."

They tucked into crepes and vol-au-vents, avocados and garlic flavoured mussels; it was when they were only half way through that Stefan realised they were still on the starters. Ho, such a thing! Stefan couldn't believe it. The table was entirely covered and yet they weren't even through to the fish.

"It's, ah, very generous helpings…"

"Very."

"D'you think that…"

"I don't know Stefan – do you think we should go?"

More and more heads were turning in their direction now. Emily toyed aggressively with her napkin.

"Do you think there's been a mistake with our order?"

"Mistake?"

"Well, there's an awful lot…"

"I know, but…"

"We can never eat all this…"

"It's fine, fine. Just eat half."

Alas, the quantities weren't easing. More and more dishes were introduced until it seemed that the poor table would collapse. Stefan was sweating heavily and looked as pale and waxy as a mushroom.

"We'll never get through all this…"

"Well, I…"

"I only wanted the tuna salad…"

"It's fine, it's fine, don't fuss…"

Secretly though, Stefan had already begun to undertake a series of complex mathematical calculations. Mentally he added the amount of cash in his pocket to the reserves of his current account and the farthest reaches of his overdraft; it still seemed some way short of filling the hole though. Even if he amalgamated his assets into one lump sum, he'd still have a very small lump indeed.

"I just need to use the little boy's room," he said. "I'll be back in a minute…"

Emily looked up at him anxiously.

"You will come back won't you?"

"Mm, I, I… Here, have some more wine…"

"Stefan…"

"I'll be right back…"

Slumped by the urinal, Stefan suffered a sudden crisis of conscience. If he tried to abscond now, then what about Emily: what about his coat? And yet he could see no other way out. How much the *Chateau Margaux?* How much the truffles? Ho, he was in a tight spot and no mistake. Even a fox knows when the chicken coop shuts…In the mirror an enormously round, puffy white face stared back at him, its visage only inches from his nose. Pale skin, bulging eyes, blank face… 'There's a face,' he thought. 'But the face of what?'

Shaken by the vision, Stefan slunk back into the restaurant deep in thought. When he looked up he could scarcely see Emily for the pile of dishes before her.

"They've served the main then," he said.

"Mm."

"The steak looks nice… is that steak?"

"I think so."

"Ah."

At that moment the maitre d' reappeared, casting an inquisitive glance in the couple's direction.

"Everything to your satisfaction sir?"

"To my satisfaction?"

"Yes, to your satisfaction?"

"Satisfaction?"

Waiter and customer gazed at each other as if striving to achieve some profound communion of the soul.

"Is there anything I can help you with sir?"

"No, no, I don't think so..."

The maitre d' knew that Stefan could not pay. Stefan knew that he knew this. And yet the maitre d' also knew that the sum involved was so huge he could not allow Stefan to inform him of such unpleasantries. What then was the solution?

"Another bottle of the *Chateaux Margaux*, sir?"

"Um, sure..."

"And maybe the dessert trolley..."

"Mm, why not?"

Waiter and customer both looked at each other and smiled. As long as Stefan kept eating everything would be okay. The main thing was not to allow him to stop.

Stefan belched and loosened the button on his trousers. 'It's true,' he thought; the joint wasn't any better off than he was. What was the way of the world after all? The waiter waited and the customer ate. As long as everybody played their parts night would turn to day and the world would keep on spinning.

'That's right! Why didn't I realise earlier?' thought Stefan. 'It's all as simple as that...'

With this in mind he returned to the dishes with a new found gusto. Pff, what had he been so worried about? Why the long face, why the clammy palms? No, as long as the courses kept on coming, there was no real reason for despair...

"Emily? Em, try the pancakes, they're really good..."

Knife and fork in hand, Stefan stared out over the enormous mountain peak of plates. There were dishes for sauces, bowls of shellfish, discarded fish bones, vol-au-vent cases. A whole extra row of cutlery awaited him, their prongs still untouched.

"Em, pour some of this sauce on, there, from that pot..."

He glanced over but the *plateau de jour* now reached up over his head. Bottles, pepper shakers, vials of oil...

"Em, Em, it's okay ... there look, have some pork..."

Stefan tried smiling and pushing his hand through the jars but couldn't seem to find her.

"Emily? Em?"

Alas, poor Stefan! Alas, the economy! A second waiter was fast approaching but his date for the night was gone.

# Venice in Blue

Where had the little bastards come from? There were bite marks in everything, punctured pages, half-eaten reports, whole chunks missing from the stationery room – not to mention all that dust. Malcolm was at a loss. Weevils, beetles, mites? Going forward, this was unacceptable: staying still, likewise. Black specks were everywhere, though whether bug, excrement or hole, was awful hard to tell. A Quality Report had come through dotted with tiny perforations, as if passed by censors during the war. Punctuation had been devoured, letters gobbled up. Some people in Finance whispered that the punctures themselves resembled letters or some kind of Hebrew text – but hey, that was Finance, right? Office workers stared at pencil shavings suspiciously. Waste paper bins were carefully inspected. Fewer and fewer people brought sandwiches to work. The general feeling was of Rome just before the fall.

"Okay, okay," said Malcolm. "I'll call Extermination."

To be honest, the last thing Malcolm needed was to have to shut the office down while some guy in a yellow suit came along and filled it with gas. Simon from Delivery was breathing down his neck. Amanda in Quality was little better. And Clive in the Pathway Hub? Better not to ask.

Things had started to slide around the time that Claire fell sick. First she was tired, then there was something wrong with her daughter, then she was signed off altogether: even her shadow looked sick. Malcolm gazed dejectedly at her work station which, like some ancient archaeological site, still bore evidence of her day to day existence. A Mummy Pig mug sat next to a nest of hair-bands, above it a picture of Venice, pinned to a board. Officially her status was 'dormant', but HR was aloof: the position was already filled, how could they fill it twice? And all the time the e-mails gathered weight and mass, like the books that killed al-Jahiz…

"Okay, I'll call Extermination," said Malcolm, "you don't have to tell me twice."

Claire's real problem, of course, was depression: whose wasn't? Her husband had disappeared the previous year, police dredging the river, sniffer dogs digging up the park. How were you supposed to care about implementing growth strategies after that? Malcolm wasn't unsympathetic. He too, sensed the meaningless of their toil. But for all that policies needed to be actioned, envisioning workshops to be held. With or without her, the team had to meet its targets: or just slightly miss them, which was also more or less okay.

"Extermination, extermination, I'm on it," said Malcolm.

The last time he had seen Claire, she seemed to have aged overnight. Her skin looked tired, her hair without bounce, strange blue circles under her eyes. Even her finger nails seemed drained. Tallulah was having 'issues' at school. There was no news about Nick. Her systems wouldn't reboot. Whenever Malcolm happened to pass, Claire would be staring at her picture of the Grand Canal, a far away look in her eyes, as if her soul were sinking deeper and deeper within. Ah, if only Malcolm could have fished her out – but from this bank the currents were too strong and his rod too short…

"Extermination, extermination, I *know*."

Extermination was called. A guy called Urbino was detached.

Urbino was a great block of a man: one could easily imagine him propping up a falling building or supporting the fly over of a motorway. Exploring under desks was more of a problem. The fella sweated just getting down on his knees.

"Hmm," he said, peering at gnawed print-outs and hollowed-out files. "Yes, yes, I see…"

The guy had a strange accent: maybe French or maybe somewhere, what, Hungarian? Unlike the pasty complexions of the office workers, his skin was olive-brown, though that might have been the spray.

"Tut, tut, Mister Malcolm," he said, peeping through the gaps in a memorandum. "This – it is a big job, you know?"

With enormous difficulty, he mounted a step ladder and peered in the air vents. Then he rolled onto all fours to take waste samples from the carpet tiles.

"Is it bad?" asked Malcolm.

"Worse than bad. A *catastrophe*!"

With his little moustache and his funny, wobbly walk, he looked like a Pictionary drawing of Poirot. And yet he seemed to know his stuff: surfaces were swabbed, openings measured, bite marks examined. "Tiny – and yet dangerous," he hissed.

Urbino and Malcolm settled themselves on Claire's desk, Urbino's ample behind resting on a pack of marker pens.

"Ho – a remarkable painting, eh?" said Urbino, plucking the picture of Venice from the cork board. "Painted by – what? A monkey?"

Malcolm looked closer: yes, the brush strokes were kind of crude. A thick blue smear for the canal, dark daubs for the buildings: was this even Venice?

"Hmm…" said Malcolm, thoughtfully. "What colour do you think that is? Cyan?"

"The devil alone knows," muttered Urbino dismissively. "The painter was either ahead of his time or of another time entirely.

255

What's this signature – Ferrard?"

Malcolm squinted but couldn't make out the squiggle: like a bird had hopped in paint. Not that the *campanile* was much better: more like someone had accidentally stepped on a tube of oils.

Urbino stared at the print with the practiced air of a critic and then tossed it aside.

"Tonight, my friend…"

"Tonight?"

"Whilst everyone away I will – what do you say? – gas the joint…"

"Mm."

"By tomorrow the infestation will be over. Poof – no more."

Malcolm nodded and played with his tie. "And in the morning, um…"

"A strong smell of sulphur, no more. Open all your windows. Don't wear your best suit…" Urbino surveyed Malcolm's shirt dismissively. "The tie is okay…"

"Well, thank you Mr Urbino, I, ah…."

"By this sign you shall know that the plague has passed," said Urbino. And with a flourish he handed over his card.

As promised, Urbino returned that very night. Emptied of all human traffic the office felt larger somehow, like a great blue print or a model version of some futuristic city. Lights clicked on and the processors hummed. A printer somewhere bleated that it needed more paper. Screensavers came and went like visions.

Urbino checked his gas canisters and his spray gun. Then he suited up and stalked the corridors like the first man on the moon.

"Precisely so," he said. "Yes indeed…"

The air conditioning had been switched off, the heating likewise. Aside from the heavy pad of Urbino's footsteps the whole place seemed set to 'pause'. An empty office was a peculiar space. Swivel chairs collected in huddles. Post-it notes stuck to the carpet. From time to time Urbino came across upended bins and knocked over coffee cups, as if the building's inhabitants had fled in panic rather than simply clocked off for the night. Over to one side the wall clock tutted.

"Foo," said Urbino. "The enemy, she hides…"

Squirting the carpets on Floor six, Urbino came to a halt by Claire's old work station, propping his gun against her desk. Ignoring the photos of Nick and Tallulah, he picked out the strange print of Venice and held it at arm's length. Yes, there was something not quite right. All those wavy blocks of the water and the heavy drips of the city – the more you stared at it the harder to tell which was which.

"Yes, yes, quite the work of art…" said Urbino, squinting at the picture. The paint had been applied in crude daubs, seemingly with fingers rather than a brush, the lines failing to meet up and no attempt at perspective. Everything – the canal, the *piazza*, the city behind – seemed of the same viscous material, more like oil than brick or stone. As for the shade of blue – turquoise? Azure? Lapis lazuli? – Urbino had never seen such a colour before in his life.

"Remarkable, hm, yes…"

As he leant in closer, he felt as if, with just a little effort, he might somehow scramble over the blobs in the foreground and miraculously enter the city, pushing his way past the inky brushstrokes to climb into the painting itself. But how odd the space, and how strangely lit! Illuminated by a blue light, was a blue *piazza*, its façade whorled like a finger print. And inside the blue house – a figure? Two?

The pest-man's eyes opened wide. As he angled the painting from side to side, the two tiny blobs seemed to chase one another, leaping from palace to tower, running across bridges and through tunnels, connected as if by some invisible wire. What kind of animation was this? Urbino brought the painting right up against his face mask and stared. Two tiny fleas, dressed in human clothing, chasing each other up and down endless indigo steps. What a sight! What a find! But how on earth had the artist done it?

"Mm…" said Urbino, pulling at the straps on his gas tank. "How peculiar! Some kind of compositional trick I suppose…"

The figures hopped, tumbled and bobbed as if putting on a show, bouncing from frame to frame on imperceptible springs. Yes, a blue maze, an enormous labyrinth: but who would want to paint such a thing and to what end?

"Well, well, I, ah…"

Scowling, Urbino squinted at the picture and rolled the shapes this way and that: yes, yes, a truly extraordinary piece of work. It certainly made the pest-man's own efforts seem rather green in comparison…

His face mask was rather steamed up by now and as Urbino replaced the picture Mummy Pig toppled to one side.

'How did Ferrand do it?' thought Urbino. 'And wherever did he find that shade of blue?'

As Urbino returned to his duties, he became aware of a low, closemouthed drone, an almost inaudible thrumming, coming from someplace nearby. The pest-man cocked one ear and listened; though his protective hood got in the way, he could just about discern some kind of chomping sound, grinding away at the very edge of his hearing.

Switching off the spray, Urbino peered at a nest of cables coiled up under a table: what was that and where it was coming from? All around him he could hear a low-pitched munching and grinding, as if a swarm of microscopic locusts were feeding upon the very fabric of the building itself.

As the sounds of digestion grew louder, the pest-man gripped his gun ever tighter. Jaws opened and mouths crunched. For a moment it seemed as if the whole office roared with the din of champing and mashing...

'What sorcery?' he mouthed. 'What manner of pestilence is this?'

Retreating toward the stairs, Urbino pointed his gun this way and that, seeking out the mandibles of the foe. The walls here were tacky as if recently painted. A vague banging sound came from the bottom of the stairs. His suit began to itch.

Something was moving at the bottom of the stairwell, the shapes writhing and biting. What kind of nest had he disturbed? The patterns flexed like the fingers of a hand.

The light in the stairwell was very bright, causing Urbino to mask his eyes. His own shadow seemed strangely distorted, more like a bear than a suit, but with a peculiar, pointed top. He waved his arms from side to side and the bear waved also, the creature shaking from side to side as if frightening bees. The shadows danced and the munching continued, unabated. To one side was a sign pointing to a fire exit, though Urbino couldn't read the language.

Below him strange black specks emerged from the nest, jaws snapping and wings sprouting. What were those things? Trying to see, the pest-man teetered on the very top of the stairs. His suit was large and cumbersome, the tanks for his spray gun awfully heavy. Urbino's footing faltered and letters seemed to float past his head. But what did they mean? Why couldn't he read? At the very last moment, the pest-man reached out and grabbed the balustrade, holding on to it for dear life. The spray gun fell but Urbino remained upright. His hot, sour breath misted his face mask and when it cleared an old guy was standing before him in a blue cap.

"Everything okay here?" said the security guy, squinting at him curiously.

"What? Yes, yes, but of course..."

"You all finished here? Can I lock up?"

"Mm, ah, yes indeed. Well, that is to say…"

Was he finished? The pest-man did not care to find out. Rather, he retrieved his spray gun, packed away his equipment, and swiftly abandoned his post. The bugs? Well, perhaps they were full. Besides, what could one man do? Eventually Time devours all things…

Urbino got back to his flat just before midnight. His pits were sweaty and his head throbbing. Fortunately a small glass of *patis* and a little broiled chicken seemed to calm him down. The apartment was dark and cramped. Canvasses and torn pages leant against care-worn furniture and unwashed dishes. The rug was smeared with paint. And yet, thinking back to that bug-ridden office, Urbino could not think of any place he'd rather be…

Seating himself before a small, blank canvas, Urbino whistled softly to himself and then began to paint. Working quickly, he sketched a building, then some water, next to it a street light, the lines thick and uneven, smeared in places by his thumb. Bridges reached over the canal, towers bent backwards, steps led both down to the water and up to the stars: Urbino didn't worry about perspective. When all was done he added two little figures, dots really, connected as if by an invisible string. Urbino stared hard at the specks, a thoughtful expression on his face. A man, woman? Foo, he could add the detail later. For now he concentrated on mixing his colours, dabbing his brush first in the purple and then the white, French navy and indigo, cyan and plum. He applied them intently, his eyes focused not on the dirt or the mess but on another world entirely.

When he looked back at the canvas he saw that he'd painted a man, woman and child, the three of them standing by the Grand Canal, eyes fixed on the water, the horizon, an ice cream, who knows? Urbino squinted but couldn't make out their features.

They were as blue as the canal, as blue as the *palazzo*, as blue as forever. The pest-man peered at the figures and rubbed his eyes. They had passed from this place to some place else: somewhere, anywhere, the place where he was not.

Urbino smacked his lips and returned to his painting, his eyes and hands moving in unison across the paper, seeking out the shapes and patterns, the perfect colour. Ho, what was that shade? How did Ferrand do it? The blue deepened, the shapes blurred, and just for a moment the gnawing of the insects seemed very far away.

### THE KNOWN AND UNKNOWN SEA
**(Cillian Press, 2014)**

This haunting and comic fable from the author of *The Sleepwalkers' Ball* is a beautiful and heartbreaking journey through memory, loss and imagination.

Rumour and suspicion engulf an eerily fog-bound town as its residents begin to receive tickets promising passage across the mist-shrouded bay to the mysterious 'other side'. For Alex and his family, this seems like the beginning of a great adventure, but as reports of a shadowy, half-glimpsed ship start to circulate, so too does the gossip and anxious speculation.

Bilton has created an alternate universe, vividly detailed but utterly ambiguous, absurd and bewildering, a dream that lingers in the mind long after the last page is turned.

'Engages the imagination ... populated as it is with such a rich cast of characters and their sea of voices' – Cath Barton, Wales Arts Review

'Mingling the darkly humorous childscapes of Roald Dahl with fantastic imagery that could have come from the early surreal silent film classic "A Trip to the Moon" by Georges Méliès, I was captivated by the mystery at the core of this book. Funny and heartbreaking, surreal and insightful, this is a brilliant work of speculative fiction. Go on the strange pilgrimage with Alex, you will not be disappointed.' – Christien Gholson, author of *A Fish Trapped Inside the Wind.*

'The word 'immersive' is a bit over-used these days, but it's hard to avoid in this case. Reading *The Known and Unknown Sea* is like falling instantly into a deep and vivid dream, a sometimes nightmarish dream - surreal, utterly convincing, impossible to wake up from' – Chris Keil, author of *Flirting at the Funeral*

Bilton's extraordinary and ground-breaking second novel takes us into a magical world: it's at once comedic, exuberant and - in a strange way - elegiac. The Welsh setting links the joy of hwyl with the pain of hiraeth, longing. The novel is an adventure story and a tale of unredeemable loss. The narrator, Alex, is a child of a warmly close family: imaginative, bright and dreamy, he records the strange events of his family's journey in a voice of great vitality. The novel's language is wildly delicious - however dark the matter it records, Bilton's prose has a virtuoso quality, presenting events as a kind of imaginative jeu-d'esprit – Stevie Davies, author of *Awakening*

Bilton is a talented writer, and this is certainly a novel to get your hands on if you have a taste for the dark, the mysterious, and the weird – Paul Cooper, New Welsh Review

## THE SLEEPWALKERS' BALL (Alcemi, 2009)

Hans is a dreamer, a waiter, a security guard, a young man tending elderly parents, a layabout, an old man scribbling his memories. Driven out in his pyjamas into a strangely black and white Scottish town, Hans sets off in search of both his girl and the one mysterious thing that will solve the riddle of his life. Clara is the art school girl with the lovely round face and ants in her pants, the crazy girl from the pub, always hindered by luggage or her dodgy innards, the sleepy waitress at the ball in the castle grounds, the blowzy dame with the world's most beautiful mouth. But can they find each other in time?

Set sometime around now, and yet also any time, this is a beautifully surreal romantic comedy wrapped around the forms of the silent film and the Gothic city ghost tour. A cross between Kafka and Mary Poppins, *The Sleepwalkers' Ball* is filmic, funny and lyrical in turns. Always moving, it follows two lives: a man and a woman, and their many attempts to hook up together.

Lightning Source UK Ltd.
Milton Keynes UK
UKOW02f1437100516

273953UK00002B/52/P